EARTH SONG

BOOK 1 IN THE EARTH SONG SERIES

NICK COOK

VOICE FROM THE CLOUDS

ABOUT THE AUTHOR

Somewhere back in the mists of time, Nick was born in the great sprawling metropolis of London. He grew up in a family where art was always a huge influence. Tapping into this, Nick finished college with a fine art degree tucked into his back pocket. Faced with the prospect of actually trying to make a living from his talents, he plunged into the emerging video game industry back in the eighties. It was the start of a long career and he produced graphics for many of the top-selling games on the early home computers, including *Aliens* and *Enduro Racer*. Those pioneering games may look crude now, but back then they were considered to be cutting edge. As the industry exploded into the one we know today, Nick's career went supernova. He worked on titles such as *X-Com*, and set up two studios, which produced

Warzone 2100 and the *Conflict: Desert Storm* series. He has around forty published titles to his name.

As great as the video game industry is, a little voice kept nagging inside Nick's head, and at the end of 2006 he was finally ready to pursue his other passion as a full-time career: writing. Many years later, he completed his first trilogy, *Cloud Riders*. And the rest, as they say, is history.

Nick has many interests, from space exploration and astronomy to travelling the world. He has flown light aircraft and microlights, an experience he used as research for *Cloud Riders*. He's always loved to cook, but then you'd expect it with his surname. His writing in many ways reflects his own curiosity about the world around him. He loves to let his imagination run riot to pose the question: *What if?*

Published worldwide by Voice from the Clouds Ltd.

www.voicefromtheclouds.com

ALSO BY NICK COOK

The Cloud Riders Trilogy (Multiverse Chronicles)

The Earth Song Series (Multiverse Chronicles)

The Fractured Light Trilogy (Multiverse Chronicles)

THE SIGNAL

Before you begin **Earth Song**, you can download the novella **The Signal**, the prequel to the **Multiverse Chronicles**, for **free.** The story features Lauren Stelleck from **Earth Song**, a radio telescope operator at Jodrell Bank who's dropped into an extraordinary first contact situation. To get your **free** copy right now, sign up to Nick Cook's newsletter here: https://www.subscribepage.com/s6z3s9_copy

In loving memory of my father-in-law, Harry Errington, a man who always seized the day. (1924-2019)

'One is never afraid of the unknown;
one is afraid of the known coming to an end.'

– Krishnamurti

CHAPTER ONE

THE CAR FERRY churned its way over the fog-covered sea, a foaming white trail eddying out across the water's surface. The icy mist numbed my face as the deck vibrated slightly through the soles of my walking boots.

The woman in the ticket office said the view of Orkney would be amazing as we approached. She said I would never forget my first sight of the island...

I peered ahead through the mist towards the sooty outline of land, screwing up my eyes as if hoping to develop X-ray vision, but the featureless grey fog still sucked the view away.

At the sound of a door closing behind me, I glanced round. An old man wearing an equally ancient and worn waterproof jacket had appeared on the deck. Earlier I'd seen him drive a knackered Saab on to the ferry. An unlit cigarette was glued to his lip by the power of saliva. He fumbled in his pocket and withdrew one of those old-fashioned flint lighters. A clunk and a click and a flame spluttered in the breeze long enough for him to light his rolled cigarette.

The guy pulled the collar of his jacket up as he took a long drag of the cigarette, which glowed like a hot coal. He let out a contented sigh as he ambled towards me across the empty deck.

Like always, my instinct flashed up a warning at his approach. Every stranger had to be treated with caution, especially since the car crash that had destroyed what remained of my old life.

The Overseers played dirty and I couldn't afford to take any chances.

I cast a subtle glance at the old guy. He seemed an unlikely recruit for the secret organisation – to my knowledge they favoured ex-military personnel. Besides, this wouldn't be the first innocent old guy to single me out. For reasons unknown to me, I seemed to be like catnip to them.

'Nice weather for it,' the man said in a warm Scottish accent as he neared.

'Yeah, sunlight is so overrated.'

He snorted. 'You're a tourist then?'

'Sort of.'

'Oh, I see. Well, Miss *Sort of Tourist*, you could've picked a better time of year to come than now.' He lifted his hand. 'I'm Patrick by the way.'

I shook his surprisingly warm hand, but I didn't offer up my own name. I, Lauren Stelleck, needed to keep off everyone's radar as much as possible, and that included revealing too much information.

Thankfully, Patrick didn't seem to be expecting me to reciprocate. Instead, he sucked on his cigarette and leant on the railing to peer out into the fog, seeming to settle for companionable silence. And with my crowded headspace at the moment, that was good.

The wind started to moan around us and, like curtains rolling back at a theatre, the fog swirled aside to reveal a looming cliff line. In front of it rose a huge pillar of rock surrounded by thousands of whirling seabirds. Even at this distance, I was almost certain that the dark birds with white chests, stubby wings and flappy flight paths were puffins.

'That view is quite something,' I said.

'The Old Man of Hoy is a grand old sight. And that whole area is a nature reserve.'

'It looks like something straight out of a *Jurassic Park* film,' I replied, allowing myself a brief smile towards this stranger.

'Sadly, you won't find any T-rexs roaming around there. Although that would be great for the tourists.'

'Maybe, but possibly less so for the birdlife, hey?'

He snorted. 'Aye, lass.'

The wind howled and whipped up the waves.

As the air started to turn bitter, Patrick took out a hip flask. 'Do you fancy a wee dram just to take the chill away?'

'A margarita is more my usual speed.'

'Maybe so, but you're here for new experiences, am I right?'

More than he realised. 'I guess I am.'

Patrick unscrewed the top of the flask, took a sip first and then handed it to me.

I held the flask for a moment. If by some miracle he was working for the Overseers, if the drink was spiked, he wouldn't have tried it first. No, on this occasion I could give my usual paranoia a short break.

I took a cautious sip and whisky fire tanged my tonsils. After the heat rush, the rich aftertaste hinted at peat and honey. The afterglow slipping down my throat was like someone had just turned a radiator on inside me – way better than porridge could ever manage. I wiped the top of the flask with my sleeve and handed it back to him.

'That's very smooth.'

'The finest single malt in all of Scotland, Orkney's very own Highland Park,' Patrick replied.

'I think I could develop a taste for it.'

He nodded. 'Whilst you're on the islands you most certainly will. It'll snare a part of your heart for ever.' He took another sip and gazed out towards Hoy.

'And you're a poet too.'

'We islanders are dreamers of every sort.'

I smiled at the mental image of a windswept island filled with hopeless romantics. The old Lauren would have fitted right in, the woman who viewed radio telescopes as a love poem from humanity to the cosmos. But that version of me had been lost six months ago when my aunt had died.

I'd been on the verge of giving up this whole business when a UFO sighting over Exmoor had caught my attention. After months of frustration, I'd decided to make one last-ditch attempt to capture evidence of a craft.

The crazy thing was, Aunt Lucy shouldn't have even been there. But she'd known how strung out I'd become whilst trying to prove that UFOs actually existed. She'd always supported me in every half-crazy dream that I'd set my heart on, even my brief attempt to be a singer in my early teens.

So she was with me for moral support as we drove along a twisty B-road through Exmoor one June day six months ago. A truck had appeared out of nowhere and rammed us from behind, forcing Aunt Lucy to lose control of her Mini. We'd crashed into a wall, but it was no accident. I knew that when a guy in black combat fatigues and a ski mask had emerged from the truck and headed towards us, a pistol in his hand.

As I'd been pinned in the crumpled Mini, I'd spotted the scar radiating from his left eye. I still remembered the cold feeling of dread that had unleashed. You see, I'd come across Mr Eye Scar before. Despite my broken arm, I'd tried to shield my aunt from what I'd known was coming.

In those last moments she'd whispered that she loved me as

she began to lose consciousness. Only then had I spotted the blood running down the side of her head from where her skull had hit the door frame.

A strange calm had filled me as I'd cradled my aunt and waited to die with her. I'd tried my best, but it was our time. Then in a split second everything had changed, when a police car had rounded the corner.

The assassin had stood stock-still for a whole second, the expression in his eyes wavering behind his mask. But then he'd run back to his truck and sped away. A police car had then screeched to a halt next to us and called for an ambulance.

But it'd been too late.

Less than a minute later, Aunt Lucy had died in my arms and my soul had shattered into a million pieces that would never be put back together.

There had been a helicopter search and temporary road-blocks across the moors, but the guy and his truck were never seen again. The police had run the truck's number plate, which had turned out to be fake – no surprise to me.

MI5 had later asked me about Mr Eye Scar. He'd led the assault team that'd stormed Jodrell Bank and murdered all those people that awful night. And the secret organisation he worked for? The Overseers, who among other things were behind the conspiracy of silence about the truth of UFOs. And they had killed my precious Aunt Lucy.

It had made this more personal than ever. I was even more determined to destroy the Overseers organisation and everything they stood for. And if I came across Mr Eye Scar again, nothing would be off the menu when it came to dishing out some well-deserved vengeance.

It was why I was here on a ferry bound for Orkney – chasing down the latest lead in my hunt for the truth.

My attention snapped back to reality as the ferry rolled down a deep trough in the waves and spray erupted over the boat. Patrick and I were doused with water as the ferry started to roll up the wave.

I shuddered as the weaknesses in my cagoule were found by watery fingers and my skin grew soaked. 'Shit, that's cold.'

Patrick raised an eyebrow at me. His waterproof dripped with seawater and his wet grey hair stuck to his head; he looked toasty warm with glowing red cheeks.

'Aye, it's getting a bit fresh,' he said. 'We may as well head back to the car deck. We'll be landing soon.'

'No car for me. I'm a foot passenger.'

'Are you now? Someone meeting you at the harbour?'

'No, I'm travelling solo for this trip. Is there Uber on Orkney?'

'Uber what?'

I smiled. 'Don't worry about it – I'll find a taxi.'

Patrick shook his head. 'No need, because I'm going to give you a lift.'

My honed survival instinct kicked in. Patrick might have looked like a harmless old man, but I hadn't managed to evade the Overseers since the crash by getting careless with strangers.

'Honestly, don't worry about it.'

'What, you think I may have wicked plans for you?' His mouth curled into a smile.

'No...but... Well, you know.' I raised a shoulder.

'You can't be too careful?'

'Sorry, just a bit wary about people I don't know.'

'I understand.' He sighed. 'Modern times, hey? Anyway, there's a taxi rank at the harbour.'

'Thanks...and sorry, especially when you're just trying to be a saint.'

Patrick's smile widened. 'It's not the first time that's been said about me.' He winked.

I laughed. 'Right.'

'So where are you staying anyway?'

For someone I'd just met, this guy was certainly asking a lot of questions. But he hadn't forced the issue when I'd refused his offer of a lift, which made me more inclined to trust him. Besides, I did need some info.

'I haven't sorted any accommodation out yet. I was going to wing it,' I said. 'I don't suppose you know anywhere to stay near Skara Brae?'

Patrick's eyes tightened on me for a fraction of second. 'Ah, the archaeological tourist hotspot.'

'That's the one.'

'But not normally so popular in the winter.'

I shrugged. 'I've come all this way especially to see it.'

'Any particular reason?'

God, this guy was nosey. I needed to shut this conversation down. Time to throw in my cover story. 'I'm writing a thesis about Skara Brae being the forerunner to Stonehenge.'

Patrick's brown eyes peered into mine like he knew I wasn't telling him the truth. 'Older than the pyramids, they say.'

'Yes...'

'No other reason then?'

Oh, Patrick so knew the real reason I was here. After all, I wouldn't be the first. The UFO boards had been filled with reports of the investigators who'd already come out here to study the outbreak of strange symbols that had been appearing all over Orkney. People were already saying it was the latest form of crop circles, another phenomenon I'd been sceptical about initially.

If you had told me a year back that I would one day know everything about crop circles, I would have laughed in your face. But that was the old Lauren. The new version of me, the one standing on a freezing ferry, was a completely different woman.

Patrick tipped his head to one side, still waiting for my

answer. 'I'm pursuing my research into Skara Brae,' I said, trying to sound convincing.

'I see...'

I could tell by the way his expression stiffened almost imperceptibly that Patrick thought I was lying. Not that it mattered. Everyone had their secrets, although mine were bigger than most.

Patrick gazed out towards Orkney with a faraway look in his eyes. Together we watched a bird, possibly a gannet, dive into the surf. A moment later it surfaced with a silver fish trapped in its beak. Patrick finally turned back to me.

'I can recommend a wonderful pub with the cosiest rooms not too far from there. The Guillemot. Great seafood and –' he tapped his flask – 'plenty more of this there too, including some from a fine fifteen-year-old cask.'

I laid on my best winning smile for him. 'That all sounds great.'

'Grand stuff. Just tell the taxi driver the Guillemot and they'll know the way. But my offer of a lift still stands.'

'Thanks, but no. I'm sure you understand.'

'I do... Like I said, sad times.'

'They are...' I gave him an apologetic smile as the ferry started to turn towards the harbour now visible in the distance.

'I'd better get back to my car. We'll be landing soon,' Patrick said. 'Anyway, nice to meet you, lass. I hope your research goes well.'

'Thanks. And thank you for introducing me to Highland Park.'

He smiled. 'Any time.' He nodded to me and then headed to the doorway.

Behind the ferry, thunderous black clouds were beginning to roll in towards the island. The forecast had mentioned something about a big storm on the way.

Rain started to patter down, rapidly intensifying. I drew my jacket in tighter round myself.

As the ferry slid towards the harbour, I grabbed my rucksack from the seat where I'd left it and prayed I wasn't chasing another dead end.

CHAPTER TWO

THE WIND HOWLED and rain bullets peppered my cagoule as I trudged the hundred metres between the pub's car park and the entrance. At least my rucksack wasn't too heavy to carry now, unlike when I'd first started my the-truth-is-out-there road trip. After almost doing my back some serious harm, I'd quickly realised I needed to shed the kilos from my pack and I'd posted the equivalent of the kitchen sink back to my old neighbour in Macclesfield. I'd asked her to look after my stuff until I returned, even though I strongly doubted that would ever happen. It would be the first place the Overseers would wait for me.

I must have seriously upset the god of weather, because the storm threw a final squall of rain at my back just before I entered the pub's porch. The backs of my jeans were now completely soaked through. I shook off as much water as I could and opened the door into a face full of cosy warmth.

Bliss.

The pub was almost empty, but had a welcoming fireplace filled with crackling logs. It was huge – big enough to roast a wild boar. The thought made me even hungrier.

I would have bagged the table in front of the fire to dry out, but a guy in his twenties with cropped dark hair nursing a pint of beer was already hogging it, a pit bull at his feet. No, I wasn't going anywhere near there.

Aside from him, the few other people in the pub turned towards me their own conversations abandoned.

Oh, here we go, the standard you're-not-from-around-these-parts reception.

But their expressions were curious rather than hostile. They each watched me trail water across the floor to the bar. I felt like a mermaid who'd been thrown up on to land by the storm whistling beyond the pub's windows.

I sat on a stool, slid my rucksack off and propped it against the wall.

A barman with thinning hair and a comb-over he really should have known better about appeared from a side door. Of course, it was at that exact moment a raindrop decided to drop off the end of my nose on to the wooden bar. But he looked concerned rather than irritated at the interloper, especially when I couldn't stifle a shiver running through me.

'Wet out then?' he asked, a smile tugging at the corners of his mouth.

I gave him a grin in return. 'How did you guess?'

He snorted and everyone returned to their conversations.

'So what will it be?' he asked.

'Please tell me you have a room? I really can't face going back out into that weather.'

'Of course we do. I'll ask my wife to turn on the radiator in it for you. But first, you settle yourself by the fire to dry out.'

I jutted my chin as discreetly as I could towards the man with the pit bull hogging the table.

'Ah, right, that won't be a problem.' The barman called across to the crop-haired guy. 'Greg, could you free up that table for this young lady? We don't want her getting pneumonia.'

The guy looked up from his phone with slitted eyes. But then he got up, pulling his suitably unimpressed dog away from the heat of fire to a table across the room.

'Thanks, I really appreciate it,' I said to him as another trickle of rain ran into my collar, making me shiver again.

'And why don't we sort you out with a drink whilst you thaw out?' the barman asked.

'A margarita if you have fresh limes.'

'Sorry, just the bottled stuff.'

'In that case, I've been recently introduced to Highland Park. Do you have any of that?'

The barman laughed, his eyes going all twinkly on me. 'I'd be run off Orkney if I didn't. A single?'

'Make it a double.'

'No problem.'

I was soon stretching out my woollen-socked feet towards the flames licking over the logs of the fireplace. My boots steamed like two boiling kettles as they dried out on the hearth.

I gazed up at the muted TV on the wall. The news channel was showing footage of the Sky Dreamer prototype mining probe, Ymir. I'd kept tabs on the mission as it had slowly closed in on an asteroid. A month ago it had successfully touched down and then drilled for deep-core samples. Going by the silent video on the screen, it had just taken off again. This was a big moment for space exploration. If the probe returned to Earth with its mined load, the next step would be to scale up the mission and launch a whole fleet of these machines. It seemed as if mining asteroids was finally about to become a real thing.

I had to give some serious kudos to A. Jefferson, the guy who ran the Sky Dreamer company. He was one of the richest people on the planet, but he kept completely out of the limelight. No one even knew what he looked like.

It had been his unwavering vision that had made this mission happen. A vision that our future as species was in the stars. He'd had many sceptics, including key players at NASA, who'd said that it couldn't be done with current technology. But despite all the odds, A. Jefferson had just raised a proverbial finger at the establishment. My sort of person.

The footage of the probe blasting off from the surface of the asteroid was replaced by a story about an MP called Alexander Langton. From what I'd read in the papers, the guy was utterly ruthless. Apparently he had his sights set on becoming prime minister, and had been plotting behind the scenes. It didn't seem particularly unusual. There always seemed to be someone like Langton lurking and plotting in the political shadows.

I returned my attention to my whisky, deciding I really could develop a taste for it, when the barman reappeared at my table with a menu.

'I can heartily recommend the special today,' he said. 'It's our rather legendary fish curry.'

'Legendary sounds good to me.'

'Oh, I promise you, it is.'

Maybe the Highland Park had loosened my tongue, or maybe it was the warmth of his smile, but before I could stop myself I was asking him *that* question.

I dropped my voice to a whisper. 'I don't suppose you know anything about the strange quartz-crystal markings that have been appearing across Orkney, do you?'

The guy's face tensed, his jaw muscles tightening. And even though I'd whispered the question, all conversation in the room died and I felt wary eyes looking my way.

'I wouldn't know anything about that,' the barman said.

'Right. But do you know anyone who might have seen them?

There are photos all over the net about them.' Perhaps I should have been slipping him a twenty-pound note and he'd be all smiles again. 'I'd particularly like to know about any markings close to Skara Brae that might have appeared recently.'

The man's expression hardened to stone. 'Look, miss, just a friendly word in your ear. I wouldn't go asking those sort of questions around here. Do you understand?'

The guy looked like I'd just threatened to burn his children, and the locals in here seemed just as hostile. Where was it all coming from?

'No problem. Maybe I'll grab a quick bath now and come back down to eat afterwards.'

But the barman's face didn't soften and instead he crossed his arms. 'Sorry, my wife just told me that we had some last-minute bookings I didn't know about. We haven't got any rooms left, I'm afraid.' He tugged his ear.

This guy was clearly lying through his teeth.

'OK... Then I'll just grab that legendary fish curry and I'll find somewhere else to stay.'

He gave a sharp shake of his head. 'Sorry, I just remembered someone ordered the last special.'

I didn't need to be a mind reader to know that whatever else I ordered would be off the menu too.

I sighed. 'I'll be on my way then.' I pulled on my boots and drained my glass. 'How much do I owe you?' I asked as I started to tie my laces.

He shook his head. 'It's on the house.'

'Thanks.' I certainly wasn't going to say no, especially when my funds were running low. Six months of trying to chase a metaphorical UFO rabbit down its hole without a paying job had taken its toll on my finances. And I had no way of accessing the inheritance from my aunt without tipping off the Overseers to my whereabouts.

Of all the things that I might have expected at that moment, it wasn't a look of regret passing over the barman's face.

'Just do yourself a favour and stay away from Skara Brae,' he said.

'Why?' I tried to hold his gaze but his eyes slid away from mine. He walked away from me back to the bar.

This wasn't hostility. It was almost as if these people were too afraid to talk, but about what? The only thing I knew for certain was that I wasn't going to find the answer in here.

I shouldered my pack and headed for the door with every-one's eyes still on me.

A moment later, I was trudging up the path with my head bent into the squalling rain. If I'd had a smartphone, I would have used it to look for a taxi. But any sort of device that could be tracked had to be avoided, especially with a GPS come-and-get-me-why-don't-you signal. On the plus side, it had done wonders to cure my previous screen addiction.

The pub door banged behind me and I heard footsteps crunch across the gravel. I turned, half expecting to see the barman with a face of apology, telling me that they had a room after all. His wife had even just found one last portion of the fish curry in the back of the fridge. But, no, it was the guy called Greg, his pit bull trotting along behind him.

I clasped the pepper spray I always kept in my pocket – ever since my last encounter with the Overseers.

'Hold up a minute,' Greg said with a strong Scottish accent.

I judged the distance, wondering if I could land a kick on his fun sacks hard enough to bring him down. 'What is it?'

'You mustn't mind them. They're afraid.' Rather than attempting to rip my leg off, his pit bull was wagging its tail at me.

So I'd been right about the fear I'd sensed in the pub. 'Is this something to do with the symbols? Is that what's making people so nervous?'

He flinched. 'I can't get into this. But there is one person who might talk to you. He doesn't give a shit about...' Greg's words trailed away.

'About?' I asked.

He just shrugged. 'Anyway, the guy you need to talk to is the Viking.'

I tried not to smile. 'Yeah, right.'

Greg read my expression. 'Look, this is no wind-up. I don't mean a guy wearing a horned helmet. He's actually an American called Jack Harper. Tall blond guy with blue eyes, hence the nickname.'

I hoped that was the only reason for his name, and not for pillaging and the rest. 'OK... So where can I find this Jack Harper guy exactly?'

'At the very place you seem to be so interested in, Skara Brae. He's the chief archaeologist on the dig going on there right now. And when I say right now, I mean it. Jack is crazy-level driven. Whatever the weather, he'll be working there every day until at least midnight – long after the rest of his team has cried off. And that's despite what happened.'

'What's that then?'

Greg looked away.

'Why won't you tell me?'

'Because you could be one of them.'

I tensed. Did this mean the Overseers were already here, and burying the truth yet again? 'One of whom, exactly?'

'Look, all I'm going to say is that it would be better for you to turn round and head home. I'll drive you back to the ferry if you like.'

'No. I'm going to Skara Brae whether anyone wants me to or not.'

Greg sighed. 'OK, cool down. If you're going to insist, I'll deliver you straight to the Viking, so you should be safe. But we never had this conversation, do you understand me?'

Safe? I didn't like the sound of that. I gave Greg a fixed smile. 'What conversation?'

'Then we understand each other.'

'I don't usually accept lifts from strangers.'

'I'm not a stranger, I'm Greg McCallister.' He thumped his chest and smirked.

I gave him a slow smile in return and thumbed my pepper spray in my pocket. However wary I was, this Jack Harper sounded like a person I had to speak to. 'Well I'm Lauren Stelleck, Greg McCallister and you talked me into it – let's go.'

'Good.' Greg pulled at his dog's lead. 'Come on, Bambi.' He towed the dog towards a beaten-up yellow Fiat Punto in the car park.

'Bambi, seriously?' I asked as I followed him.

He flashed me a grin. 'Wouldn't hurt a fly, would you, boy?'

Bambi wagged his tail as Greg opened the back door for him. Bambi leapt on to the seats, circled once and then settled down on a blanket covered in dog hairs.

I dropped my rucksack alongside Bambi and jumped into the passenger seat.

As Greg started the car and we headed off into the storm lashing the island, a pulse of excitement ran through me. After all my research, I was finally about to see Skara Brae, the Neolithic site at the very epicentre of the riddle. I could feel with every fibre of my being that I was closing in on something huge. And if the Overseers were already here, then I would just have to deal with that too.

CHAPTER THREE

THE WIND THREW thick grey sheets of rain across the road, which was barely illuminated by the Punto's feeble headlights. Greg had driven me towards Skara Brae to the music of Dire Straits, 'Money for Nothing' thumping out of the car's stereo since we'd left the pub. Before that I would have bet good money on him being a thrash metal fan.

Bambi had zonked out on the back seat, seemingly unfazed by the rain hammering on the car's roof like a barrage of ball bearings.

'So is the weather normally this gorgeous around here?' I asked.

'At this time of year this is pretty typical,' Greg replied. 'The gales blow straight in off the Atlantic. But to be honest, this squall is nothing compared to what we can get.'

'I bet they're spectacular.'

'Waves five metres high hitting the island? Yeah, you could say that.'

We headed towards a bend and Greg dropped down a gear to the accompaniment of metal graunching against metal.

He winced and cast me a sideways glance. 'Needs a new clutch.'

'You don't say.'

He caught my smile and shook his head.

As we rounded the bend headlights appeared in the distance. A vehicle was heading towards us down the narrow road. Thanks to the crash, my instincts kicked in. Lone road – check. No other witnesses – check.

It seemed I was not alone in my concern because Greg clutched the wheel hard, peering over it like a granny with a bad case of astigmatism. He pulled into a lay-by to let the vehicle pass us, then sat back, his expression taut. 'Lauren, get down. You don't want to be seen by the people in that car.'

'Who—'

Before I could finish my question, Greg grabbed my arm and pulled me towards him. I caught a brief glimpse of a silver SUV closing in before my head ended up in his lap.

'Hey, I'm not that sort of girl,' I said, trying to inject some humour into the situation to disguise the worry spiking through me.

'Funny, but just keep down until they're past.'

Headlights skimmed the Punto's side windows as the vehicle flashed by.

My tensed jaw muscles relaxed as I realised they weren't going to ram us.

Greg let out a sigh and released me.

I sat up and peered at him. 'So what was that all about?'

'You just don't want those people to take notice of you.'

'Right, on the dark side of a stormy night and inside a car? How do you think they would have spotted me? Because of my sunny deposition shining out like a lighthouse?'

'The thing is that strangers get noticed at the moment. Take the reaction to you in the pub. People are scared.'

'And whomever it was in that vehicle is part of the reason that people are scared? Why no one will talk to me?'

'I'd rather not say, Lauren.'

I gazed out of the windscreen. So who were they? MI5, or was my paranoia right and the Overseers were already here? I turned the suspicion over in my head.

In my old life I'd been a radio telescope operator at Jodrell Bank. I'd been there the night we'd captured a fast radio burst – an FRB signal – that had contained the code for an alien AI called Sentinel. MI5 had quickly turned up to investigate as Sentinel had hacked his way into sensitive databases around the world, heading us towards World War Three. And then things had got even crazier. An Overseers assault team had arrived, led by Mr Eye Scar himself, and they'd shot the MI5 agents. They'd tried to seize the computer containing Sentinel's core code, something that I'd personally helped put a stop to. Ever since then, the Overseers and how I could bring them down had dominated almost every waking moment of my life. And in the pursuit of that obsession it had been a long, torturous road. One that had led me to Orkney.

I'd sounded out some of the key figures in the UFO community who I could trust to talk to about the secret organisation. The few that knew anything and were prepared to talk had told me that the Overseers were a powerful oligarchy that operated outside the rule of law and weren't answerable to any government. They were old money with major interests in fuel, transportation, pharmaceuticals, utilities and even whole economies. Hence their desire to suppress the knowledge about UFOs and more specifically the advanced systems that powered the craft. The rumour was that advanced anti-grav tech had been reverse-engineered from recovered UFOs. If revealed to the science community and general population, that technology would outdate oil and even nuclear power in a heartbeat. Something that would lose the Overseers an awful lot of money, power and influence.

So that was how I'd found myself up against the secret organisation that no one was meant to know about – know about and live at least. I'd crossed that line in my pursuit of the truth and my aunt had been caught in the crossfire. Now I wanted both truth and vengeance.

But Overseers or not, whoever was behind the paranoia on the island, had done a great job to make people clam up about the runic symbols that had spread across the internet like the proverbial wildfire. And that was despite zero coverage on the main news channels. That wasn't a surprise, of course, since the Overseers also owned most of the world's press.

The lack of official coverage about the markings had only heightened my suspicions. Especially when what little did leak out was through an editorial puff piece describing them as yet another crackpot hoax, despite the very unique characteristic that differentiated these from crop circles. These symbols were formed from quartz. And each new set of markings had appeared etched into the ground overnight – when no one was watching. That, combined with the fact they were Angelus symbols, the alien race that'd built Sentinel, had more than caught my interest. I'd decided that whatever was happening on Orkney had to be worth further investigation.

Of course, it might not be the Overseers suppressing information about these latest phenomena, but MI5. From my previous experience with the intelligence organisation, I knew they were more than capable of killing a story if it wasn't seen to be in the national interest. I'd learnt that much from Kiera, an MI5 field officer, before she'd been killed by Mr Eye Scar.

'Nearly there,' Greg said, breaking my train of thought.

The Punto's dim headlights picked out a sign to Skara Brae pointing off the main road.

Greg turned the car on to a single-track road. Fields stretched away around us, bordered by low stone walls just visible in the gloom. We followed another sign for Skara Brae, taking us through a gate and into a small car park. At the end of it was a single-storey horseshoe-shaped stone building.

I pointed to it. 'I'm guessing that's not Skara Brae, unless you're about to tell me that Neolithic builders had mastered the art of double-glazed windows.'

He snorted. 'That's the visitor centre. Skara Brae is just beyond it. Be warned, though, the site itself is almost hidden until you're on top of it, thanks to the mounds surrounding it. Anyway, I'll take you to the Viking in person. He'll be under the floodlights – he had them set up so he can work well into the night.'

'Thanks for the info, Greg. But you don't have to come. I can look after myself.'

'I couldn't live with myself if...'

Whatever Greg was about to say was lost as his eyes tightened on a silver SUV similar to the one that'd passed us on the road. It was parked next to a Land Rover in the otherwise empty car park.

Greg started to turn the Punto round.

'Hey, what the hell are you doing?'

'Getting us both away from here. I can't afford any trouble with anyone official, Lauren. What with my parole and everything.'

'Parole?'

He stared straight ahead. 'Yeah...'

'So when were you going to tell me about your dodgy criminal lifestyle?'

'Less with the dodgy, hey? More like an entrepreneur.' He rubbed his neck. 'I may have steered a bit too far away from the letter of the law sometimes.'

'How far is *far* exactly?'

'Just a bit of harmless smuggling across Europe, but nothing too serious.'

I face-palmed him. 'Stop there. I don't want or need to know any more.'

Greg shook his head. 'Your choice.' He graunched the gearbox again and swore about the parenthood of the mechanics who'd built the Punto.

As he turned the car back towards the entrance, I wrapped my fingers round the door handle. 'Right, pull up here and let me out.'

'Because I'm a dodgy criminal type?'

'Nooo,' I said, rolling the 'o'. 'Because I need to meet this Jack Harper guy and I'm going to see him with or without you.'

Greg sighed. 'Have it your way, Lauren.' He stopped the car and jumped out to get my rucksack from the back seat. Bambi raised his head to give his master a sleepy look.

I opened my door and heard the rumble of crashing waves in the distance.

As Greg handed me my rucksack, I tried one last time to get some more information out of him. 'Are you sure you don't want to tell me what's got people so worked up?'

'Let's just say that the symbols-in-the-ground phenomenon isn't the only weird shit that's been happening around here. Then the men in the SUVs turned up, sticking their noses in and upsetting a lot of people.'

'And the other weird shit?'

'All I'm going to say is that it started happening a week ago and close to where the symbols appeared. Look, are you sure you're going to be OK?'

'Probably not, but I'm doing this anyway. If you see me on any missing person's poster, you'll know it all went south from here.'

'Well, know that you can stay with me if you need a mate.

But I really think—' Greg froze and peered past me into the hammering rain.

'What?' I turned to see two pops of light in a distant field.

My heart raced. *Bloody hell!* Could this be it, my first honest-to-god UFO encounter? But my initial euphoria washed away as I took in Greg's panicked expression.

He leapt into the Punto and floored the accelerator. Oily smoke billowed out of the exhaust as the car shot back up the lane. So much for him looking out for me. Whatever it was we'd just seen had put the fear of god into the guy.

A police officer had once told me you were either a runner or a chaser after I'd tackled a man who'd snatched an old lady's handbag. I'd wrestled the guy to the ground before I'd had a chance to think about what I was doing. I was a chaser, and Greg was obviously a runner.

I scowled at the retreating vehicle and returned my attention to the bursts of light on the gentle hillside. Could it really be this easy? The intensity of the rain combined with the darkness made it near impossible to see what was going on over there. And there was only one answer to that.

My heart sped up as I skirted a field along a low-lying stone wall, ready to throw myself flat on my face at the first sign of trouble.

The rain streamed into my eyes, making the bursts of light blur as if I were looking at them through a waterfall. I eventually drew less than a hundred metres away, and disappointment swirled within me. Whatever this was, it definitely wasn't my first shiny UFO. Three men were silhouetted in the gloom, gathered round a large boulder. Their head torches flickered over the rock in front of them. A flashgun burst came from a camera held by one of the figures and I found myself staring at a cow lying dead on its side.

Could it be...?

My mouth tanged with adrenaline as I shuffled along the stone wall, wind howling over the top of it.

I drew level with the group on the other side, slowly raised my head and the air caught in my lungs. Christmas had just arrived early and I wasn't talking about a knitted jumper, but rather the keys to a shiny new sports car.

Caught in the beam of the men's head torches was the cow's flank, with a missing circular plug of flesh half a metre wide. Exposed entrails had been cut cleanly like snipped sections of hosepipe. The incisions looked millimetre-perfect too, like a laser had carved straight through flesh and bone.

My healthy obsession with hospital drama reruns stopped me from hurling what was left of my breakfast. That and the giddy state of euphoria now flooding through me.

A whole year of dead ends, but this time I had a real lead.

And then things got even better.

On the ground between me and the cow was a triangular symbol with a circle on it, similar in design to the geometrical symbols that Sentinel had used to communicate with me. And here it was almost on top of Skara Brae. Was that significant?

Its surface glittered silver as the light from the men's head torches kept catching it. Was this a message from the AI? I'd heard nothing from him since he'd vanished. But if so, what the hell was the mutilated cow about?

From my vantage point, it looked like the quartz surface of the symbol had pushed up from the turf, its perfect symmetrical edges cutting through the grass.

One of the men withdrew a syringe full of blood from the cow and stood up.

'We need to get this sample back to the lab and analysed,' he said. 'We also need to get a team here to clean this up.'

The other two men nodded. They began to strip off their forensic suits and stuff them into a holdall. I ducked down as they started along the hill towards where I was hiding. Thankfully the storm made me hard to spot and I didn't hear them shout any challenge. I kept still as they opened a gate and descended the field towards the shoreline. For the first time I took in the flood-lights illuminating the undulating mounds of earth and recognised it immediately from the photos – Skara Brae, the ancient Neolithic site. And if Greg was right, Jack Harper would be working there, making it my next destination, but first...

I waited a good five minutes as the team walked directly towards the mounds before I risked moving. Then I headed quickly towards the symbol.

If anything, the quartz rune exceeded all my expectations. A photo on a forum was one thing, but seeing a symbol for myself was on another level. The circular geometric rune was beyond perfect. Everyone in the UFO community was certain these things weren't a hoax and seeing it for myself I had to agree. The amount of effort needed to create something like this would have been ridiculous.

I knelt by the symbol and placed my hand on its milky quartz surface. It felt warm to the touch. That had to be significant. Beside it was a small hole I assumed the men had dug, which exposed a root of the same crystal material. It appeared to be burrowing into the ground almost like a tree would. Could this thing have grown from the earth somehow?

I took out my waterproof camera and began to take pictures of the symbol from every angle. I shot at least a hundred photos before I stopped. But I had something else to record too. With a deep breath, I headed over to the cow.

I felt a wave of sadness sweep over me as I gazed down at the dead animal. The cow looked serene, considering half of its flank was missing. Whatever had killed it, it must have been quick, going by the lack of fear in the cow's expression. Hopefully that meant the poor animal hadn't realised what was happening.

I leant in for a closer look. The wound itself had been seared, the edges of the neat incision burned black. Behind the faint smell of charred flesh there was also a distinct whiff of ammonia in the air.

Movement at the far end of the field caught my eye. I got ready to run but then made out the shapes. A herd of cows had their bodies pushed right up against the wall, as far away from their fallen friend as possible. I wasn't an animal psychologist, but their behaviour suggested that they were well and truly freaked out by what had happened.

So this was it. I'd found my first gold nugget of truth. Now I needed to check out Skara Brae itself and see if my detective work would bear fruit there too.

Pocketing my camera, I placed my hand on the cow. Its flesh was still soft. No rigor mortis yet. So had this just happened, maybe only a few hours ago? And was its death linked somehow to the symbol's appearance?

I needed to talk this through with the UFO experts on the forums – people with experience of this sort of phenomenon. When I'd found a secure connection, one I couldn't be traced on, I'd reach out for their help.

Silhouettes of people moved in front of the floodlights down at the Skara Brae site. No doubt government investigators, probably MI5 going by my past experience, would be talking to Jack Harper to find out if he'd witnessed anything.

I patted the cow, feeling another tug of sadness for the fallen animal. I turned away, rain swirling around me. I kept low again as I stole down the sloping hill towards the ancient Neolithic site beside the shoreline. Hopefully there I'd discover more answers.

CHAPTER FOUR

THE RUMBLE of breaking surf grew louder as I worked my way towards the rolling mounds of the 5,000-year-old Skara Brae. My toes were beginning to grow numb in boots that had given up the fight to try to keep my feet dry ages ago.

But even with every discomfort and encounter with wary locals thrown in, this trip was still going to be worth it. When I'd charted the appearance of the Angelus symbols on the Orkney Islands, I'd noticed a pattern to their arrangement. The final missing part of that puzzle had been completed when a diver had found a crystal symbol on the seabed a few miles out from here a couple of weeks ago. It meant that Skara Brae was bang in the middle of a tightening spiral along which the different symbol sites were located. If I'd thought there might still be an element of chance at play here, that'd been swept away by the discovery of the mutilated cow and the latest symbol. I knew Skara Brae was significant, and I needed to find out why.

I knew from pictures of the site I'd studied that the mounds ahead of me were actually the outside grass-covered walls of a network of ruined rooms. Their roofs long gone, the Neolithic rooms were exposed to the elements.

Sheets of rain squalled in the beams from the floodlights that picked out a group of people on the mounds. I lost sight of them as they stepped down into the ruins.

It took me a moment to take in the scene. It was certainly easy to see why some people thought that these turf-covered buildings were the inspiration for J. R. R. Tolkien's famous hobbit holes. All I knew was that the comfort-loving Bilbo Baggins would have seriously hated this weather.

I crept silently towards one of the lower walls ringing the mounds, not that anyone could have heard me over the snarling wind.

I pulled myself slowly on to the grass ledge above the wall. The chilled earth sucked out what little body heat I had left. I crawled flat to the ground up the slope and peered over the edge. My the-truth-is-out-there mission was all well and good, but a hot bath needed to be in my immediate future after all this.

Below me was a network of roofless rooms, their stone walls partly broken down. The rooms were arranged in a random petal shape round a central courtyard area.

A huddle of people stood at the far end. Three of them I recognised as those who'd been examining the mutilated cow. They were talking to a guy whose neatly bearded face I could just see beneath the hood of his cagoule. Next to him stood a man who was almost a head taller. His blond hair whipped around in the wind, but he stood like an oak tree against the elements whistling past him. He *had* to be the Viking. The nickname certainly really suited him – all the guy needed was a horned helmet and he'd be set.

Whatever their conversation, I was curious to hear it, especially if it related to the cow and the symbol.

I began to shuffle my way along the top of the wall, using my elbows and knees in a snake-like crawl. Metre by metre I closed on the group, and as I neared the ledge above the people I began to make out their conversation.

'We've taken blood from the cow, Robert,' the man who'd taken the sample said.

The bearded man nodded. 'Then we'll need to run the usual battery of tests. Have you ordered a recovery team in yet?'

'Already on their way, although in this storm they won't be able to get a helicopter out here. They might have to wait until tomorrow.'

'Then tomorrow it will have to be. In the meantime, order our reconnaissance teams across the island to get back here and form a secure perimeter a mile out around this entire site. With the notable exception of Mr Jack Harper here, as long as he signs the confidentiality agreement, I don't want anyone else entering or leaving Skara Brae without my express permission. We'll tell the locals that an unexploded bomb has been discovered. That shouldn't be too much of stretch for them to believe with the amount of ordinance that was dropped on these islands during World War Two.'

A secure perimeter sounded like bad news for my escape, but I'd worry about getting through that once I learnt what I could here.

The Viking, aka Jack Harper, scowled at Robert over the top of a waterproofed iPad he'd just been handed.

The forensic team headed towards a series of steps that led up on to the ridge where I was lying. With no time to go anywhere else, I pressed myself flat into the coarse, wet grass. The smell of earthy peat filled my nose. I didn't breathe, didn't so much as move a millimetre, as the men reached the top of the surrounding wall. Luckily, they were too busy trying to stay upright in the howling wind to notice me. Even so, I waited until they had disappeared round the corner of the visitor centre before risking raising my head again.

Robert was gesturing towards the tablet that Jack was still holding and frowning at. 'Let's just get this formality out of the way and sign the bloody thing.'

Jack drummed his fingers on the side of the tablet. 'Why should I sign your MI5 gagging order?' he said in a mid-west American accent.

'I can assure you that you have no option but to sign this, Mr Harper. The alternative will be very unpleasant for you.'

There it was, although I had half suspected it already: MI5 already had feet on the ground here and were making threats as usual... Just like Kiera had rough-handed me and the others back at Jodrell Bank after we'd intercepted the Sentinel signal.

'Hey, I'm not even a British citizen, so what gives you the right to pressure me like this, buddy?'

'That may be true, Mr Harper, but, as I'm sure you're aware, our two nations have always worked closely together, especially on areas that are considered to be of national security. So even though you might not be one of our own, rest assured that the US authorities will follow our lead and take all necessary steps to make sure your silence is maintained.'

God, this guy was just as hard-nosed as Kiera had been with me. She'd had a job to do, just like Robert here had. What that job was exactly became more intriguing with every passing second.

Jack's knuckles stood out as he gripped the tablet harder. 'Are you trying to threaten me?'

Robert shook his head. 'Not so much threaten you, but make you a promise that your career will take a spectacular nosedive if you don't cooperate. So let's make this easy for both of us and just sign it.'

Jack held Robert's gaze for a moment, shook his head,

unclipped a stylus from the side of the iPad's case and scribbled his signature on the screen.

He handed the tablet and stylus back to Robert. 'And you know where you can shove that.'

Robert gave him a thin smile. 'Seeing as we're now such good friends, you have my word that you can continue with your work here uninterrupted. Just keep clear of our area of interest in the field where the cow and symbol were discovered. As a sign of my country's appreciation, the government will be sending a very generous contribution to Harvard University to help you continue your research work there. I also will do what I can to find out about your friend Mike. You see, we look after our friends.'

Jack tipped his chin up a fraction towards Robert. Going by the way he had planted his feet slightly apart and clenched and unclenched his hands, I got the distinct impression that he was fighting the urge to thump Robert in the face.

Fortunately for the MI5 officer, who was also probably reading Jack's body language, he turned round and headed off after his team.

I sprawled flat on the grass once again as Robert passed me.

A moment later, I heard the scrape of metal. I edged forward and peeked down to see Jack using a trowel to scrape away a shallow impression in the middle of the roofless room.

Greg hadn't been exaggerating about this guy being driven. Here he was working on a winter's night in a full-blown gale, with MI5 officers crawling all over the place and a cow carved up like a biology experiment gone badly wrong. It seemed none of that was going to deter Jack from continuing his excavation. And I recognised that sort of determination in the dark-haired woman who stared back at me from the mirror every morning. Hopefully that shared trait would make this next bit go as well as it possibly could. Time to announce my presence.

I stood up and the wind immediately shoved into my back, trying to tip me head first into the site. I leant into the gale as I walked round the lip of the mound until I reached the stairs.

Here went nothing.

'Hey there,' I said.

The Viking turned round and his shoulders slumped as he saw me. 'Hell, what now?'

'My name is Lauren Stelleck and I'd just like to ask you a few questions.' I followed that with my best winning smile.

'I've already wasted enough time tonight talking to you people, miss, to last me several lifetimes. That Robert Lloyd guy promised me I wouldn't be bothered any more.'

'You don't understand. I'm not with them.'

His eyes narrowed on me. 'You're not?'

'No, but I do have a personal interest in what's been happening around here.'

His eyes widened. 'You're here about Mike?'

'Who?'

'Oh...I thought you might be an old girlfriend looking out for him.' He shook his head. 'But don't tell me, you're a journalist after a scoop about what happened in the field over there.' He gestured towards where the cow had been found.

'Not that either.' I gave him a small shrug in the way of an apology, preparing to hit him with the next bit because I knew just how crazy it would sound.

His cobalt-blue eyes locked on to mine as his blond hair fluttered in the wind. I pictured him standing at the stern of a Viking longboat as it charged towards a beach for a raid. God, the guy was seriously gorgeous. In other circumstances... I shook my head to keep myself focused.

He groaned. 'Oh no, not another friggin' one.'

'Another what?'

'You're another damned UFO chaser, aren't you?'

I would have reacted exactly like this a year ago. But then I'd encountered Sentinel and my life had changed.

'I've had personal experience of strange phenomena,' I said, 'if that's what you're getting at.'

'What, they did the whole rectal-probing thing on you and now you're a true believer, right?'

I glowered at the guy. What an absolute arse. I lowered my gaze, trying to keep my anger in check. I noticed his wedding band. Poor woman to live with a dickhead like this. Then I met his eyes again. 'For your information, Jack Harper, I've had access to some highly classified information about UFOs. And if it kills me, I'm determined to get the truth out there.'

Jack stared off into space over my left shoulder. 'Yeah right.'

This was going so well, but I pushed on anyway. Even if this guy was a twenty-carat gold-plated jerk, I still needed to find out if he knew anything.

'Look, just answer my questions and I'll get out of your way. Do you know anything about how the crystal marking appeared in that field?'

'No, not a thing. All I know is that it appeared about a week ago in the middle of the night.'

'And the cow mutilation?'

'That only happened yesterday. Again, I didn't see a thing, just like I told the others.'

'And this Mike guy you mentioned. Am I right in guessing that something happened to him?'

Jack crossed his arms. 'If you don't know, I'm not going to say.'

'So in other words, you're letting that MI5 officer get to you with his threats.'

He glared at me. 'Look, I've got work to do. And I'm in a bad enough mood already. So just do me a favour and go back to whatever hole you crawled out of.'

Anger surged through my limbs as he turned his back on me. 'Oh, you can fuck right off.' I pointed at the gold band on his finger, which glistened with raindrops. 'And whomever your wife is, she has the patience of a saint to put up with an idiot like you.'

Jack whirled round, his face a snarl.

I instinctively took a half step back, recognising I'd crossed some sort of line. Thankfully Jack funnelled his fury at the trowel near his feet and kicked out at it, sending it over the ground and striking the stone wall with a loud clang.

Jack glowered at me. 'Get out of here now before I do something stupid!'

But I barely noticed what he was saying because the clanging sound bouncing off the broken walls rang in my ears, growing louder until it drowned out even the screaming storm.

I squeezed my hands over my ears but that did nothing to stop the deafening noise. The floor and walls began to vibrate as the sound grew deeper, a bass note so powerful I was sure it could have cracked the world into two. The Neolithic site started to blur around me.

But Jack didn't seem to be reacting at all. Instead, he was looking at me with something approaching concern in his eyes. His lips moved but I couldn't hear what he was saying over the thundering noise.

With a shudder, every surface was bathed in brilliant light, casting Jack and the site into monochrome brilliance. Then geometrical patterns began to rush around me, locking into place around the ruins. Squares, triangles and circles now covered every surface like a hologram overlay. Angelus symbols.

The patterns faded away to be replaced by countless points of lights floating in a disc shape with spiral arms centred on the courtyard.

My mind barely had a chance to register the galaxy pattern as the image started to zoom in, the stars skimming past me as the view focused on a region near the tip of one of the spiral arms. Planets sped by – a large gas giant with rings, another gas giant with a big storm spot...

Jupiter!

My brain felt like it was being boiled from the inside out as Mars rushed by and the view hurtled to Earth. I briefly registered the hologram of our own moon passing straight through Jack's body. He didn't so much as flinch as he stared at me. Part of my mind realised that he wouldn't be seeing any of this light show.

The view pitched over and plummeted down towards Earth, towards Scotland, towards the Orkneys, towards Skara Brae...

I screamed as searing pain roared through my mind. I crashed on to the floor as blackness flooded my thoughts and the world vanished around me.

CHAPTER FIVE

I OPENED my eyes and found myself in a room with grey daylight leaking through a gap in the checked curtains. Around me the shelves were lined with what looked to be mostly archaeology books.

Where the hell am I?

As the numbness of my unconsciousness fell away, the rush of previous events flooded my head. I'd been at the Skara Brae site where I'd met Jack Harper, the guy who'd given me all that attitude. He'd kicked that trowel at the ground in a hissy fit, the sound of it striking rock triggering my synaesthesia and... I shook my head at the memory...a holographic display of the Milky Way had appeared.

Shit!

This whole wild experience had all the fingerprints of the Angelus on it, the race that had created Sentinel.

And whatever grinding pain that my head had suffered, I didn't have even the hint of a headache now. But before I could mentally process this further, I heard footsteps on the other side of the closed bedroom door.

I sat up and realised I was wearing only my bra and knickers beneath the soft duvet. Someone must have undressed me after I'd passed out. I scanned the room but couldn't see my clothes anywhere.

Oh, double shit!

So had Jack carried me to wherever this was, probably his house, after I'd passed out? I took a mental breath as I quickly pulled the duvet up to my chin as I sat up

Just chill, Lauren. It was probably his long-suffering wife who undressed you.

The bedroom door opened and Jack entered carrying a super-sized mug swirling with steam.

Was that the hint of a smile on his face as he saw me clutch the duvet to me like a defensive shield?

Bastard!

'Relax, it's nothing I haven't seen before,' Jack said, setting the mug down on the bedside cabinet.

I felt my face flame. 'Not *my* body you haven't, mister.'

Again he gave that quick infuriating smile of his. 'Maybe not.'

I narrowed my gaze on him. 'Please tell me your wife undressed me?'

Instead of a smile, this time I caught a brief look of pain flicker through Jack's face before he shook his head. 'I undressed you.' He held up his hands. 'And before you let loose at me, I didn't have a choice. You were unconscious. I had to get you out of your wet clothes before you caught pneumonia. Your body temperature was through the floor.'

So this complete stranger had seen way more of me than anyone before a third date was ever allowed.

Despite my embarrassment, I found my gaze lingering on Jack. He'd transformed from the wild Viking of the previous night into someone who'd looked, well...just a bit hot actually.

My eyes wandered over him without any conscious

command from me. He was wearing a thick lumberjack-style blue checked shirt, the sleeves rolled up to reveal well-toned forearms. His hands were slightly rough and calloused, no doubt due to all the archaeological digging, but delicate too, with the fingers of a pianist. But it was those cobalt-blue eyes he kept flashing my way that seemed to be directly linked to the swirly feeling in my stomach. And all that framed by neatly groomed shoulder-length blond hair. Yep, seriously hot...

Good grief, woman, you saw something incredible last night and all you can do is get it bad for a married man. Get a grip, Lauren.

'So what does your wife have to say about you having a gorgeous half-naked woman in your spare bedroom?'

Once again I saw a slight flicker in his expression. Shit, I'd put my foot in it again, like I had last night. Maybe Jack was divorced and I was picking at an old emotional scar. I mentally frowned at the highly inappropriate ripples in my stomach resulting from the prospect that this guy might be on the market.

'Actually, this is my room,' Jack said.

My brain went straight to the inevitable conclusion: unconscious me plus hot guy equals...

My horror was obviously written in big neon letters across my face because Jack quickly shook his head.

'Lauren, relax. I slept downstairs on the couch.'

My shoulders dropped from where they'd shot up round my neck. 'Good...' I ignored the twinge of disappointment.

'Anyway, haven't we got more important things to discuss than our sleeping arrangements last night?' Jack said as he sat in a chair at the end of the bed.

I was glad one of us had their priorities straight. I nodded. 'Where do you want to kick off?'

'Let's start with what happened to you. One moment you were all Miss Sarcastic and in my face. The next you were sprawled out unconscious. I checked your vitals but they seemed fine, apart from your body temperature being sub-zero. That's why I immediately brought you back here to get you warmed up.'

'Please tell me you managed to do that without tipping off those MI5 guys I was there?'

'Chill. They weren't in the car park when I put you into the back of my Land Rover.'

'Oh, thank Christ.'

Jack's eyes probed mine. 'So I'm guessing you're trying to keep a low profile with them?'

'Let's just say I had to sign a similar gagging order as the one Robert made you sign. You see, I wasn't meant to pursue anything I'd found out at Jodrell Bank – the place I used to work – including proof that aliens are real.'

His gaze widened a fraction. 'Right... And that's the radio telescope place, correct?'

'Yes. And, look, I know I probably sound like a conspiracy nutter to you, but the more I've investigated since quitting my job, the more I've come to believe that at least five per cent of sightings are real and can't be explained away.'

He shrugged. 'Each to their own.'

'Look, I'm not here to convince you of anything. But anyway, thank you for looking out for me last night.'

'No problem. Someone needed to. If I hadn't seen an improvement this morning, it would have been an ambulance for you and a CT scan at the local hospital.'

'You sound like you have some medical training?'

'Something like that. So what do you think caused your blackout?'

I gazed at Jack, trying to work him out. He wasn't a Viking in any sense of the word. No, Jack Harper was an archaeologist and a university academic. And a guy who'd done me a massive favour.

My attitude towards him started to soften. After all, I'd crashed his dig site and thrown weird questions at him. The cherry on the cake was me swooning to the floor. Despite all that, he had helped me, rather than turn me straight over to MI5. Yes, he was one of the good guys.

Maybe me feeling more than a touch vulnerable, not helped by my lack of clothes, was what made me just blurt the truth out about what I'd seen.

'OK, if you really want to know what happened, it went like this. When you kicked your trowel across the floor and it made a clanging sound, it triggered something inside me.'

'An epileptic fit?'

'Nothing like that. But the noise kept growing louder in my head. I'm guessing that you didn't hear any of it?'

Jack shook his head. 'Beyond the initial sound of the trowel hitting, nothing else.' He peered at me. 'You haven't had any sort of head trauma recently?'

'No, I'm fine, both physically and mentally – just in case you're getting at it being some sort of psychotic break.'

He gave me a guilty look. 'You can't blame me.'

'No, I can't, because I would do the same in your position. But if you really want to know, here it is...' I took big mental breath. This was my opportunity to reveal my unusual gift, getting it out of the way to make everything easier to explain. 'I have something known as synaesthesia. Basically, certain sounds trigger light patterns in my vision.'

'Synaesthesia...and a visual manifestation. Interesting.'

'You sound like you know something about it?'

'Yeah, I do... What sort of things do you see when it's triggered, Lauren?'

I was taken aback by Jack's calm response and the fact he wasn't staring at me like some sort of freak. Normally I'd have to go into a lengthy explanation about how my brain combined my senses in a unique way. Most people immediately assumed I was a bit of a psycho until I stepped them through it. But with Jack, it had been effortless. Maybe he knew somebody with the same condition?

With one hand holding the duvet up above my chest to maintain some semblance of modesty, I picked up the mug of tea with the other and took a sip. It quickly worked its magic and I felt myself relax even further.

'I have to say this makes a refreshing change to the usual reaction I get.'

'I guess I've encountered a few things in my life to make me open-minded. Anyway, I'm interested to hear what happened to you last night.'

'In that case, I'll skip straight to when my synaesthesia kicked off. Jack, I saw something incredible...really incredible...'

'What flavour of incredible?'

I took another slurp of tea. This guy could certainly make a good brew. Another box ticked. Handsome and with great tea-making abilities.

Focus, Lauren... I inwardly sighed at myself again.

'The only way I can describe it is that it was like a hologram of the Milky Way conjured up within the ruins of Skara Brae. The hologram zoomed into our solar system and kept on going until it reached Earth.'

'You're seriously trying to tell me that you saw some sort of galactic star chart in the ruins of a Neolithic site?'

'I am. And all the crazy doesn't stop there, Jack. You see, the hologram continued to zoom in on Skara Brae, which was ringed with a red circle.'

'Which means what?'

'I wish I knew.'

Jack tipped his head to one side as he peered at me. 'Now don't go off at the deep end on me again, but it was you who raised the subject of a psychotic break. Do you have any history of mental health issues in your family?'

I crossed my arms, furious that he would even think that. The duvet slipped down to expose black bra. I just stared at him out, mentally challenging him to stare at my tits. But whatever else Jack Harper was, he seemed to be a decent guy – his eyes stayed firmly on mine, not once straying south.

I made a huffing sound as I pulled the duvet back up to cover myself back up. 'No, I'm as sane as you are, mate.'

'You're certain about what you saw?' Jack asked, his expression now unreadable.

'Of course I am. I wouldn't be telling you otherwise, because of exactly this kind of reaction. Oh, and there was this vibration running through the site during the whole experience too.'

Jack did the last thing I expected him to do. He leapt up and started pacing the room.

'I fucking knew it! This all fits, Lauren. Mike would have been all over this.'

'And that would that be because?'

'Mike's an amateur geophysicist – when he isn't working in a surfing shop on the other side of the island. He's been studying a strange vibration that had been reported throughout Orkney. With his equipment he tracked the seismic activity to its epicentre at Skara Brae, which is how I got to know him.'

'You're telling me that earthquakes have been hitting Orkney?'

'Nothing as dramatic as that. More like a vibration so faint that most people can't sense it. But birds, cats, dogs and livestock across the island have all been going crazy. Even shoals of fish have vanished, upsetting the fishermen. What with that and the more recent bout of cattle mutilations, you can imagine what the locals are saying.'

'That aliens like fish and chips, with a steak on the side?'

His dazzling smile flashed my way again before it vanished. 'Let's just say I have heard some people who should know better referring to it as witchcraft.'

'Seriously?'

'Yep, but you know what people are like. Superstition can quickly take over from rational thought. Anyway, the vibration that Mike was studying has to have something to do with what you saw and felt. I mean, it can't be a coincidence that Skara Brae seems to be the source of the vibration and it triggered your synaesthesia in such a unique way.'

'You sound like you're starting to open up to what I saw...'

'Maybe, but it's still a stretch from there to little green aliens.'

'I didn't say that's what it was.'

'So what is it then?'

'I wish I knew. Did Mike discover where this vibration was coming from exactly? A sort of geological fault beneath the island – something like that?'

'That's what he was working on at Skara Brae, installing all his kit and running a battery of tests. He was also interested in the geology behind the crystal markings, and told me that there was no way the quartz should be able to form anything within a matter of hours. His hunch was that the vibration had to be linked to the markings' appearances somehow, even though it flew in the face of normal geology.'

'This Mike sounds like an interesting guy. An amateur geophysicist, you said?'

'Something like that, although Mike was always vague when I asked anything more about it. Anyway, this is where his story gets truly freaky. His computer-modelling software indicated that there was a sine-wave pattern to the vibrations at Skara Brae, almost like the beat of a very slow drum. The program he wrote predicted the next beat in that pulse was due to happen again a few days ago. Mike was there by himself monitoring the site when it happened.'

I sat up straighter in the bed. 'Did Mike witness something?'

'Much more than that, Lauren. I'd left him to it on the site and was heading back home. But I'd only driven about a mile away when I saw an intense flash of light in my rear-view mirror. I immediately turned round, thinking there'd been some sort of explosion. But by the time I got back there was no sign of any damage. And no sign of Mike either. That was when I called the authorities. Problem was, the police drew a complete blank and said Mike being missing was an unexplained disappearance. But everything changed the next day when that symbol appeared in the field next to the site. Last night we had the cow mutilation thrown into the mix and MI5 turned up this morning, asking me if I'd seen any other phenomena.'

'Such as?'

He pointed to the sky and raised his eyebrows at me.

'Seriously, after everything you said, MI5 actually asked you whether you saw a UFO?'

'Well, they called it a UAP – an unexplained aerial phenomenon.'

'Same difference.'

'So why go off at the deep end with me when I suggested alien involvement?'

'Look, Lauren. I'm a rational guy. I don't go in much for flights of fantasy, even one being investigated by your UK security services. But now you turn up and claim to have seen sort of galactic map at the archaeological site that Mike was investigating. Mike who is now missing. Combine that with all the quartz symbols, markings whose origins no one can explain, plus the cattle mutilations, then maybe I'm prepared to open my mind up to the possibility that something weird has been happening on Orkney.'

So Jack really was starting to believe me. If I'd had a few more clothes on, I would have jumped out of bed and flung my arms round this guy. Some days I found myself questioning my own sanity, but he was listening to me. And even if I didn't understand the connections yet, everything Jack had just told me suggested that I was definitely in the right place.

I lifted the mug of tea and took a large sip, its taste sharpening my mind. 'So you say you saw a flash of light. Any ideas about what that might have been?'

'I know what you think it was.'

'It's hard not to, Jack. With the cattle mutilations and the rest, we're into classic abduction territory here.'

'Apart from the fact I didn't actually see a flying saucer and Mike being levitated into it by a beam of light.'

'So what do you think it was then?'

'Maybe the flash was part of Mike's kit blowing up.' Jack rubbed the back of his neck. 'Hell, I don't know, Lauren. Maybe Mike staged it all and had a massive life insurance policy ready to pay out. The guy was seriously short of cash, hence him working in a surf shop.'

'But I thought an insurance company would need a body for a payout?'

'Yeah, I guess they normally do.' He sighed. 'I wish I had an explanation. It's been slowly driving me crazy.'

'If you're not there yet, this next bit may tip you over the edge. You see, there's another part of this puzzle I haven't told you.'

'Hit me with it.'

'My own research into what's been happening suggests that either the Skara Brae site, or at least its location, is significant.'

'How so?'

'The crystal symbols form a spiral when linked together, which centres exactly on Skara Brae.'

'You're saying there's a direct link?' Jack asked.

'My instinct says yes, but I have no idea how. I sense we're glimpsing parts of a much bigger truth here. What that truth is, and whether it somehow might be linked to alien activity, will be down to us to uncover and tell the world.'

'Hey, what's with this *us* thing? I don't remember agreeing to join your little-green-aliens crusade?' Jack said.

'You do want to know what's going on, though, don't you? You want to know what's happened to Mike?'

'Yeah, when you put it like that, I guess I do.'

'In that case, you get the coffee on whilst I grab a shower,' I said.

'No problem, but your clothes are still drying out. You're more than welcome to wear some of my wife's old things. You're about the same size and build, so her clothes should fit you.'

'That would be great, if it won't cause any problems?'

'It won't. I'll leave some things out for you.'

What was the situation here? I was desperate to find out more. 'She certainly must be an understanding woman. Especially after you bring a strange girl home with you last night – one who is about to start parading around your house in her clothes.'

'It won't be an issue. My wife is no longer here.' Jack's face clouded again. Without another word he headed towards the door and closed it behind him.

So my initial hunch had been right. Jack was divorced or separated and obviously taking it badly. I stared after him. I'd asked a question too far and scratched at his wound. Even talking about her was clearly still painful to him. I brought my knees up, rested my head against them and groaned.

Idiot!

CHAPTER SIX

Sporting Jack's wife's jeans and an old sports top, I slowly walked Jack through what had happened back at Jodrell Bank whilst we ate breakfast. How, during the graveyard shift, we'd captured an FRB signal with Lovell's dish that had originated in a parallel universe, so we'd found out. If Jack looked shell-shocked by that particular revelation, it was nothing compared to when I told him that the signal had contained the code for an alien AI called Sentinel – the discovery of which had inadvertently dragged the world towards the brink of World War Three.

And then I hit him with the punchline about how Sentinel had been created by an alien race called the Angelus. I explained that once the code for the AI had finished compiling on our systems, Sentinel had immediately begun trawling for information about experiments into dark energy called the Dark Energy Collector, or DEC. It had later been on the news when it'd blown up the following week and had taken out a whole science park with it. If that'd been a bad or good thing, I had no idea. But as a result of the AI's research, during which he'd hacked into highly classified government files, he had inadvertently revealed that

UFO phenomena were real, a truth that had been suppressed since the 1950s. I then hit Jack with the fact that the geometrical symbols on Orkney bore a strong resemblance to the ones that Sentinel had used to communicate with me.

After all that, Jack stared at me with his jaw literally hanging open.

Minutes later we were in the Land Rover, a bent and bruised vehicle that had definitely passed its sell-by date, bouncing down the track away from his cottage towards the main road. Above us the low winter sun shone in a clear blue sky, the storm of the previous night now a distant memory.

'I still say I'm concerned about you trying this again, Lauren,' Jack said, giving me a sideways glance.

I finished off the last of the drink laced with electrolytes. Jack had insisted on giving it to me straight after my coffee. 'Will you please stop worrying? I'm going to be fine. Anyway, if it gets too much for me, you can always drag me off the site before I pass out. Whatever happens, this is going to be worth it. This is huge, Jack. It doesn't get much bigger than discovering solid evidence that an alien intelligence was involved in some way with an ancient site such as Skara Brae, especially when you add the hologram into the mix.'

'If it is true, the implications for our world are massive. Everything from history to science to religion would be shaken up.'

'Jack, if I can prove it, the world as we know it will be changed for ever.'

'And how will you prove it?'

'I'll try to conjure up that hologram again to see if we can learn any more. We know my last encounter didn't do me any permanent harm, so it's certainly worth trying again.'

'We *think* it didn't do you any lasting harm,' Jack said. 'For all we know it could be frying your brain. Only a CRT scan would confirm that one way or the other.'

'Look, will you stop fussing? You've already shone a torch into my eyes. And as cute as you are, I'm not ready to start playing doctors and nurses with you just yet.'

Jack glanced across at me again. 'You think I'm cute?'

I arranged my face into a neutral expression. 'If you're into the whole wild Viking look, I guess so...but I'm really not. Anyway, what were you looking for in my eyes – my soul or something?'

A small smile lifted the corners of his mouth. 'That was to check for your pupil dilation response. It's the first indicator of a problem with the brain.'

'Do you have medical training, or is it too much time watching medical dramas like me?'

He shrugged. 'A bit of both. Anyway, any ideas about how we are going to replicate what happened to you last night? Assuming that you didn't have some sort of huge psychotic episode after all?'

'Thank you for that vote of confidence. To answer your question, the sound that you made with the trowel seemed to have acted as an acoustic trigger. My guess is that the site was somehow designed to create a visual response in somebody with an audio synaesthetic ability like mine. You just happened upon the right key to unlock, which of course had no effect on you.'

Jack pulled a face. 'Oh, come on, Lauren. You're telling me that our Neolithic ancestors worked with these Angelus to create some sort of acoustic map of the cosmos at Skara Brae – one that could be used by someone with synaesthesia? Seriously?'

'The famous sci-fi author Arthur C. Clarke once said. "Any sufficiently advanced technology is indistinguishable from magic." And the Angelus certainly have the tech to pull off what I witnessed. After all, Sentinel was able to communicate with me using my synaesthesia to create symbols. And I saw those same symbols at the start of the boot-up sequence last night. That supports the theory that the Skara Brae site is directly linked to the Angelus.'

'I'm sorry, but that still doesn't make sense. If we run with your idea that the original buildings were designed in such a unique way, why is it still working after thousands of years?'

'Angelus have really good batteries running their abandoned tech?' I raised my eyebrows a fraction.

Jack snorted. 'I didn't mean what's powering it, although that's an intriguing question in itself. I meant, if Skara Brae was designed to reflect sound in order to run some sort of high-tech celestial observatory, how can it still be working when the buildings are not much more than rubble?'

'I've no idea. But for whatever reason, it is. Maybe that's how we'll discover the answer to your question. Maybe there's a handy help file somewhere.'

Jack drummed the steering wheel with his fingers. 'You do know I'm having a real problem processing all of this. It sounds like a whole lot of crazy and part of me is wondering whether this is all some big wind-up on your part.'

'And I understand why you think that, Jack. I'd certainly be wondering the same in your shoes. But I promise you that everything I've told you is the absolute truth. Besides which, don't forget you saw a flash of light from Skara Brae the night that Mike disappeared. That has to be linked somehow.'

'Someone disappearing in odd circumstances is one thing. But you're seriously suggesting that Skara Brae was effectively the local drive-in for an alien race visiting Earth? Not to mention that they left us with some sort of galactic map that still works. Even a true believer like you must realise that this is something of a stretch for anyone to take on-board.'

'I know exactly how you feel, Jack. I was where you are a year ago. My view of the world was torn to shreds when Sentinel crashed into my life. And now I hang out on UFO forums. Go figure. All I ask is that you keep an open mind. And if you want to follow me down this rabbit hole, then that's great. If not, I get it. But the thing that I could do with most right now is a rational second opinion. If only to make sure that I'm really not losing my mind.'

'You haven't got anyone else that can help you with this?'

'Not anyone I don't want to expose to some very real danger.'

Jack stared at me. 'You're talking about MI5?'

'If only. There's an organisation that's far more dangerous and directly involved in the cover-up of UFOs – a cover-up that's been going on for decades.'

'And they are?'

'The Overseers, the hidden power that really runs this world. There's every chance they'll be interested in Skara Brae too, if they're not here already.'

'Oh, wow, I should've known, yet another conspiracy. I bet your bookshelf makes for fascinating reading.'

'It does. But that doesn't mean what I'm telling you isn't the utter truth.'

'And these Overseers, I suppose they're dangerous, right?'

'Very.'

'So you don't mind putting *me* in harm's way.'

'For goodness' sake, you look like a Viking. I'm sure you can handle yourself. Besides, you were in the wrong place at the right time, so you sort of got yourself into this.'

'Oh, so it's my fault now?'

'Wrong place, right time. Welcome to my world.'

'And you've been alone in this search for a while now?'

I nodded. 'A whole year.'

'That must have been quite a load at times.'

Losing Aunt Lucy, my old life destroyed, practically penniless... 'More than you can imagine.'

Jack sucked his cheeks and slowly nodded. 'OK, let's be honest. We got off on the wrong foot with each other.'

'That's a bit of understatement.'

'Yeah, it is. Anyway, I'm going to help you in any way I can, Lauren. Partly because I want to know what the hell happened to Mike. Also, you have more than caught my attention with everything you've told me. But more than any of that, I know what such a sense of isolation from the world can feel like. I'm on-board with this for as long as it takes.'

'Thank you...' Of course Jack knew what being alone felt like. He'd separated from his wife, a woman he still clearly loved, and had probably spent too many years solo since then. I'd been forced to abandon my friends in case the Overseers got to them. Then Aunt Lucy had been killed, the woman I'd been closest to, the person who had adopted that troubled child who used to wet the bed. I had no one either.

'You've gone quiet on me,' Jack said.

'Just thinking that I could certainly do with your support.'

'That's sorted then. But there is one thing you need to do for me now that I've signed up to this mad UFO-believers road trip.'

'Name it?'

'Can you get into the back and pull that green tarpaulin over your head? We'll be arriving at Skara Brae any moment and you don't want any of Robert's people to see you.'

'No problem.'

I unbuckled my seat belt and clambered over the seats. I wiggled down into a gap between several large canvas bags and crates filled with archaeological kit. Then I pulled a green plastic tarpaulin over the top of me. I breathed in the scent of earth, oil and damp, but I guessed this wouldn't be for too long. Plus Jack was right. If MI5 discovered I was here, I would have a hard time explaining my presence. Besides which, as the Overseers had managed to infiltrate MI5 once, why not again? I didn't much fancy another direct encounter with Mr Eye Scar, or anyone else who worked for them.

'Here we go – there are signs everywhere about their unexploded bomb and warnings to keep clear of the area,' Jack said. 'They've even set up a checkpoint at the gate.'

'You can't say that MI5 aren't efficient when it comes to a cover story.'

Jack snorted. 'But they're still amateurs when it comes to the CIA.'

'Probably.'

'OK, not a word until we arrive now and I give you the signal,' Jack said. 'Then we'll slip away from the car towards the dig site.'

'Got it.'

My blood thumped in my ears as the Land Rover began to slow. We came to a stop and a moment later I heard a tapping sound on glass. I listened to the Land Rover's window being wound down by hand on the old-school no-frills vehicle.

'Hi, I'm Jack Harper. I was told by your boss that I was still allowed access to Skara Brae.'

'Of course, Mr Harper,' a man's voice replied. 'You have been cleared to proceed. However, please restrict your movement to your immediate dig site whilst we carry on our investigations.'

'For that unexploded bomb, right?'

A chuckle. 'Precisely, Mr Harper.'

Seconds later we were on the move again.

'Respect to your MI5. They don't mess around,' Jack said. 'There's a Chinook in the field and a team of people are loading that cow on to it. At least it gets to travel out of here in style.'

'I suspect it would be happier to still be alive and munching grass,' I said.

'I assume the Angelus are responsible for that too?'

'Not necessarily. One theory on the UFO forums is that

cattle mutilations are a form of misdirection by the government to encourage people to be afraid of aliens.'

'You're saying MI5 are deliberately slaughtering livestock to give aliens bad PR?'

'Well, I'm not sure that theory fits here. Why would they bother to take blood samples if they did it? No, if someone is responsible, it's not them.'

'Who then? These mysterious Overseers of yours?'

'I certainly hope not. If they are already involved here, things could get seriously ugly.'

'People-getting-killed ugly, like what happened back at Jodrell Bank?'

'Exactly...' So far I'd skipped telling Jack about Aunt Lucy being a victim as well. That was still too raw for me to talk about.

The Land Rover came to a stop. 'Right, we're in the car park, but you'll need to lie low for a bit longer because that MI5 guy Robert is approaching.'

'Understood,' I whispered back.

I heard the door opening and Jack getting out.

'So how are you on this glorious day, Mr Harper?' I heard Robert ask him.

'Still annoyed because of all your disruptions to my work here,' Jack replied.

'Well, you'll be pleased to know we'll be out of your hair within the hour. We're heading over to the other side of the island to investigate the first crystal symbol that appeared there. However, I'm afraid we'll need to keep the cover story of the unexploded bomb going for a little while longer to make it convincing for the islanders. We will have a bomb disposal team fake a detonation on the beach for the full effect.'

'Don't forget that additional funding,' Jack said.

'I can assure you, Mr Harper, I am a man of my word.'

I heard footsteps walking away and then the back door of the Land Rover being pulled open.

'He's still watching me, so don't bring your head up yet and don't say anything,' Jack whispered as he started moving boxes around me.

I kept silent. It was a good three minutes later that Jack finally lifted the tarp.

I blinked in the bright sunlight. 'All good?'

'Yep,' Jack replied. 'They've headed up towards the Chinook, so we can go over to the dig site.'

'Thank god for that,' I said as I rubbed my back and climbed out. I slipped round to the far side of the Land Rover, using it to shield me from view.

'Stick to me, Lauren, and we should be able to make it to the site without you being spotted.'

'I'll be your shadow.'

Keeping Jack between myself and the men in the distant field, we headed towards Skara Brae. I glanced over at the Chinook. At least twenty people were gathered round the heli-copter, with Robert coordinating the loading of the pallet holding the cow. The beast was slowly being hauled over the grass by a winch into the back of the waiting Chinook.

'I'd love to see the forensic results for that cow's death,' I said.

'Wouldn't we all.'

We approached the rolling mounds of Skara Brae. Excite-ment pulsed through me as we stepped up on to the ridge over-looking the broken buildings and descended into the basin of the former Neolithic settlement. Had the Angelus really visited this site 5,000 years ago? Just thinking about it gave me the shivers.

When we entered the ruined room where I'd first seen the galactic map, my pulse kicked up, half expecting the world to explode with rainbow light. But nothing happened, and in the bright sunshine with the cry of gulls and murmur of the waves in the air, the vision of the previous night seemed like an impossible fantasy.

Jack turned to me. 'So let's get a few ground rules ironed out first, before you try again.'

'Such as?'

'That if it gets too much for you, we stop this immediately.'

'Yep. Anything else?'

'That you tell me exactly what you're seeing. Not all of us have your ability.'

'Glad to know that you're starting to treat synaesthesia as the gift that it is.'

'Seems that I am. So how are we going to replicate what happened last night? Should I strike the trowel on a stone again?'

'Maybe with a bit less attitude on both our parts this time,' I replied.

His smile lingered a bit longer than usual. 'Good plan.'

My brain noted that Jack seemed to be warming to me, as he picked up the trowel and squatted on the stone floor.

'Are you ready?' he said.

'Born that way,' I replied.

My heart threatened to burst out of my chest as he raised the trowel. I just knew I was on the edge of something that would change everything. For me, for Jack and, as we'd already discussed, maybe even the whole world.

CHAPTER SEVEN

THE TROWEL BLURRED as Jack struck it on the stone and my synaesthesia ignited. Like a ring of spreading flames, orange light cascaded out around the ruined room and symbols started to appear, hovering in mid-air. The ringing tone of the trowel began to fade.

I grinned at Jack. 'It's working...' But the symbols started to disappear as the sound grew softer. 'Shit, spoke too soon. We need to try again.'

'Got it,' Jack replied. He struck the trowel down on to the rock once more and the same metallic clang rang out. The symbols shimmered back into life but then vanished again as the sound faded.

'Same thing happened. The sound isn't ramping up in my head like it did before.'

'Like when you strike a match and it keeps blowing out in the wind?'

'I guess so.'

'In that case, we need to protect our metaphorical flame.'

'How exactly?'

Jack took out his phone and opened a voice memo app. Rather than hold it to his mouth, he moved it next to the stone he'd been hitting and pressed record. He struck the stone with the trowel again, but as soon as the clang started to fade, he hit the stop button. Jack pressed the loop function and a moment later the note was playing over and over.

My vision erupted with kaleidoscopic light.

'Working now?' Jack asked.

Excitement ratcheted up inside me as the symbols steadied and locked into place. 'Oh god, yes, and it's not stopping this time either.'

A flock of floating particles coalesced to form a miniature architectural hologram of Skara Brae hanging in the air before me. I barely had a chance to take in the incredible detail that even showed the tumbling stone from the walls before the image started to shrink away as the view zoomed upwards. The site receded to a dot and soon the whole globe of Earth was revealed. It was as if I were on a fast rollercoaster as our planet shrank into the distance, followed shortly by our entire solar system, until the view finally slowed to a stop.

'My god, it's full of stars,' I whispered.

'2001: *A Space Odyssey*, right?'

'You are so on my wavelength, Jack.' I grinned, a sense of elation sweeping over me as I took in the hologram equivalent of an orrery view of our solar system.

'Don't forget the running commentary you're meant to be giving me,' Jack said.

'Yes, sorry. It's the galactic map again. The view has shot away from Earth again and has moved above the orbital plane.'

'The what?'

'The plane that our planets orbit the sun around.'

'Got it,' Jack replied. 'So how is your head doing this time round? Any danger of passing out again?'

I hadn't even thought about how I was feeling, I'd been so caught up in the phenomenon I was witnessing. I did a physical inventory and everything came up green.

'Great, actually. But if that changes, I'll say.'

'Make sure you do.'

The hologram began to zoom out until I was hovering over a spiral arm of the Milky Way. I could see Earth's sun among a number of neighbouring stars picked out with a green marker. A solid red line between the sun and a star I recognised as the relatively nearby Tau Ceti had appeared too. As spectacular as this was, I didn't understand why I was seeing this.

As if in answer, the view started to hurtle in towards the Tau Ceti system. Four rocky planets shot into my vision, all looking very barren and dead. I recalled hearing that there were M-class planets in this system – the same category as Earth and which might sustain life. There'd even been talk about sending probes there on the off-chance it might be a planet we could one day colonise. But so much for that idea based on what I was seeing because the system looked devoid of life sustaining planets. However, I knew several astronomers who would sell their grandmothers to see this – probably their entire family in fact.

I pressed my lips together as the hologram shimmered throughout the ruins of Skara Brae. The implications of this technology were vast. If I could find a way to control this, humanity had basically been handed the keys to the astronomical secrets of our galaxy, perhaps others too. I'd spent my life studying the secrets of the cosmos, and here they all were just waiting to be unlocked.

A wave of emotion washed over me and tears threatened. It was all so overwhelming.

Keep it together, Lauren, especially in front of Jack.

But the revelations weren't over yet – not by a long way.

The view centred on the fourth planet – a dead world with

no hint of an atmosphere, orbited by a mottled brown moon. Maybe this planet had leaked most of their atmospheres like our own Mars had. Certainly it didn't look capable of sustaining any form of life without the help of a spacesuit.

I walked around the hologram, examining every angle of the planet.

Jack's gaze narrowed on me. 'Lauren, you've gone awfully quiet again, what's going on?'

I broke eye contact with the world to glance across at him. 'I just wish you could see this for yourself, Jack. The galactic map has taken me on a trip over to Tau Ceti, one of our nearest neighbouring star systems.'

'Sounds cool.'

'Oh, it's so much more than that. My mind is practically dribbling out of my ears looking at this. I could definitely spend a lifetime writing papers about it.'

'I'll look forward to watching the movie about your discovery they're going to have to make one day.'

'Me too.' I gazed at the planet slowly rotating. Something on the far side was coming into view. 'Hang on a minute...'

'What is it?'

'Not sure...' I walked around the planet and peered at a strange mountain rising from the surface of the world. Everything about it looked wrong for any normal geological structure; it was far too big in proportion to the planet. Whatever it was had to be artificial – and the red line, now dotted, led directly to it.

The hologram began panning away along the dotted line and focused in on a cylindrical asteroid, marked by a red diamond symbol. Ahead of the asteroid, the line became solid again. Was the red line a projected flight path?

My blood iced as an awful possibility struck me. Was this hologram trying to show us that this asteroid was on a collision path with Earth? Our solar system had certainly experienced its fair share of interstellar asteroids passing through it. The 'Oumuamua asteroid was one famous example, a huge chunk of rock that had spun its way end over end through our solar system before exiting again. But even if this Tau Ceti asteroid did escape the gravity well of the star, it would still take it hundreds and hundreds of years to reach our world. So if this was a warning of a possible collision, the human species had a very long time to prepare.

I tapped my fingers on my lips. 'I don't get it...'

'What?'

'Just give me a moment and I'll explain everything I'm seeing...'

Something felt off about this, but what I wasn't sure. I walked right up to the asteroid and lowered my head until it was at eye level. That was when I spotted the metallic domes with large radiating fins dotted across the surface of the rock.

I put my hands on top of my head. 'Holy shit sticks.'

Jack peered at me. 'Will you just tell me already?'

'Sorry, yes. OK, hold on because this is going to be quite a rush. Have you ever come across the concept of an asteroid that's been turned into a ship?'

'Yeah, of course. It's a classic idea in science fiction.'

'Well, a ship like that is just leaving the Tau Ceti system and is on its way to Earth.'

'For real?' Jack asked, his mid-west American accent thickening.

'For real.'

'Shit... So this is more hard evidence that humans really aren't alone in the universe,' he said.

I gestured around me at the hologram. 'Just added to all that's been left here for us to discover. Not to mention the top-secret UFO documents I've seen and my own encounter with Sentinel.'

'You do realise that all I can see is you staring off into empty air, don't you?'

'I know I'm asking a lot of you to believe everything I'm telling you.'

'That's quite the understatement, Lauren. Everything I thought I knew is being thrown into question. And if that's true for me, it's going to be the same for an awful lot of people.'

'And that's exactly why I'm doing this, Jack. People deserve to know the truth – a truth that's been kept suppressed for years by our governments. Or do you think people would prefer to live in happy ignorance?'

'Now there's a question,' he said.

Before I could reply, I was distracted by a huge flash of light coming from the top of the strange mountain on the Tau Ceti planet. A blue lance of energy shot out from its summit, straight towards the asteroid ship. For a moment I thought it was some sort of Death-Star-like weapon and that the ship was about to be vaporised. But instead of destroying it, the beam shot straight through the middle of the craft.

I crouched for a better look at the asteroid's axis. The inside was hollowed out along its length and a huge lens had been mounted within it, spreading the cone of light that exited the far end of the ship, striking...

I peered closer at what was in front of the asteroid... An enormous ghostly solar sail was tethered to the ship.

'Oh sweet god!'

Jack frowned at me. 'What now?'

'Sorry. There's some sort of huge laser built on the planet that seems to have been constructed to power that asteroid ship.'

'How can a beam of light power a ship?'

'By using a solar sail. We've theorised about the same idea in order to send probes out to Alpha Centauri with the Breakthrough Starshot programme, although on a much smaller scale to what I'm looking at here.'

'I think I read about Starshot somewhere. A laser on Earth will be used to power the solar sail, right?'

'That's it. Eventually the laser should be able to propel the probe to twenty per cent of the speed of light. Accounting for acceleration and deceleration times, it would take around twenty years for the probe to cover the four light years between us and Alpha Centauri.'

'So how long for this asteroid ship?'

'Tau Ceti is about twelve light years away from Earth. And the laser I'm seeing is of Death Star proportions. So if it reached around eighty per cent of the speed of light, say, then we're probably talking about fifteen years before it arrives on our doorstep.'

'Hang on. If governments have been suppressing information about aliens, do they already know about this? And if so, why not tell anyone? Fifteen years isn't that far away really.'

I stared at the hologram of the dead-looking Tau Ceti planet. 'Jack, what if they don't come in peace? What if this is an invasion ship on its way to Earth? Maybe the reason governments aren't telling people is to prevent mass panic?'

'Crap. That makes sense even though I don't want it to. But why choose Skara Brae to tell us –' Jack made air quotes – '"By the way, humanity, you're screwed because you're going to be invaded one day."'

'You of all people know how significant Skara Brae is from an archaeological perspective. We're talking about the forerunner to Stonehenge here. Maybe the Angelus chose this place because among the people who originally occupied this site were people like me – people with synaesthesia. And maybe they were trained by the Angelus to use this map as a sort of celestial observatory as you suggested before. For it to act as an early-warning lookout. But maybe the knowledge became lost over the millennia? It certainly wouldn't be the first time in human history that's happened.'

Jack pressed his lips together. 'That's quite a stretch, Lauren. Aliens visiting this site and we're only discovering all this now? I have to say, as an archaeologist, I would have expected to come across some evidence for this long before now.'

'But what if there has been evidence? After all, the Overseers tried to suppress the truth about Sentinel. Who knows what other ancient information they might have buried too?'

Before Jack could fire off another question at me, I held up my hand to silence him because the view was starting to move again. It began to zoom away from Tau Ceti and back towards Earth. A moment later it was over Skara Brae, but this time with a notable difference. The hologram was now overlaid across the archaeological site. If I turned my head, the painted-light version of it matched exactly. And what it showed was incredible: the entire original structure, complete with a roof shimmering over our heads where it had once been.

'Holy shit, I wish you could witness this, Jack. I'm seeing Skara Brae as it used to be when it was intact.'

'That's it. When this is over, I want you to draw exactly what you've seen. It could provide invaluable information for my research.'

I nodded as I noticed something beyond him in the far corner of the room opposite us – a green orb was pulsing within the hologram. I headed over for a closer look.

'What now?'

'Not sure yet...'

Jack followed me whilst holding on to his phone that still looped with the clanging sound.

As I neared the ghostly orb I could see it was about the size of a small apple and covered with a number of nodules that formed a regular geometric pattern of bumps.

As I crouched down by it and my perspective of it shifted, I realised the object wasn't *on* the floor but was *beneath* it.

I pointed at the spot on the ground. 'Jack, I think there's something buried at this exact spot – a ball thing with patterns over it.'

Jack gawped at me. 'You have to be shitting me.'

'You know what this is?'

'You're basically describing a carved stone ball. We've already found a number of them here at Skara Brae. Others have been discovered at other Neolithic sites across the country. Nobody knows what they're for. Some have suggested they may have been used to play a game, others that they might have been an early way of visualising mathematics.'

'Are they rare then?'

'Relatively,' Jack replied.

'And do you think that what this hologram is showing me is really there?'

'Only one way to find that out...' Jack took some thin blue latex gloves out of his pocket, pulled them on and unhooked a trowel from his belt. 'If we do find something down there, it will definitely confirm one thing at least.'

'What's that?'

'That you're not crazy, or simply imagining all of this.'

'Oh ye, of little faith.'

'I hope we do, Lauren, because I really want this all to be true.'

'You and me both.'

As Jack began to dig, carefully scraping the soil back, the hologram of the orb didn't waver. He worked frustratingly slowly, moving the dirt a fraction at a time.

I tapped my foot. 'Can't you go any faster?'

'This is the speed a good archaeologist always works at. Slow and steady wins the race.'

'Give me the bloody trowel and I'll hurry things up for you.'

'You'll have to prise it out of my cold dead hand first.'

'That can be arranged.' I grinned at him and then stood on tiptoes to peer over the embankment towards the Chinook. The cow was now out of sight. One of Robert's team seemed to be chiselling samples from the crystal itself whilst a woman was waving something like a metal detector over it. The important thing was that none of the team looked like they'd be heading our way anytime soon.

Jack continued to scrape away at the dirt, his hair hanging around his face, his eyes bright. An archaeologist on the hunt. I just prayed that this wasn't a bust and he'd end up labelling me as a lunatic. But then the softest chink came from the tip of the trowel.

We exchanged a long stare, then Jack blinked several times.

'Let's go for broke,' he said. He took a brush out of his pocket and started to dust away the powdered earth.

My heart leapt as the top of a grey stone ball was revealed, its form perfectly matching its hologram counterpart.

'Will you look at that,' Jack said as he carefully prised the stone orb loose to cradle it in his hands.

'Didn't I tell you?'

'You did. But this is still all crazy.'

'A synaesthetic hologram triggered by sound used as an X-marks-the-spot on a map? Of course it's crazy.'

'I don't mean like that. We've done ground radar surveys throughout the site which should have definitely picked this stone orb up before now. But I guess that's another thing we're going to have to puzzle over.'

I felt a little thrill inside at the use of *we*. 'Do you mind if I hold it?'

'Knock yourself out, but please wear these first.' Jack dug

another set of blue gloves out of his pocket and handed them to me.

I slipped them on and took the weight of the stone ball, surprisingly heavy for such a small object. My thrill only increased as the green holographic tracked the stone ball exactly as I picked it up and changed in colour to bright amber.

If I thought that was significant, it was nothing compared to the cobweb of geometrical symbols springing out from the orb to radiate around it like moons orbiting a planet. Some were spirals, some squares, others circles with radiating lines.

'Um, Jack? Something seems to be very special about this particular stone ball.'

'What sort of special?'

'Hang on, let me try something.' I began to rotate the orb and the icons spun round.

'I'm not certain, but the stone seems to be interacting with the hologram, which is conjuring up these icons around it.'

'You are seriously telling me that the stone ball is acting like, what, some sort of control?'

'Could be. But if so, to do what?'

'I guess you'll have to keep experimenting to find out,' he said.

He leant closer and I breathed in his smell. Not aftershave, but just a pleasant soapy scent. At least he had a good hygiene routine for a Viking. I smiled to myself as he gave me a sideways look.

I bit back my grin as I continued to experiment with the sphere, rotating it this way and that. I twisted my wrist and a new outer set of symbols appeared around the first lot. A green eye symbol framed in a box was at the top. I brought the orb up to my face and rolled my wrist back for a better angle to examine it. At once, a pulse of green blazed out from the stone orb and cascaded away through the site with a ripple of light.

'Whoa, that was new,' I said.

'What flavour of new?'

A vibration shuddered in the ground.

I stared at him. 'That to start with. Please tell me you can feel the ground shaking?'

Jack slowly nodded. Then his eyes widened on me as the walls started to vibrate too. 'What did you do?'

In the distance we could hear Robert's team shouting to each other as the stone walls groaned around us.

'I have no bloody idea!'

'Whatever you're doing, stop it, Lauren, or Skara Brae will be torn apart.'

A strong tingling sensation like a static shock flowed up my arm from the ball and I jammed my jaw together. I tried to release the ball, but my hands wouldn't obey and my fingers spasmed even harder round it.

'I can't let go,' I said through gritted teeth.

As Jack tried to pull my hand free, Robert and a woman crested the mound and stared down at us. Then Skara Brae disappeared around us in a blaze of light.

CHAPTER EIGHT

As the light faded, I saw a transformed world. Skara Brae, where we'd been standing just a moment ago – a world made of sky, sea, stone and turf – now shimmered like a mirage that couldn't quite make up its mind what it wanted to be. The tumbling stone walls and mounds wavered in and out of focus as light danced over their surfaces. Robert and the female officer were still above us on the mound, but frozen like statues.

Jack looked around, slack-jawed, his body blurring like somebody who had moved during a slow-exposure photograph. I looked down at my own hands going in and out of focus.

It was like the real world had turned into a hologram that wasn't working properly.

'What the hell, Lauren?' Jack asked, his eyes the only constant feature in the otherwise shifting form of his head.

I fought the feeling of vertigo making me want to vomit. 'You know that bit in *Alice in Wonderland* where she falls down the rabbit and it all goes a bit weird? I think we may have done just that.'

'Or maybe we were hit by the concussion wave of a blast

caused by the alien tech you've been messing with going wrong. Maybe we're both lying on the ground unconscious and this is all just part of my hallucination.'

'If it's a hallucination, then it's one we're sharing.'

'Yeah, but in my hallucination you would say that.'

The floor undulated like it had been turned to water. I reached out to steady myself on the wall and my fingers brushed straight through the surface.

Jack gawped at my hand. 'Fuck!'

'Exactly.' I examined my blurring fingers. 'So maybe we're dead and we're now some sort of ghosts?'

'Not sure about that. Look now.' Jack pointed to the people above us, though his arm looked more like a column of smoke than a limb.

Robert and the woman had begun moving again. Slowly at first, but then soon at normal speed, blinking and rubbing their eyes with blurring hands.

'Where the hell did Harper and that woman just go?' Robert asked.

'No idea, sir, but it looked as if they let off some sort of flash-bang grenade. They must have slipped away under its cover.'

'Then start an immediate sweep of the area,' Robert replied. 'Whatever that tremor was, something tells me those two will be able to cast some light on it.'

The female officer nodded and disappeared behind the mound as Robert descended into the site.

'We're really the other side of the mirror, aren't we?' Jack said. 'It's obvious they can't see us.'

'It would seem so,' I replied.

Jack and I watched Robert approach us in the fluctuating alternative version of Skara Brae. His gaze scanned the site but never lingered on us even once. He closed to within a metre of where we were standing and Jack waved his hands in front of his face. Not so much as a flicker.

'So what is this place, Lauren?' Jack asked.

'Whatever this is, it's beyond me. All I can tell you is that I was rotating that stone ball and then one of the hovering icons around it slotted into place.'

'You're really trying to tell me that a five-thousand-year-old artefact is responsible for all of this?'

I looked at the orb still clutched in my hand for the first time since we'd arrived in this alternative world. I examined the stone ball, which wasn't ghosting like everything else. The floating icons had disappeared around it, but the round shapes carved into the stone were now edged with green light.

'Whatever this device is and however it got us here, it's obviously way beyond Neolithic levels of tool technology,' I said. 'So that leads us to one conclusion – well, two, actually. One, this could be some sort of top-secret human tech.'

'That doesn't make sense of why it's in the middle of an ancient archaeological site. It seems like a weird place to bury it.'

I nodded. 'Exactly. Or two, and which is much more likely...'

'That this really is Angelus alien tech,' Jack replied.

'It's the only thing that makes sense.'

'I know. But every fibre of my archaeologist being screams out that I didn't sign up to reinforce the beliefs of people who live on the fringe of society.'

'Once again, I've got the T-shirt for where you are now. Don't forget I'm a trained radio telescope operator. And I've found myself pitched into god knows what alternative reality.'

'So how do we get back through the looking glass, Alice?'

'Which makes you the Mad Hatter, I suppose.'

His smile wavered within his blurring face. 'I can live with that. So what do we do now?'

'This all started when I manipulated the stone ball, again suggesting that it's some sort of control.'

'So the question is, can you reverse what you did?'

'That's a billion-dollar question.' I examined the orb again and gave it a shake but nothing happened.

Jack pointed skywards. 'Hey, Lauren, did you just do that?'

I looked up to see a point of light high overhead, growing large fast. 'Not that I know of.'

'Is that...' Jack's eyes hung on to mine in this crazy alternative world.

I spread my blurring hands wide in the way of an answer as the UFO – because every instinct was screaming at me that it was that – ate up the distance.

Cold raw fear surged through my veins as the craft closed in on us, my mind tilting.

Jack's hand sought out mine, a tingle of energy as our fingers shimmered over each other. We stood side by side staring at the alien thing hurtling towards us. At the speed it was going it would make the massive Winslow impact crater in northern Arizona look like a pinprick and we'd soon be reduced to no more than stardust in this strange alternate version of our world.

But then the silent craft came to a sudden and absolute stop a hundred metres up, like the rules of momentum didn't apply to it. One moment it had been travelling at thousands of miles per hour and the next it simply wasn't.

Adrenaline swelled in me. We might actually live through this after all. I took in the shape and the hairs on my neck rose. It felt like all my Christmases had come at once.

The tetrahedron-shaped craft hung like an inverted pyramid in the sky. It had to be at least a hundred metres tall and was hovering directly over our heads. The craft's surface seemed to be made from some sort of translucent crystal, through which I could see a steady blue light at its heart.

'Holy fuck,' Jack said, staring up at it. 'Lauren, talk to me. Is this the ship your alien AI buddy showed to you in those classified files?'

'Yes, yes, it is...'

Jack gestured across at Robert who was now examining a toolbox. 'Going by his distinct lack of crapping his pants, this craft can't be seen in our world?'

'Maybe not normally, but don't forget I've seen photos of UFOs like this that Sentinel showed me.'

'Then it must have some serious stealth tech that makes it invisible to our radars, even visually.'

What Jack was saying made sense, but something told me stealth tech wasn't quite what we were dealing with here. Then I caught a glint of light in the tip of the nose of the craft. The three-sided point seemed to be folding in on itself to reveal a bright white triangle of light. A harmonica-like note filled the sky. Then the ground started to vibrate beneath our feet again. A few stones began to float upwards.

'I'll need to see a seriously good shrink after this joyride,' Jack said as we started to drift up too. He grabbed on to me to stop me floating away from him. Meanwhile Robert stayed firmly anchored by gravity. This tractor beam, or whatever it was, had an effect localised to this alternative world.

With a crackle like a welder's torch, a beam of light a good metre wide lanced down from the craft's nose straight into the middle of Skara Brae. Then gravity sucked at us again and we, together with the rest of the flotsam, slammed back to the ground.

'Maybe it would be easier to mentally deal with this if we accept we have both gone mad?' I said as I stood shakily on the still vibrating floor.

But Jack didn't answer. He was staring straight past me. I turned round and my heart immediately crowded my throat.

Within the shimmering column of light, a blurry naked man

was lying in a foetal position on his side. The energy beam around him shut off. Then, in perfect silence, the ship evaporated into the sky like it had never been there.

'Mike!' Jack shouted. He raced over to him and placed his fingers on his neck. 'No pulse, but he's still warm, so there may be a chance to save him.' He rolled Mike on to his back and placed his hands on his shimmering chest.

'God, is he going to be OK?' I said.

'Working on it! One, two, three...' Jack counted as he pressed his palms down on to the man's sternum. Then he tipped Mike's blurry head back before pinching his nose and opening his mouth. With a gentle exhale, Jack inflated the guy's lungs. He repeated the procedure three more times then gave me a grim look. 'Can you get us back to our world? I need the defibrillator in the back of my Land Rover.'

'How come you have one of those?' I asked.

'Action first, answers later, Lauren.'

My mind raced. I needed to find a solution and fast to help save Mike's life. Whatever this place was that I'd pitched us into, it had to be something to do with the specific icon I'd selected round the stone orb. The problem was, there were no icons to select this time. But there was one thing I hadn't tried...

I gently squeezed the stone orb itself.

The green lit edges turned amber and symbols leapt out from the orb to resume their orbits. Like a computer, the bloody thing had entered snooze mode. I began to rapidly rotate my wrist and the ring of icons spun to match.

Jack glanced across at it as he continued to work on Mike. 'It looks like some sort of menu system.'

'You can see this?' I asked.

'Yes...'

Interesting, but my immediate priority was remembering the sequence that I'd stumbled on before. The eye symbol flashed into my mind. I hunted through the icons and spotted it at the bottom. I rolled my wrist until the eye symbol had aligned itself within a top rectangle that stayed put and the icon glowed slightly brighter.

'Will you hurry this up?' Jack said as he continued to work on Mike.

'Doing my best...' I fought the panic threatening to unleash inside me and tried to think my way through this. A man's life depended on me.

If this was some sort of menu system, there had to be a way to select an option. Squeezing the ball harder had no effect. I lifted the ball and moved my hand to examine it. I rolled my fist forward like I was controlling a motorbike accelerator and the green eye grew larger. Then a new line on the outer icons sprang into existence around the first.

A submenu!

I scanned the new set of symbols. They looked a lot like Egyptian hieroglyphics. So many, and so complicated. But then one snagged my gaze: three wavy lines stacked on top of each other and blinking. I rotated the orb until they had moved to the top and then rolled my hand forward again. The icon turned into a single dot and everything flared with white light.

In a rush of reality, we were suddenly back in Skara Brae, everything including us no longer a mirage but certain again.

Robert dropped Jack's trowel. 'What the hell. You just appeared out of thin air!'

Jack ignored him and heaved Mike up on to his shoulder in a fireman's lift. Neck muscles cabling, he started forward past Robert and towards the steps, me right behind him.

The MI5 officer rushed past us and blocked our path. 'What the hell is going on here?'

I squared up to Robert. 'Mike is going to die unless Jack gets him to a defibrillator.'

Robert peered at the unconscious man on Jack's shoulder. 'Mike, that's the man who disappeared?'

'In one,' I said. 'We can talk about everything later after Jack saves his bloody life.'

Jack didn't say a word, but shoved past Robert and headed up the steps on to the ridge and down the other side. I raced after him as the female officer spotted us and raised her pistol.

'Hold your fire!' Robert shouted.

The woman lowered her weapon.

A few moments later, we'd all reached the Land Rover. Jack carefully lowered Mike to the ground as I yanked open the back door. He grabbed a crate from the vehicle, tipping its contents everywhere, and began hunting through the mound of contents. He pulled out a bright red box with 'defibrillator' written on it and threw it open to reveal a machine with two paddles connected by wires.

'Charging – stand clear!' Jack shouted.

We pulled back as the defibrillator whined as it charged. As soon as the green light pinged on, Jack pushed the paddles to Mike's chest and pressed the button. Mike's body shook as the jolt of energy passed through him, but became motionless again as the shock ended.

'Come on, Mike, fight,' I said.

Jack pressed the paddles to Mike's chest again. The machine whined once more.

'Clear!' Jack shouted.

Mike's body shook as electricity poured into him. And then he gasped, arched his back and began to shake.

'Oh, thank god,' I said, sagging into myself.

But Jack was shaking his head. 'We're not out of the woods yet – he's going back into arrest. Lauren, grab my medical bag from over there.'

Medical bag? I shook the thought from my mind and raced

over to scoop up a battered brown-leather bag from the middle of the heap.

'Hurry up – we haven't got much time!' Jack called out to me.

I ran back to him, already opening the bag, revealing a stethoscope, boxes of drugs and everything else you would expect a doctor to have.

So maybe Jack was a GP when he wasn't poking around in holes in the ground?

He grabbed the bag from me, tore a syringe from its wrapper and pulled away the needle's cover. He stuck it into a small bottle of clear liquid and pulled up the plunger.

'What are you doing?' Robert asked as Jack leant over Mike.

'I'm going for a Hail Mary,' Jack replied.

'Which is what exactly?' I asked.

'I'm going to inject adrenaline directly into his heart.'

'You're going to do what?'

'Trust me, I know what I'm doing.'

I turned to Robert. 'We've got to get Mike to hospital.'

He nodded and walked away, talking rapidly into his radio set.

Jack's hand shook slightly as he hovered the syringe over Mike's chest, his other hand probing for a gap between his ribs. A bead of sweat ran down his forehead.

I gently placed a hand on Jack's tensed shoulder. 'You've got this.'

He gave me a sideways glance and then nodded. 'Yes...' Grimacing, he brought the syringe down and drove the needle into Mike's chest.

My heart lurched in sympathy as Mike gasped and his eyes flew open, locking on to mine.

Before I knew what was happening, Mike had grabbed my wrists with a steel-like grip. He stared at me his jaw muscles cabling and shouted, 'Earth Song!' Then his eyes rolled up into his head and he slumped to the ground as he let go of me.

I stared at Jack. 'Please tell me he's going to live?'

Jack pressed his fingers to Mike's neck. 'He's got a pulse, but I need to get him to an ICU immediately.'

Robert put away his radio. 'Five minutes and you will be, Jack.' He made a spinning sign with his fingers towards the Chinook. At once, the helicopter's engine roared as its rotors began spinning up to speed.

I grabbed a blanket from the back of the Land Rover and draped it over Mike. Together with Jack, I pulled him to his feet, as Robert rushed ahead of us shouting instructions to his team.

The few minutes it took us to carry Mike to the Chinook felt like a lifetime, but at last we were climbing into the back of the helicopter with Robert as its rotors blasted a small hurricane down on to us. We squeezed alongside the dead cow tied on to the pallet. One of the pilots began strapping Mike on to a bench seat.

I glanced at Jack as he sat next to me. 'Is Mike going to be OK?'

'I hope so...'

I gently patted his hand. 'No one could have done anything more.'

Jack just stared across at Mike, his expression unreadable.

Robert turned towards us as the rear ramp began to close, shutting away the view of Skara Brae. 'I need to interview both of you about what happened here.'

'First I need to make sure Mike is OK,' Jack replied as the Chinook shuddered.

Robert gave Jack a long look as the helicopter rose quickly into the sky and then nodded.

And that just left me.

CHAPTER NINE

ONE OF THE MI5 OFFICERS, doing a good impression of a bouncer at a seedy nightclub, had escorted me into a small office in the hospital with an internal window with a closed venetian blind to stop prying eyes from the corridor outside. He shut the door behind me. Three hours had passed since we'd arrived in the Chinook and it was now dark. The worst thing was no one had said a word to me about how Mike was doing. The last I'd seen, Jack had rushed off with him, under escort. The longer the lack of news went on, the more worried I became. Robert had at last turned up and now sat watching me with his fingers steepled together, as if I were a tricky crossword puzzle he was trying to solve.

The contents of my rucksack had been emptied on the desk between us. It was the detritus of a young woman's life, from old receipts and hair bands to an emergency lipstick in case I ever needed to make myself look half decent. There was a Swiss army knife that Aunt Lucy had given me one Christmas and a map of Orkney, which I'd been annotating with the locations of the reported appearances of the crystal markings. But of course the item that stood out was the carved stone ball, nestled on top of an old scarf.

Robert gestured to the chair opposite him and I sat down. I gazed at my opponent over my belongings as if we were about to begin a game of chess. In a sense we were. The question was, how was I going to play this?

I tried to look anywhere but at the stone orb. The one thing I knew for certain was that if I let slip what the ancient artefact could do, it would almost certainly be the last time I'd see it. All governments loved their secrets. But here was the oddest thing – I felt a strange bond to the lump of carved stone. It was as if the bloody thing was calling out to me and it was as much as I could do not to clutch it to my chest, whispering, 'My precious.'

I sat back, trying to look as relaxed as I could. Still neither of us said anything. The MI5 chief and the amateur UFO sleuth considering their moves before committing to a strategy. The silence in the room lingered and the tension notched up as Robert's eyes narrowed on me.

I felt myself tempted to start gabbling. *You see, Robert, I stumbled into this alternative universe with Jack, and, no, we hadn't taken any illicit substances first...* It was the truth, but I wasn't sure how well it would play out for us. No, maybe it'd be best to feel my way into this dance and to hear what Robert said before volunteering any information.

He drummed his fingers on the table, caterpillar moves through each digit, then tilted his head left and right.

I could almost hear his mental cogs grinding together as he deliberately let the silence continue, probably hoping the truth would spill out of my mouth. *Bastard.*

But I didn't blink and finally his nostrils flared.

Here it came – his first move. I sat back in my chair.

'Would you care to explain your presence at Skara Brae, Lauren?' Robert asked.

As good a place to start as any, but how did he know who I was? I made sure I didn't travel with any ID for exactly this reason. Maybe he'd already grabbed a chance to speak to Jack, and if so, how much had the guy spilt?

I tried to force my face muscles to stay relaxed. 'First, tell me how Mike's getting on.'

'Stable, but still unconscious.'

'And have you spoken to Jack?'

'No, because he's still assisting with the treatment of Michael Palmer.'

'Is Jack a doctor or something?'

'You mean you don't know about his former life?'

'It's been less than twenty-four hours since we met, and we haven't exactly had the chance to swap life stories.'

'Well, Jack is a former field-trauma surgeon. He worked on the battlefield until five years ago. Then he left the army.'

'To become an archaeologist?'

'Precisely.'

'That's quite a career shift, isn't it?'

'That's as may be, but I'm not here to discuss Jack's life story with you.'

'Of course...' The mental box I'd placed Jack in really would have to be rethought. This guy had a past, and an interesting one at that.

I leant forward. 'So how do you know who I am, Robert?'

'No need to be modest, Lauren. You're quite the celebrity within the security services and our government's inner circle. After all, you were instrumental in averting an international disaster during the Event.'

The Event – the catchy little title that referred to the moment Sentinel had arrived and almost pitched our planet into World War Three. If it were down to me, I'd rename it the Thank-God-We're-Still-Here Event.

'Oh, I see.' I rested my hands on the table, once again resisting the urge to grab the orb. 'I was never the same after what happened. None of us were after those soldiers attacked.' I made sure not to use the name 'Overseers'. The less MI5 thought I knew about that organisation, the better. 'And I'm really sorry about what happened to your officers, especially Kiera Owen. She didn't deserve to die like that.'

Robert's gaze softened a fraction. 'Kiera was a rising star in the service.'

'Did you know her personally?'

'Yes, I did actually – she was a good friend and colleague. She always put her country first, to the extent that it eventually cost Kiera her life.'

The old sadness for someone I'd barely known squeezed my heart. Kiera had sacrificed everything to protect us when we'd been attacked by the Overseers.

'Yes, she was one in a million. I owe her my life... I don't suppose you have any leads on who did it?' I couldn't resist the urge to fish for any update he might have about the Overseers.

'Let's just say that investigations into the group responsible for the attack on Jodrell Bank and the murder of my officers is ongoing. Of course we also have the later incident involving the attempt on your life.'

I gave the guy a wary look. Where was he going with this?

Robert looked at his notes. 'I'm sorry for your loss. I know Lucy Jacobs adopted you when you were nine and she was your only family. Her death must have hit you hard.'

'Deeply...' I felt the cracks in the centre of my being threatening to open up again.

'And you are still certain that the masked man who led the raid was the same person who rammed your vehicle?'

The tears that had been gathering were replaced by the heat of anger. 'I'm sure of it. I'd recognise his scar anywhere. But why are we talking about this? It's old ground. I said all this during the interviews at the time.'

Was Robert deliberately trying to unsettle me so I'd spill the truth? Was this another move from his MI5 playbook?

But actually, when I looked at Robert, there was concern in his expression. 'I'm sorry to bring this up because it's obviously painful for you,' he said. 'I'm even sorrier that we haven't brought the man responsible to justice. We followed every lead, but they were all dead ends. Even the chassis number on his vehicle we later recovered had been filed off. Everything about it has the hallmarks of a professional hit. The question then – and now – is why would this man specifically target you and leave the others who were with you that night at Jodrell Bank alone?'

Because it was me who'd been investigating the richest families and corporations of the world – those who had the most to lose from a revelation that UFOs were real. Instead, I served up my excuse from my original interview.

'Probably because the guy who ran that assault team took it personally that I shot one of his people and blew his mission. If you do ever track his team down, I hope you find and shoot every last one of them.'

'We'll have to see about that...' Robert's face settled into a neutral expression. 'So now we have all that out of the way, we need to discuss the real reason we're both here in this room together. And I want the full truth – no spin stories, Lauren – because I can smell horse shit from a mile away. To begin with, can you please tell me why you turned up at a location of significant interest to MI5?'

'Lucky coincidence?'

Robert folded his arms.

'Maybe it's just my magnetic personality, attracting weird shit to me like a bunch of paperclips.' He gave the tiniest hint of a smile, suggesting that the guy wasn't a complete robot.

Robert drummed his fingers on the desk. 'So you're telling me you haven't been in contact with any of your old colleagues at Jodrell Bank?'

'No, I haven't actually. And what's that got to do with anything anyway?'

'Just ruling out a possible line of enquiry...'

What was that meant to mean?

Robert wrote something down on a pad in front of him, probably noting he should interview every single member of the team at Jodrell Bank to see if they would confirm that. But his question suggested there might be a link between Skara Brae and the radio telescope site. Maybe something to do with Sentinel? I made a mental note to ring Steve, my old boss...that was if Robert was ever going to release me.

'So back to why you're here, Lauren.' The MI5 officer fixed me with a piercing, unblinking stare.

Aunt Lucy had used a similar technique on me and it was just as effective as an adult, coming from Robert, as it had been as a nine-year-old child, delivered by Aunt Lucy.

I threw up my hands. 'OK, here is the absolute truth. I heard a rumour that brought me out here.'

'About?'

'About the strange symbols appearing over Orkney.'

'I see... And why did you turn up at Skara Brae specifically? Did you have some previous contact with Jack Harper? Did he inform you of the latest appearance of a symbol near the site?'

'No. As I already made clear, I've known Jack less than a day.'

'Why Skara Brae then?'

I gave him the longest look. There was little point in ducking this particular truth, but I needed to leave our trip to the twilight zone out of it. 'If you give me that map and a pen, I'll show you.'

Robert took a pen from a pot on the desk and gave it to me.

I smoothed the paper out. 'I've marked this up with all the

known symbols on or around the Orkney Islands. They form a pattern – watch.' I began to link the points together with the pen. As I worked, Robert's eyebrows rose up his forehead.

I finished and put down the pen. 'As you can see, when you link all the locations together, it creates a pattern. I wasn't certain until the underwater one was found by that diver last week. But each symbol has been closing in on a specific location. And if we add the latest one...' I drew a final 'X' roughly at the position of the latest symbol in the field and then linked it to the others. 'The symbols create a spiral, centred on Skara Brae.'

Robert sat back. 'Why didn't our experts spot that? It's so obvious now you point it out.'

'Maybe because you were concentrating on the phenomenon itself rather than the pattern the symbols were creating?'

'So what's the significance of this shape?'

'It could be a way to get our attention and make us look at Skara Brae.'

'Look for what precisely?'

I sucked my lip. Maybe I should tell him about the stone ball and what had happened? The only thing I knew for certain was that this game of chess was getting complicated, not least because I didn't even know what we were playing for.

'Is this something to do with Sentinel? Did he set you off on some sort of private mission?' Robert continued.

That was a good question. Although the AI hadn't specifically tasked me with it, he'd been the one who'd revealed the conspiracy of silence over UFOs and specifically the photographs of tetrahedron-shaped craft. But, no, that wasn't it. The reason I'd chased the trail of breadcrumbs to Skara Brae was my own desire to get to the truth. Certainly, carrying on with my life and working at Jodrell Bank wasn't an option after what I'd seen. As awful as Aunt Lucy's death had been, it had made me even more determined.

I settled on giving Robert just a shrug.

'Lauren, there's no need to be so evasive.'

I gazed at him, trying to judge the man. But there was little point in denying what was screamingly obvious. I was an amateur Mulder and that was the end of it. And I'd dived in with both feet, following a hunch. Definitely not the more measured approach that Scully would have taken. The endless circle of guilt and self-recrimination cycled through my head for the billionth time. If I had played this more cautiously, maybe Aunt Lucy would still be alive.

I exhaled through my thinly pursed lips. 'No, Sentinel didn't tell me to do any of this. Talking of which, any news about my old friend?'

'That's classified information, I'm afraid.'

It sounded as if there was something. Not that Robert would give it up.

'Right...' I replied, feeling a stab of disappointment. I'd often wondered what had happened to Sentinel after he'd uploaded himself to a satellite from the Lovell dish and if he was linked to the explosion at that lab. If so, had he been destroyed with it as he attempted to fulfil his mission?

Robert's brown eyes locked on to mine. 'But your presence here is linked somehow, though, isn't it, Lauren?'

Tenacious was this guy's middle name. I had to give him something.

'You're right,' I said. 'What happened back at Jodrell Bank changed my world view for ever, considering Sentinel told me that aliens were real. And I'm desperate to discover any further evidence of previous alien incursions into our world.' That would have to do. I certainly wouldn't let the MI5 officer know that I had a head full of UFO evidence from the classified files that Sentinel had hacked into.

'That's more like it, Lauren. So why don't we carry on down

this path now you're starting to be straight with me? Tell me exactly what happened at Skara Brae. To start with, what caused that tremor? And exactly how did you disappear and then materialise out of thin air in front of me? I'd also like to know where you found Mike.'

There was no ducking past this line of questioning. Robert had witnessed at least part of it with his own eyes. I made extra sure I didn't glance at the orb.

My worry, and a very real one in my head at least, was if the Overseers had infiltrated MI5 once, they might do so again. There was a chance that the man sitting opposite me worked for them. If I told Robert what really happened, it could well be the last anyone saw of Jack, Mike and me. But I needed to give him something, at least until I worked out whether he was on the level or not.

I clutched my hands together, trying to look as earnest as possible. 'OK, this is what happened, Robert. I was asking Jack if he'd seen anything unusual at Skara Brae.'

'Having first managed to slip past my officers?'

He really didn't need to know that Jack had smuggled me in. 'Yes, I'm resourceful like that. Maybe they need some more training. Anyway, Jack and I were talking when the ground started to shake and there was an intense flash of light. I must have blanked out for a few moments because the next thing I know there is a butt-naked guy lying on the ground and Jack is fighting to save his life.'

'That's it? You don't remember anything else?'

'Not that I can recall.'

'So do you have any theories about how you all appeared from nowhere?'

'None whatsoever. You?'

'Not yet, but once I report in, our experts will be investigating the matter further and will probably want to examine you.'

Was that code for interrogate the shit out of us? I frowned at him.

Before Robert could ask me anything else, the door flew open and the bouncer-like MI5 officer entered, talking rapidly into his phone.

He then thrust out his phone to Robert. 'There's been a development, sir.'

Robert took the mobile. His face paled as he listened to what sounded like a woman on the other end.

'Implement an immediate lockdown,' he said. 'No one enters or exits this hospital without my express order.' He handed the phone back to the officer.

'What's happened?' I asked.

'It seems someone entered the CT suite where they were treating Mike and shot the attending doctors.'

I was instantly on my feet. 'They killed Jack?'

'No, one of my agents, who was injured in the firefight but survived, has reported that Jack was taken hostage, along with Mike who was still unconscious.'

'But they're both alive?'

'It seems that way, at least for now. However, the question remains, who targeted them and why?'

'I wish I knew.' But this had the smell of the Overseers all over it. And if they were here, just as I knew would happen eventually, things would get nasty fast. But how the hell had they found out about Skara Brae? Another leak at MI5?

Robert's eyes bored into mine. I was sure he could tell I knew who it was. He gave me the slightest headshake. 'Whomever it is, you'll appreciate that you're probably also a target if Jack and Mike are. So once again, is there anything you're not telling me, Lauren?'

'I...' But I still couldn't cross that line. This could all be a deliberate ploy. Robert might be playing me. He could be that inside man. I shook my head.

'In that case, remain in this room whilst I join the rest of my officers to try to locate Jack and Mike before they're spirited away.' He turned to the officer. 'I'll leave you to stand guard over Lauren. She is to stay in this room whatever happens.'

'Of course, sir,' the officer replied.

Robert held my eyes with his. 'When I return, Lauren, we're going to continue our conversation and you're going to tell me what really happened. So far what you've served is a long way off full disclosure, I know that much. And one way or another you're going to bloody well tell me everything.'

My heart clenched as he left and his officer took up guard outside the room.

CHAPTER TEN

I PACED UP and down the small office, my fingers interlocked round the back of my neck. If Jack and Mike had been taken hostage by the Overseers, Robert was right, I'd almost certainly be a target too. Having my own personal MI5 bouncer was all well and good, but I wasn't sure he would be anywhere near powerful enough to protect me if I was in the Overseers' sights again and they were here on the island.

I crossed the window and glanced down from the third-storey floor of the ultra-modern curve-shaped hospital. I had a direct view of the main entrance below. The immediate very disturbing thing was that it was eerily quiet out there. The only two people I could see were members of Robert's team that I recognised from Skara Brae. That almost certainly meant MI5 would have the other exits covered too. At least whoever had abducted Jack and Mike would find it difficult to leave without being spotted. However, the Overseers would have planned for not being able to waltz out of the hospital unchallenged and would be heavily armed – if their assault on Jodrell Bank was anything to go by.

I turned into the room again and gazed at the back of the

well-groomed head of the MI5 officer through the window in the door. Even with this bodyguard out in the corridor, I still didn't feel safe. I picked up the stone orb and it felt warm to the touch. My mind tingled with possibilities. Maybe I could pull off my Alice routine again, and step out of this world for a moment to be invisible and maybe even pass through the solid walls?

I looked around the room for anything that could be substituted for an archaeologist's trowel and spotted a metal ruler in a desk organiser. It was certainly worth a go.

I gave the desk a gentle strike with it so not to alert my guard to what I was up to. A dull metallic *twang* came from the ruler, but nothing else happened. I tried a second time, then a third, but the same result occurred. So either the sound wasn't at the right frequency or it only worked within the Skara Brae site. The latter seemed more than likely. This was it, I was stuck and the Overseers were coming for me. Fear prickled my skin.

The door opened and the MI5 officer poked his head through. His expression grim, he placed his phone back in his pocket. 'A lone gunman has been spotted on this floor and is headed this way. Whatever happens, you're not to emerge from this office until I give the all-clear. Then we'll move you to an alternative location.'

'I'm not going to just stay here and wait for someone to grab me.'

'So that's why I'll do my best to protect you and make sure that doesn't happen. Just find somewhere to hide in here...just in case.'

The lights flickered and died, plunging the room and outside corridor into darkness.

I exchanged a stare with the officer.

'Now!' he said.

Before I could argue with him, he closed the door and I heard it being locked. A moment later, his shadow moved past the other side of the office's venetian blinds as he stalked off down the corridor, the silhouette of his pistol raised in his hand.

A few moments later, the unmistakable crackle of gunfire echoed along the corridor, followed by shouting. Another shot, then a third... A crashing sound...and utter silence.

Goosebumps rippled over my skin.

Fuckity fuck...

I crept to the blinds and opened them a fraction. My heart twisted as I saw the MI5 officer lying at the end of the corridor, blood pooling out across the floor. A man dressed in a black army gear and a ski mask stepped over his body, his firearm raised.

Fear lapped around my stomach as the guy approached an office several rooms along and tried the door. With a scowl he stood back and with one kick smashed the door open.

A man's voice came from inside, and although I couldn't hear the words, I could make out the pleading tone. But the guy still aimed his pistol, and there was a flash of light and muffled crack of a bullet. The pleading stopped dead. I guessed the gun was fitted with a silencer.

My blood tingled. I tried the door handle, thinking I'd try to slip away, but it was definitely locked. And if I smashed my way out, the sound would only alert the soldier to my presence.

I forced myself to take a deep breath. *Pull yourself together, girl. You've survived worst.*

And I had. What had happened at Jodrell Bank had changed me for ever. I needed a plan and fast. Somehow I needed to alert Robert to what was happening...if he was even still alive.

I had no mobile, but there was a landline on the desk. I grabbed the receiver. Not so much as a click. It seemed that along with the power, the hospital's phone lines had been killed too. I bet they were using a jammer to deal with mobile signals as well.

I grabbed a chair, and as quietly as I could stuck it at an angle under the door handle. Although it wasn't a very effective barricade, hopefully it would still slow the soldier down a bit.

The crash of another door being kicked in echoed along the corridor.

I stared at the desk, the only thing I could hide under, but the soldier was bound to check under there. My eyes zipped around for any escape route or defence idea. Was there anything I could use as a weapon against a guy with a gun? Maybe I could hit him over the head with the chair? But going by what I'd already seen, I was dealing with a trained assassin here.

My eyes fell on the window. I didn't have any other choice. Mind instantly made up, I became laser-focused and moved before common sense stopped me.

My gaze locked on to the stone orb and I grabbed it and stuffed into my rucksack. There was no way I would let that fall into their hands – at least not whilst I was still breathing.

I headed to the window, threw the catch and slid it up. It jammed into a stopper in the frame, leaving only a tiny gap that wouldn't even fit a child.

Bloody health and safety!

I examined the metal stop. It was fastened to the frame by a Phillips screw. I tore back to the desk and grabbed my Swiss army knife. I had been seriously underwhelmed when Aunt Lucy had given it to me a lifetime ago in my teens, but now I could have kissed her. I headed back to the window, unfolding the screwdriver attachment out from between the other tools.

I fumbled with the screwdriver and, after a couple of attempts, fixed it into the screw. Way too many turns later, I had the stop off.

The crash of a door being kicked came from the next room.

'Don't! Don't!' I heard a woman crying.

Then there was the hiss of a silenced bullet and the unmistakable thud of a body hitting the floor.

I slid the window up and looked down. A tiny ledge was just beneath it. My bowels felt as if they'd turned to water as I squeezed through the gap and lowered my feet on to that narrow lip of stone.

A shadow moved across the other side the blinds, heading towards my door.

I quickly slid the window shut behind me. With my heart racing so fast that I thought I was going to vomit, I grabbed the grooves between the blocks of the wall, fingernails breaking on the stone. My toes clawed the tiny ledge as the heels of my boots hung out over empty air. I was all too aware of the massive drop to the tarmac below.

I began to shuffle sideways and, not for the first time in my life, I cursed myself for having size seven feet.

I waved at the two MI5 officers on the ground, but they weren't looking up. I was about to call out to them when a crash came from the office I'd just vacated. I moved to the side of the window just in time.

Through the glass I watched the soldier entering the room, his pistol sweeping ahead of him. He looked down at my belongings still scattered over the desk. They looked wrong – like someone had left in a hurry. His gaze begun to hunt around the room.

I gripped my fingertips even harder on the tiny grooves between the brickwork and shuffled my way along the ledge towards the offices in which he'd already been.

The hiss of three bullets made my stomach drop. Then I realised the shot hadn't come from the window but from below. I glanced down and saw Robert's two officers lying dead on the floor.

Another soldier in black walked casually across the car park towards the entrance, his automatic weapon slung from his shoulder. The guy was speaking into a mic on a headset as he headed for one of the parked ambulances.

Another soldier emerged from the shadows and jogged into the entrance. A moment later, distant cries and shouts drifted up to me as flashes of light filled the foyer area.

My stomach became a lead weight. All those innocent people. And this wasn't a lone wolf attack either, but a highly organised op, just like the Overseers mission at Jodrell Bank. Being prepared to murder a small team that ran a radio telescope was one thing, but attacking a hospital full of people was in a completely different league. Apart from the sheer number of potential casualties, for an organisation that went out of its way to avoid publicity, how could the Overseers hope to hush this up?

I reached the next office window and felt a huge wave of relief when I realised it was already partly open. But then I saw the reason why and bile rose to my mouth. A young female doctor had been shot in the back and was lying on her side, one hand still clamped on the sill where she'd tried to push the window up, just like I had.

A cold fury filled me. Give me a gun and I'd make that bastard pay.

I examined the window, but of course the metal stop was in my way.

With the screwdriver extended from the knife, I stretched my arm in through the gap and up towards the metal stop. Holding the Swiss army knife by the tips of my fingers, I finally managed to locate the screw head after several attempts. Carefully, I began to rotate the screw a quarter turn at a time, my wrist cramping as I worked the screw at a strange angle. Then at last it came loose and dropped on to the floor, the gentle thud on the carpeted tiles sounding impossibly loud to me.

I slowly raised the window with my breath held until the gap was big enough for me to crawl through. As quietly as I could, I slipped through it and dropped down next to the dead doctor. She was young and pretty, wearing trainers and with her hair scooped back in a ponytail. This woman, probably in her late twenties like me, had been someone with their whole life to look forward to. But now she was dead because of the Overseers. And just like Aunt Lucy, inadvertently because of me?

Maybe if I handed myself over, I could stop this. But would it really end? The Overseers didn't play by the rules and probably wouldn't want any witnesses...

My determination strengthened and I stood slowly and made for the door.

Then my plan, what there was of it, fell apart in a second. I'd only taken two steps towards the door when it swung open and the soldier pointed his pistol directly at my chest.

'Oh, just fuck off,' I said. 'You weren't meant to double back.'

'You've watched too many movies if you thought you'd escape that way,' the guy replied. 'Anyway, where is it, Lauren?'

So he knew my name. But at least he hadn't shot me on sight. I just hoped he wasn't asking for what I thought he was.

I put on my best poker face. 'What, exactly?'

'The spherical object you retrieved from Skara Brae.'

Damn it, they must have got Jack to talk. 'Don't know what you talking about, mate.'

'There is no point in lying. We have been monitoring the site for a while now from a military satellite parked in stationary orbit directly above.'

Bloody hell, these guys didn't mess around. I tried to keep my expression relaxed. 'And why would you do that?'

'Because we've detected neutrino bursts at Skara Brae.'

I stared at him. 'Neutrino bursts, as in radiation?'

'Not enough to kill someone, if that's what you're worried about. Anyway, hand over the artefact.'

I shook my head. 'I still don't know what you're talking about.'

'Look, we have a 121 megapixel camera on the satellite monitoring that site – enough resolution to catch an ant scratching its arse. And it recorded you and Dr Jack Harper recovering a round object the size of an apple. More interestingly, it then witnessed you both disappear in a flash of light before then reappearing at the same location a short while later.' He extended his hand. 'Just hand it over and this will go easier for you.'

Like a-bullet-in-the-head easier?

My pulse raced as I slipped my day bag off and opened it. But as I put my hand in and clasped the orb my gaze snagged on the dead doctor. A fresh sense of determination surged through me. I hadn't survived a full-blown attack at Jodrell Bank just to give them the key to an incredible ancient artefact now. And I wanted – no, needed – payback for what they'd done to Aunt Lucy.

The soldier's eyes locked on to the stone orb in my fingers as I turned back towards him. He waggled his fingers for it.

I gave the man a thin smile and tightened my grip. 'You really want this?' I'd always been brilliant baseball pitcher – ever since my days at the all girls' school in Oxford that Aunt Lucy had enrolled me into when I went to live with her. This orb might be heavier than the balls I was used to, but it would still do nicely for what I had in mind.

As his hand extended forward to take it, I whipped my arm back and threw it with all my strength straight at the guy's smug face. There was a satisfying crack of splintering bone and a spurt of blood from his nose. He toppled backwards like a felled tree.

The stone ball rolled back to me. I picked it up, ready to use it again, but when I looked up I found myself staring at the silencer on his pistol.

The soldier clutched the doorway as he pulled himself back up. 'You really shouldn't have done that, bitch.'

I closed my eyes as he started to squeeze the trigger and flinched as a loud shot echoed through the room.

But a loud shot on a silenced pistol? And no accompanying spike of pain in my skull and shaft of celestial light for me to head towards?

I cracked my eyes open to see the guy had crumpled to the floor for a second time. Only now a lump of his skull was missing from the side of his head.

Robert stood behind him, staring at me, his own pistol in his hand. 'Don't just stand there, Lauren. We need to get you out of here before more of his people arrive.' He stooped down and pulled the soldier's pistol from his hand and stuck it into the waistband of his trousers.

'What's been going on out there?' I said, trying to surreptitiously stuff the stone orb back into my day bag.

'A full-blown siege and a hostage situation, that's what. Anyway, come on – we need to get you to a safe location, Lauren.'

'And what about all the innocent people here?'

'We're doing what we can. But if you're worried about them, the best way to draw these soldiers off is to spirit you away. So get a bloody move on.'

I nodded and together we crept along the corridor.

CHAPTER ELEVEN

THE CORRIDOR WAS BUILT to the same curved profile as the hospital and we made our way along its bend, Robert with his pistol drawn. It was eerily quiet, with not a person to be seen anywhere.

'Where is everyone?' I whispered.

'The hospital is on lockdown,' Robert replied. 'Patients are being kept in their rooms and staff members have to remain where they are until they get the all-clear.'

'They'll be frightened out of their wits. But what I don't get is why anyone would launch an attack when there are so many witnesses. Why not take a much more low-profile approach, like ambushing you when trying to leave with us?'

'That's what's got me worried as well,' Robert replied. 'It's almost as though they are going out of their way to kill as many people as possible. And that makes me think that whoever is behind this wants the world to think of it as some sort of terrorist attack...'

'But surely the government wouldn't allow them to spin something like that to the media?'

'You might think that...'

'You mean the government would be prepared to be complicit? And that's despite Orkney being the most unlikely terrorist target on the planet.'

'You're overlooking the fact that the islands are geographically near an awful lot of North Sea oil-drilling platforms. That could provide the perfect cover story if someone wanted to claim that what happened here was a demonstration of just how vulnerable the West's petrochemical resources are to an attack.'

'Oh, come on. You're telling me that MI5 will roll over and accept that as a cover story?'

Robert paused for a moment and glanced back at me. 'That won't be an issue on this occasion, as I doubt I or any of my team will be allowed to leave the hospital alive. Whoever is responsible won't want anything out there that can challenge that terrorist narrative. Which includes leaving intelligence officers alive to argue against it.'

'So you're saying this is it? What about calling for backup?'

'All communication between Orkney and the outside world has been cut. Even the satellite phones we use during field operations have been taken offline.'

'Damn it. The guy you shot said they'd been monitoring Skara Brae with a military spy satellite. So if they have access to that sort of tech, of course they'd be able to kill all communication.'

'You don't sound surprised about any of this, Lauren.' Robert paused for a moment in the corridor. 'Why is that exactly?'

Robert knew I was holding back. I made a quick mental calculation and figured there was nothing to be gained by not talking to him about whom I believed our attackers to be. Not when we could both die at any moment.

'Look, let's stop sidestepping the issue,' I said. 'We both know who is really responsible here. This has the Overseers' smell all over it.'

'How the hell do you known about them?'

'Kiera told me all about them before she died. There was also the small matter of one of your own being a double agent working for them.'

Robert stared at me. 'That's as maybe, but Kiera had no business telling you about any of it.'

'Well, she did, so get over it already. The question is, do you think this is an Overseers' operation or not?'

He sighed. 'Yes, I do, Lauren. And that leads me to another obvious conclusion. We know that the Overseers tried to grab the Sentinel AI and the most obvious link there is you. Something strange happened at Skara Brae, that much is obvious. The Overseers clearly think it is significant enough to warrant a full-blown assault on a hospital packed with people. And rather than simply kill you as they did before, they must be trying to seize you and the others. They want you alive.'

'Not so sure about the *trying* part of that statement when they already have Jack and Mike.'

'So we'll have to make sure they don't score the hat trick, won't we? And let me worry about your friends. If we manage to live through this, you can tell me the whole truth rather than the edited highlights.'

There was my problem. By the time Robert had dealt with the hospital siege, even if we did survive, Jack and Mike would be long gone, possibly even dead.

I spotted the wide, frightened eyes of a guy staring at us from an internal window. He ducked down when he saw the pistol in Robert's hand.

So many lives were being threatened by this attack. And my feeling of powerlessness was only increasing by the minute.

Robert headed towards the lift and pressed the button. Nothing happened. 'As I suspected, as part of the hospital's lock-down procedure it has shut down the lifts. At least that will slow down the Overseers' soldiers.'

'Surely their people will just use the stairs instead?'

'Yes, but it will take them longer. Even a few seconds could mean the difference between life and death.'

'So what's our plan?'

For the first time I saw the MI5 officer smile.

'Please tell me you haven't got some crazy *Die Hard*-style plan in mind, like using a lift shaft?' I asked.

'Relax. There's another way...' He set off down the next corridor, with me close behind.

'Which is?'

'There's a sloping roof on the south side of the hospital, just above the ambulance bay. We can use that to get to ground level. Then we need to get to a safe location as soon as possible.'

'I am not going to abandon the others.'

'You may not want to, but you have no choice, Lauren. For whatever reason, you've become a target to the Overseers – a target that's endangering the lives of each man, woman and child in this hospital. So the sooner we get you out of here, the sooner these fake terrorists will hopefully see continuing their assault on this place is unnecessary.'

'Then it's a plan. Lead the way.'

Robert cast me a sideways glance. 'For a civilian, you've certainly got the right attitude to be a very effective MI5 field agent, Lauren.'

'Maybe in another life.'

He raised his eyebrows at me as we reached a door and he put his hand on the handle. 'Good – we've made it without drawing any unwanted attention. If I'm correct, the room beyond this door should give us access to the roof over the ambulance bay.' He tried the door but it was locked.

'I thought this was starting to look too easy,' I said.

'This isn't going to be a problem.'

Robert took a small cylindrical device from his pocket and inserted it into the keyhole. He pressed a button and a whining sound started up, followed by three green LEDs that lit one after the other. A snick came from the lock and Robert tried the handle again. The door opened.

'I so need one of those. I was always locking myself out of my flat back in Macclesfield.'

'I'm afraid they're MI5-issue only. Something that might make interviewing for us more tempting maybe.'

'I'll keep that in mind,' I replied.

We entered an empty meeting room and crossed to the large window at the far wall. Through it the sloping roof below us was clearly visible.

'I love it when a plan comes together,' I said.

'You're not the only one.' Robert started to raise window, but like the one I'd encountered, it jammed on its safety stop.

I took out my Swiss army knife and started to pull out the screwdriver.

But Robert shook his head and hitched up the back of his jacket to reveal the silenced pistol he'd stuffed into the waistband. 'Stand back, Lauren.' He held his hand up to shield his face and aimed the weapon directly at the metal stop. The bullet hissed and the stop flew off sideways without even cracking the window.

'Nice shot,' I said.

'All that time on the target course has its benefits,' Robert replied as he slid the window upwards.

We both peered down at the roof again. It was only a few metres, but certainly enough to turn an ankle or worse, if either of us misjudged it.

Robert clambered out of the window first and lowered himself out of view until just his hands were visible on the ledge. Then he let go and vanished. I heard a dull thud and leant out to see him standing on the roof looking up at me, his finger to his lips. He gestured to the roof below him and I heard the murmur of voices. I nodded. I needed to do this as silently as possible and pray our luck held out.

I followed Robert's lead and sat on the windowsill. Twisting round, I grabbed hold of the frame and lowered myself down until my feet were dangling over empty air. Although it was a relatively short drop, someone needed to tell my legs that because they were hollowing out. I had to mentally force my fingers to let go. The wall skimmed past and I absorbed as much of the impact as I could in a cat-like landing, but there was still a quiet thud as my boots hit the roof.

We traded glances, but no challenging shout came from below. Robert gestured forward and we started to creep towards the far end of the roof. We reached it and peered over the edge.

Two men in black combat fatigues stood guarding the ambulance bay, both wearing the obligatory ski masks. More menacing were the large automatic weapons they held. However, luckily for us, their attention was focused on the entrance to the A & E department. Around them, a number of vehicles had been abandoned.

My heart twisted as I saw an ambulance driver sprawled from the door of his vehicle. Bullet holes peppered his windscreen.

'Bastards,' I whispered.

Robert didn't say a word. Instead, he took out the silenced pistol and aimed it at the first of the two men. His shoulders slowly rose as he steadied himself to take the shot. Then I heard shouting coming from inside the A & E department as the doors opened.

'Keep your fucking hands off me!' Jack's voice shouted.

A huge wave of relief rolled through me. He was alive.

A group of men headed out of the doors.

'Prepare an ambulance!' a masked man at the head of the group called out in a Spanish accent.

The soldiers already in the bay rushed to the ambulance with the dead driver. One of them hauled him out, dumping him on the tarmac like rubbish.

Heat rose through my blood. Who did these bloody people think they were?

Meanwhile another soldier headed to the back of the ambulance and threw open the rear doors. A moment later Jack came into view, his hands on his head as a guy wearing a ski mask and goggles pushed Jack forward with the tip of his rifle in his back. Another two soldiers followed, pushing a trolley carrying Mike, a drip line still connected to his arm.

'We need to stop them whilst we still can,' I said.

Robert shook his head. 'Not yet. There are too many of them and they're heavily armed. We need to pick our moment.'

A sinking feeling filled me as first Jack and then Mike, unconscious, disappeared into the back of the ambulance.

The guy who'd barked the order at the others pulled a walkie-talkie off his webbing strap. 'We're clear. Blow the charges.'

Robert pushed me flat. A second later a series of explosions rattled the building behind us, vibrating the roof we were lying on. I rolled over to see three balls of flame rolling up into the sky from the far side of the hospital. Any sense of numbness was swept away by the white-hot fury coursing through my veins.

'Give me one of your bloody guns and I will shoot that bastard myself,' I said.

Robert shook his head. 'I know how angry you're feeling, Lauren, but attack now and we'll just be throwing our lives away.'

I glowered at him, anger still swirling through me, but now it was teamed with guilt. If I hadn't been so tenacious in searching for the truth, all these people would still be alive. Was anything worth all this suffering?

The Overseers leader climbed into the driver's seat of the ambulance as the group with him fled into the back and shut the doors.

I stared down at the ambulance, knowing that in a second it would be gone. The Overseers would interrogate Jack until they broke him to get all the information they needed. Then they would simply kill him. As for Mike, who knew what they had planned, but it would be nothing good.

The ambulance started to pull away. My heart rose to my mouth. 'Do something, Robert.'

'Don't you worry, I'm planning to.'

With its lights flashing, the ambulance headed towards the main road. It was the perfect getaway vehicle – after all, who would stop an emergency vehicle speeding along the roads?

Robert settled himself once again, his face pure focus as he ignored the fire now blazing on the other side of the hospital. He sighted the two men who'd been guarding the ambulance bay along his pistol, who were now heading towards a black Audi estate.

Robert pulled the trigger and the man on the right crumpled to the ground. Robert was already swinging the pistol round towards the second soldier, but he was rolling sideways, bringing his weapon up and spitting out automatic fire. Bullets blazed up through the roof, sending sparks flying around us.

I ducked, but Robert returned fire without so much as flinch-ing. I heard the unmistakable sickening impact of a bullet into flesh. Robert let out a stifled cry and spun sideways, clutching his shoulder.

'Damn it,' he hissed. Blood pooled around his fingers as he pressed his palm into the wound.

The still-active soldier headed beneath the cover of the roof and fired straight up as he ran. Bullets lanced holes across the roof all around us.

'You need to get yourself out of here, Lauren,' Robert said, gritting his teeth.

'What about your injury?'

He gestured at the hospital. 'I think I'm already in the best place possible to deal with that.'

'Then just give me a sodding gun already.'

'Maybe you wouldn't make such great agent if you can't follow orders.'

'Now we're starting to understand each other. Hand it over!'

Robert passed me the silenced gun as more bullets whistled up into the air. 'Good luck.'

'You too...'

Another ambulance was parked just under the edge of the roof. That would have to do. Could I make it down to the ground where I would get a clear shot at the guy? I didn't give myself time to think and allow my fear to kick in. Instead, I sprinted forward and leapt on to the ambulance's roof.

As the clang of my boots on metal rang out, the soldier spun round to face me and raised his gun.

I aimed the pistol as his bullets raked the ambulance working their way towards me as he corrected his aim. I breathed out as I'd seen Robert do, and fired a single shot.

Time stood still. Then a single bullet hole appeared in the soldier's forehead. He gave me a surprised look as he dropped his automatic weapon and collapsed to the ground. But I didn't allow myself the luxury of processing what happened, only dropped down the side of the ambulance and raced over to him.

Within a moment, and trying to ignore his lifeless staring

eyes, I had his automatic weapon and perhaps more importantly his car key.

I rushed over to the Audi estate, pressing the unlock button on the remote fob as I ran. The vehicle's indicators flashed. The next minute, I was heading away from the hospital chasing after the bastards who'd taken Jack and Mike.

CHAPTER TWELVE

EVEN THOUGH I didn't have a direct line of sight on the ambulance and had deliberately kept my distance in the early gloom of the dawn, its strobing emergency lights were acting as a useful homing beacon. They illuminated the surrounding countryside in shades of blue as the world crept towards a grey, rainy dawn.

I kept my distance as I pursued the vehicle. The trauma of what had happened back at the hospital should have been looping through my mind, but it was strangely absent, like some part of my brain had shut down. Maybe it was a combination of survival instinct and adrenaline making me feel like a robot. More likely was that the Overseers attack on Jodrell Bank, the murder of my aunt and now all these innocent people at the hospital had numbed me. My attitude towards vengeance had been rewired. 'Kill or be killed' was my new personal motto. To underline that new philosophy, my day bag now bulged with extra ammo magazines and even some flash-bangs and smoke grenades I'd found in the glove compartment of the Audi.

My brain was occupied by thinking about the neutrino burst

that the Overseers soldier had mentioned. Neutrinos equalled radiation and it wouldn't be good for any of us who'd been at Skara Brae, even if it hadn't been a lethal dose. But how was it linked to popping over to the twilight zone exactly? I needed more data to draw a conclusion. Maybe the Overseers knew something that we didn't. I glanced across at the holdall I'd found in the car and that I already quickly looked through. Maybe there were some clues in there I'd missed? A radiation detector badge maybe, that sort of thing?

With one hand on the wheel, I reached across and began to hunt through the rucksack.

It was full of clothes, presumably belonging to one of the Overseers soldiers, but nothing of interest in the main compartment.

I unzipped a side pocket and discovered an old-fashioned flip phone. The Overseers soldier had presumably chosen this very un-smart phone because it didn't have a GPS chip and so couldn't be easily located. Holding it, I realised I really needed to ring someone who might be able to help me formulate the answer to what had caused the neutrino bursts and find out just how powerful they had been. Maybe an extended exposure had sent Mike into a coma-like state, which would have explained why he'd been missing for over a week.

I surprised myself when my fingers instinctively remembered an old mobile number. I began to dial. After just three rings the phone was picked up.

'I don't recognise your number,' Steve said. 'If you going to tell me you can help me claim for a car accident I never had, you can bloody well sod off right now.'

My eyes immediately stung at hearing the voice of my friend and colleague from Jodrell Bank. It had been over a year.

'Steve, it's me, Lauren.'

A pause and then a gasp. 'Bloody hell, Lauren. Are you OK?'

'Despite what life has been throwing at me recently, I'm doing all right.'

A concerned edge tinged his tone as he said, 'Why, what's happened?'

'It's best that you don't know.'

'That sounds serious?'

'It really is, but I can't tell you anything.'

'I see...' He sighed. 'It's great to hear your voice anyway. You do realise I've been worried sick about you since hearing about your aunt?'

'You know why, Steve. It was safer for you that I didn't make contact.'

'But now? You certainly sound different...' His words trailed away.

A lump filled my throat. Different how? Harder? A woman who was becoming numb to violence? But with Aunt Lucy gone, Steve was the one person on this planet who cared about how I was doing.

I gripped the mobile tighter. 'Hey, at least I'm getting plenty of fresh air rather than being stuck in that control room with you.'

Steve snorted. 'You make that sound like the worst thing on Earth.'

'No, they will always be some of the happiest moments of my life, and you know that.'

I rounded a bend and saw the ambulance turn on to a track. The emergency vehicle headed towards a run-down farm at the end of it. I slowed the Audi to a crawl.

'So come back to us,' Steve said. 'You know your old job is waiting for you. All those pulsars are still there for you to visually trip out on.'

'I can't, Steve. You know that. Whatever is going on is too big for me to turn my back on now, especially since Aunt Lucy...'

'Yes...' Another sigh. 'God, I so miss your sunny disposition around here.'

'I miss you too, Steve.'

'But you would only have reached out to me if there was a pressing reason.'

'You know me too bloody well, you know that?'

'I do.'

The ambulance disappeared behind a complex of dilapidated farm buildings with broken tiled roofs. They looked distinctly abandoned. I slowly headed past the track leading to them, and pulled up in the gated entrance to a field and killed the engine.

'So how can I help, Lauren?' Steve asked.

'I need to know about any neutrino activity that's been captured, particularly over the last two weeks.'

'What, you're looking for supernovas?'

'Not exactly, more like a source closer to home. Is there anyone you can think of who could supply me with a list of unexplained bursts without a known origin and also a measurement of their power?'

'Yes, there is, actually. The project leader at the IceCube Neutrino Observatory in Antarctica is an old friend of mine. They monitor everything from that facility – from supernovas to atmospheric activity.'

'Do you think you could get me a copy of their data from the last couple of weeks?'

'Yes, that shouldn't be a problem. But why are you interested? Is it something to do with your little green aliens search?'

'Maybe. I can't say any more. But before I go, can I ask you one more thing? Have you any idea why MI5 would ask me if I'd been in contact with you?'

'Ah...I'm not really meant to say anything about that.'

'Come on, Steve. It's me you're talking to.'

'OK...but you didn't hear this from me. It's being referred to as the Earth Song investigation, and it's got a lot of people freaked out.'

I gripped the phone harder. This was what Mike had said when he'd come round at Skara Brae...

'Shit, seriously?' I said.

'Yes, why? Do you know something about this?'

'Nothing other than the name.'

'Ah, right. So here's the deal. You've heard those NASA recordings of the random radio sounds that Earth makes?'

'Of course. They're really haunting, especially when they trigger an accompanying light show for me.'

'Well, this is the thing you obviously don't know. About a year ago, just after you left, the random tones became a lot less random and a regular recurring pattern started to emerge.'

'You mean there's a strong radio source operating at the same frequency that's swamping everything else out?'

'That was one initial thought. Maybe some sort of experimental energy research screwing with the atmosphere like that HAARP experiment that none of us are meant to know about.'

'HAARP?'

'The High Frequency Active Auroral Research Program. It's a US-military-funded programme using high-power, high-frequency transmitters in the ionosphere to investigate radio communications. There were a number of reports some time ago of weird sounds coming from the sky. Back then people thought they might be linked to what they were up to at the HAARP research station in Gakona, Alaska. But the US military have denied any involvement in it.'

'The usual response even when it's an outright lie.'

'Of course, same old.'

'So what about a location for this high-powered radio source?' I asked.

'That's the thing, Lauren. We can't locate just one – it's operating across multiple frequencies and seems to be coming from everywhere at once.'

'Hang on, that sounds like the omnidirectional signal from a parallel-world transmission that sent Sentinel to us.'

'Exactly.'

'And is it?'

'No. The radio source contained no data we can discern, unlike the Sentinel broadcast. However, GCHQ seemed to think it was a possibility and hence MI5's renewed interest in us. We've all been interviewed again to see if Sentinel has made any further contact. Which he hasn't. But whatever did cause this, the radio song Earth sings out into the cosmos has permanently changed. Hence the project title "Earth Song". And Jodrell Bank is now part of a secret global effort to research it.'

'And that's all you know?'

'For now.'

'Well, if that changes, make sure you tell me the moment you find anything out. You can ring me on this number, but don't leave a voicemail if I don't pick up. And don't forget that information about the neutrino activity.'

'I won't, but it will have to be off the record.'

'Of course.' I glanced across at the farm. 'It's been great talking to you, Steve, but I've got to go.'

'Lauren, please take care.'

'I always try to.' I cradled the mobile for a moment, not wanting the call to end. But I also had lives to save.

'Speak soon, Steve...' I pressed the end call icon before he could ask me any more. An ache for my old life pulsed inside me.

I climbed out of the Audi, the morning air icy on my face after the warmth of the car. I drew my jacket in round me, slid the pistol into the waistband of my jeans and grabbed the silenced automatic rifle along with two extra magazines.

It was probably just as well that Steve couldn't see me right now. I shouldered my day bag with the orb, extra ammo, flash-bangs and smoke grenades inside, and climbed up on to the gate. With a calming breath, I jumped down the other side and headed towards the farm buildings. Here went nothing.

CHAPTER THIRTEEN

THE WIND MOANED round the far buildings as I neared them. The brief respite of clear weather rapidly disappeared as another bank of storm clouds rolled in to paint the sky with metallic greys. It was a perfect metaphor for the growing sense of dread I felt inside.

I reached the first stone outbuilding and began to creep along its rear wall. My fingers played over the rough surface until I finally reached the corner. I poked the nozzle of the automatic rifle round the edge first. When no one shouted a challenge, I followed the gun with my head.

In the courtyard the ambulance had been parked alongside a black pickup truck. I scanned the dilapidated buildings around me. The windows were long gone and many of the doors were hanging off their hinges. A pile of scaffolding poles lay in a pile. At some point Orkney's very own Banksy had graffitied a giant red penis on the wall. Zero out of ten for originality there.

I scanned the buildings for any sign of activity, but spotted none.

Too damn quiet...

Then I noticed a slit of light escaping between the closed doors of a corrugated cattle shed at the far end of the courtyard. OK, this was more like it. But the smart move wouldn't be to use the main doors. That would be like entering a bar in a western, ready for a showdown with the bad guys. And this situation was unfortunately anything but Hollywood. The reality would almost certainly mean being killed, and pretty quickly too. No, a much better alternative was to find another way to sneak in and hopefully take them by surprise. Then I'd free Jack and we'd escape in the Audi. Easy...

My brain slid past the in-between part of that plan, pretending there wasn't a gaping hole in it. I had another thing to worry about too. Could I really stop these people? I'd discover the answer to that soon I guessed.

I manoeuvred round the back of the shed and spotted a door hanging on one hinge squeaking as it swung in the wind. My way in.

As I approached I heard the faint sound of voices from inside.

'You're only delaying the inevitable, Dr Harper,' a familiar voice with a Spanish accent said.

The Overseers man in charge of the team at the hospital. I tightened my finger on the trigger of my automatic weapon.

'I suggest you talk now and you'll save yourself a lot of pain,' the voice continued.

'You'll not get anything from me, arsehole,' I heard Jack reply.

My heart filled my chest. God, the guy had guts.

I slipped through the broken door and found myself in a gloomy room filled with tools and a bench. There was an open internal door at the far end where the voices were coming from. I unhitched my day bag and took out the extra ammo magazines and flash-bangs for my full-on *Matrix*-style attack...in my head at least. I placed my bag under the bench and covered it with an old rotten sack. If this went badly, and it probably would, the last thing I wanted was the stone orb falling into the Overseers' hands.

OK, this is it, Lauren Stelleck. You might be frightened to death, but you're going to do this anyway.

I edged forward and peered round the edge of the door frame into the gloomy interior of cattle shed.

A group of Overseers soldiers were in the middle of the room, watching a guy standing over Jack. He'd been lashed to some railings and his shirt had been torn open. His chest was a ribbon of cuts. Rivulets of blood ran from the wounds down over his abdomen.

I fought the nausea spiking through my guts. I had to stay strong and not lose it if I was serious about saving them.

The soldier prowled around Jack. He was wearing surgical gloves and had a scalpel in his hand. 'You're going to talk eventually,' he said. Then he turned enough for me to see his face and time stood still.

My gaze locked on to his crystal-blue eyes and the scar radiating from his left eye. This was the same bastard who'd led the Overseers assault on Jodrell Bank. He was responsible for all these fresh deaths. But most of all he was the man who had murdered Aunt Lucy.

White-hot fury rose through me as the arrogant shit stopped in front of Jack and casually pressed the scalpel slowly into his stomach.

My hand tightened on my automatic rifle as Jack hissed with pain. Mr Eye Scar withdrew the scalpel's blade and a fresh trickle of blood joined the others.

Jack glowered up at his tormentor through the fringe of his sweat-soaked hair. 'I'm going to stuff that thing right up your fucking shithole, Colonel Alvarez.'

The man narrowed his gaze on him. 'How do you know my name, Dr Harper?'

'I overheard one of your mercs talking with you.'

'I see... Not that it matters. You will be dead soon anyway. And if you want to take this scalpel from me, you can be my guest.' Alvarez spread his hands wide and smirked.

An image of a bullet appearing in this guy's head filled my imagination.

Jack strained against the plastic ties that lashed his hands, but his bonds didn't break.

Alvarez sneered. 'Didn't think so.'

His soldiers grinned at each other as they enjoyed the floor show.

I resolved to make the bastard pay, but I could taste the danger in the air. One of the soldiers cupped his hand round a cigarette as he lit it and I spotted what was behind him: Mike on the trolley, still very much dead to the world. And he and Jack would be dead soon permanently unless I stepped in.

There were five Overseers mercenaries including Alvarez, making me very outnumbered, but even so I had to seize control of this situation. The alternative was too awful to consider.

Alvarez looked at his watch and sighed. 'Look, Dr Harper, I'm a busy man. I haven't got time for you to act out your you-are-never-going-to-break-me stance. So I think I'll get started on Mike instead and maybe that will loosen your tongue.'

'Just leave him fucking alone,' Jack replied.

'I don't think so.' The colonel turned to a nearby bench and opened a case. He took something out of it, but his back blocked my view as he crossed over to Mike.

Keeping low, I crept behind a mouldering hay bale and rested my machine gun on top.

'Leave him alone!' Jack shouted at the colonel.

'Unfortunately, that's not an option. You see, I need Mike awake for questioning. What you won't tell me, maybe he will.' Alvarez raised his hand to reveal a syringe full of clear liquid.

Before I could react, he plunged the syringe into Mike's arm and pushed the stop all the way down. Mike immediately started to fit.

'What the fuck did you do to him?' Jack shouted.

'A shot of adrenaline to bring him round,' Alvarez replied.

'But the CT scan was inconclusive. That could kill him.'

'Then that's what'll happen. And then I will have to set to work on you with some bolt cutters on your fingers.'

I grabbed the pin of a flash-bang, ready to pull it, just as Mike arched his back on the trolley, his mouth wide as his eyes shot open.

'Earth Song is our only hope!' he shouted. Then his eyes fluttered shut and he slumped back on to the trolley.

I stared at him. Had Mike been abducted by the UFO in the twilight zone? Is that how he knew the phrase?

'What's he talking about, Dr Harper?' Alvarez asked.

'Even if I did know, which I don't, I wouldn't tell you. So you might as well get it over with and kill me.'

'Are you really in such a hurry to die?'

Jack twitched his shoulders up in a shrug. 'Why not, asshole?'

'Everything comes to those who wait, Jack. But first another shot of adrenaline should be enough to keep Mike conscious long enough for us to extract the information we need.'

My heart thundered in my chest as Jack rattled the railings he was tied to, trying to break his straps yet again.

This was it. I had to act now.

Do it and don't think...

I pulled the pin and pitched the grenade in an arc over the hay bale I was using as cover. Jack's eyes widened as he spotted the flash-bang bounce and roll into the middle of the group of soldiers beyond him. He snapped his eyes shut and averted his head.

I dived flat and clamped my hands over my ears. The flash of light burned through my closed eyelids as an impossibly loud bang rattled my covered ears. Without even looking, I lobbed a smoke grenade.

Act fast whilst you have the element of surprise...

I brought my head up, my automatic gun ready.

Smoke billowed from the grenade and the soldiers lay dazed on the floor near the flash-bang, blood trickling from their ears. But not all of them...

Shit!

Alvarez, blood trickling from his ears as the smoke thickened around him, slowly raised his pistol towards me with a shaking hand.

Time to make good on my promise. I took aim and squeezed the trigger on my weapon... It wouldn't budge.

Alvarez blinked and steadied one hand with the other.

Sheer unadulterated panic surged through me as I squeezed the trigger a second time. Same bloody thing. A bullet whistled past my head, Alvarez grimacing behind it. He took aim again as he started to disappear behind the wall of smoke. And then my stupid mind caught up with what was happening.

The safety! I reached up with my thumb and flicked the safety off, but it was too late. A bullet sliced through my left bicep with a hiss and sickening thud as molten metal levels of burning pain seared through my arm. My weapon clattered to the ground.

Alvarez gave me a twisted grin as he emerged from the smoke like some sort of demon.

My rescue attempt had gone to shit because I hadn't bloody remembered to check the safety. Instinctively I tensed, ready to die as Alvarez stood over me and took aim for the final shot.

Then a figure loomed out of the fog behind him, already swinging the box that had been full of syringes in a large arc. With a crack, the box smashed into the back of Alvarez's head and the colonel sprawled to the floor.

Mike stood over Alvarez, his hospital gown flapping open at the back and showing me his arse as he panted.

I shook myself back into action, standing up. 'You're awake!'

Mike pointed at the blood trickling out of his ears and shook his head.

Of course, he'd been deafened by the flash-bang. But what about Jack?

Nursing my shoulder, I picked up my automatic rifle. I trailed it behind me, heading into the smoke towards where Jack had been. A vague shape appeared ahead – he was alive, tied to the barrier and staring at me.

'You?' he said.

'In person, although that rescue attempt didn't go as well as I'd planned.'

With my hand shaking as warm blood trickled down my chilled arm, I fished my Swiss army knife out and selected the blade. In two cuts, I'd freed Jack from the plastic ties bonding his wrists to the barrier.

'Where the hell did you come from?' Jack asked.

'You must be dreaming and hallucinated me up,' I replied.

Despite his injuries, a small smile filled his face. 'Right.'

I pointed to his ears. 'And you can hear me despite the flash-bang?'

'I've got perforated eardrums from a diving accident. I think that helped with the concussion wave.'

'At least that's one unexpected positive.' I grabbed Jack's arm to steady him as he took two tottering steps.

Mike loomed out of the fog in front of us. 'What the fuck is going on?' he whispered as men started to groan hidden somewhere in the smoke.

His question was answered by the hiss of a bullet speeding over our heads.

I swung my automatic weapon round and opened fire,

spraying bullets in an arc into the smoke. A cry came out of the fog, followed by a thud.

'And who the hell are you? Lara Croft?' Mike asked.

'It's not the first time I've been called that,' I replied with a tight smile. 'But introductions later, let's focus on escape first. So follow me.'

Mike exchanged a look with Jack that was obviously asking who the hell this woman was. I was starting to wonder that myself.

More gunfire hissed out of the gloom.

'Come on,' I whispered as I supported Jack with my good arm and led him and Mike out through the workshop. 'Hang on a moment...' I leant down, pain pulsing from my wound, and grabbed my day bag from its hiding place before starting forward again.

I sucked in the clean air as we emerged outside.

Gunfire still reverberated through the building as men shouted and smoke billowed out between the panels of the corrugated panels.

'With any luck they might shoot each other in the confusion,' Jack said.

We rounded the corner of the building and Jack pointed to the ambulance and pickup truck. 'I don't suppose you've got the keys for either of those, Lauren?'

'No, but I have an Audi I stole from some other Overseers. It's parked up near the main road.'

'Whoever you are, you're quite something,' Mike said.

'She is,' Jack said. 'But now we have the chance, let's grab the medical kit from the ambulance so I can deal with your bullet wound and then my injuries. I also want to give you a thorough check-up, Mike. Let's slow them down a little...' Hanging on to me, Jack picked up a scaffolding pole from the ground and stuffed it through the handles of the double doors into the cattle shed.

'There is still the back door, you know,' I said.

'By the time they work that out, hopefully we'll be long gone,' Jack replied.

We crossed to the ambulance and Jack, now steadier on his feet, hunted inside the vehicle. He reappeared a moment later with a green medical bag and several boxes of drugs.

I'd started to move away when I remembered the Swiss army knife still clutched in my hand. 'Hang on a sec.'

I raced back to the vehicles and stuck the blade into each of the tyres with satisfying hisses.

'You really are Lara bloody Croft,' Mike said, staring at me as I rejoined them.

I shot him a smile. But then a huge clang came from the cattle shed doors and the handles shook against the scaffolding pole lock.

'Get these fucking doors open!' Alvarez shouted from inside.

Jack extended his hand and gestured for my machine gun. 'Do you mind?'

'Knock yourself out.'

He took it from me and sprayed the doors with bullets. The clanging stopped fast after that.

'Damn, that felt good. I hope I got the bastards, Alvarez specifically,' Jack said.

'Me too, because that dickhead had it coming,' I replied.

Together, our ragtag group limped across the field towards the Audi.

CHAPTER FOURTEEN

We sped along a country lane as heavy rain smeared the world through the Audi's windows. Jack, despite his injuries, had insisted on driving, not that any of us were in great shape.

'So what's the plan? Mike asked from the back seat. He'd been constantly shaking since the moment we climbed into the vehicle despite me cranking the temperature up to max. Probably everything to do with shock taking over as the adrenaline started to work its way out of his system.

I pressed the bandage that Jack had given me hard into my bullet wound. It had gone straight through my bicep.

'There's no way we can head back to your place,' Jack said. 'It's bound to be crawling with Alvarez's soldiers by now.'

'We could try to contact Robert to ask for protection?' I said.

'You saw for yourself how well that played out back at the hospital,' Jack replied.

'Why, what happened?' Mike asked.

'Yet another thing we need to brief you on. It wasn't good,' I said.

'So maybe we should just get ourselves off the island,' Jack suggested.

I shook my head. 'I doubt that's going to be an option. They're bound to be watching all the ports.'

'My place is a no-go too – it's the obvious place to look for us along with Jack's cottage,' Mike said. 'So what about yours, Lauren?'

'The only place I've stayed on this island has been Jack's cottage.'

'Is it now?' Mike grinned at the back of Jack's head.

'Nothing happened!' I said.

'Of course not.' Mike's grin widened.

I rolled my eyes at him but also caught the stiffening in Jack's expression. As subtle as it was, he couldn't have made it clearer to me that he wasn't in the right headspace for getting involved with another woman.

'I have a surfing mate who has a caravan on a pitch near Rackwick Beach,' Mike continued. 'I store some of my crap there when I'm surfing.' He gestured to his hospital gown. 'And I for one really need a shower and a change of clothes. I'm tired of showing you my derrière, Lauren.'

'Then that makes two of us,' I replied, shaking my head.

'Hey, some ladies would be honoured to see my booty.'

'Well, I'm sadly not one of them.'

Mike's chuckle turned into a teeth chatter.

'How are you doing there?' I asked.

'I'm concentrating on the plus point that I'm alive rather than the fact my skull feels as if it's been split in two and stuck back together with superglue.'

Jack peered at him through the rear-view mirror. 'Being brought round with a shot of adrenaline is going to do that to you. But the question is, what knocked you into that comatose state in the first place? Presumably it had something to do with your disappearance?'

I started to open my mouth, but Jack gave me a quick sideways glance with the slightest headshake.

I picked up on Jack's strategy and stopped the prompt I was about to give Mike. Getting him to tell us that he'd been abducted by an alien craft, rather than for us to leap in and suggest it, was the best approach. The alternative would probably mean he'd label us both as crazy.

'I wish I could remember. All I have is a big, fat mile-wide gap in my memory,' Mike replied. 'One moment I was running an acoustic test as I waited for the next pulse of seismic activity and the next there was a huge flash of light. The next thing I remember is coming round to see that you'd stabbed me in the heart with a syringe, Jack. Then I blacked out again.'

'Jack saved your life,' I said.

Mike gazed at Jack. 'You did?'

Jack raised his shoulders. 'Your heart had stopped, although there's no need to make a big deal of it. You can buy me a drink later. But you really don't remember what happened after that flash of light?'

Jack gave me another loaded he-doesn't-remember-being-abducted look to which I nodded.

'Nothing,' Mike replied. 'Not until I came round with that Alvarez guy's back to me. I saw the state of you, Jack, and the needle in my arm, and quickly realised we were both in serious trouble. So I pretended to be knocked out still, and waited for my moment. Then I saw Alvarez about to shoot some woman trying to help us, and I knew I had to act.'

'Something for which I will always be in your debt, Mike. You saved my life today, like Jack did yours.'

'I think we all pretty much saved each other's arses, so that makes us equal in the grand scheme of things,' Jack replied.

'Another thing we can certainly drink to,' Mike said.

Now to mention the thing that I'd been dying to ask him. 'So what about what you said about Earth Song being our only hope?'

'I did?' Mike replied. 'Did I say anything else?'

'That was it,' Jack said.

'Sorry. Earth Song being our only hope? It doesn't mean anything to me. I don't remember it.'

I tried to keep the disappointment off my face. It seemed I would have to rely on Steve for any further insight there. There was certainly no point in pursuing it with Mike, at least not until if and when he remembered anything about his joyride in a strange UFO.

'What's the reason for the acoustic tests you were running at Skara Brae?' I asked.

'I've been trying to pinpoint the cause of all the low-level seismic activity across the island,' Mike said. 'I'm something of an amateur geophysicist among other things. And there have been some strange seismic waves rippling around the world. Have either of you heard about them?'

'I think I read a report about one,' Jack said. 'Scientists picked up a weird tremor off an island in the Indian Ocean that didn't fit the normal earthquake criteria.'

'That's it,' Mike said. 'The first one was detected off the coast of Mayotte, the island you're talking about. It was a wave picked up over twelve thousand miles away. No one knows for sure what caused it as it was monochromatic, which means across a single frequency, whereas normal earthquakes are multi-frequency. There is one theory that it was linked to slow-moving lava beneath Earth's crust, but I have another idea.'

'Hang on. Do you think it's linked somehow to the recent seismic activity around Orkney?' I asked.

'You nailed it.'

'It can't be coincidence,' Jack said.

'What do you mean?' Mike asked.

'For now, let's just say that Skara Brae is the epicentre of strange activity, which includes your disappearance,' I said.

'Yes, and of course there are the crystal markings too,' Mike said. 'I've been studying them, but they defy any known form of quartz formation due to their rapid formation. The one thing that's for certain is something very weird is going on here.'

I glanced across at Jack. 'We really need to tell Mike everything.'

'Tell me what?' Mike asked, sitting up straighter.

'First things first,' Jack said. 'I don't want you to freak out on us when we tell you where we found you.'

'I'm not sure I like the sound of where this is headed, but go on,' Mike replied.

'Passing the baton to you here, Lauren,' Jack said.

'Thanks for nothing,' I replied. I turned round to face Mike. 'I'm going to do this explanation fast to lessen the pain, a bit like ripping off a plaster, OK?'

'Just tell me already,' Mike said.

I took a breath. 'Right. So hear me out to the end before you ask anything. It's like this. My research revealed a pattern to the crystal symbols that have been appearing across Orkney. Basically they form a spiral that centres on Skara Brae. I was with Jack at the site yesterday when we discovered a buried stone orb – some sort of ancient device, almost certainly alien in origin, and could be triggered by sound.'

Mike opened his mouth to ask a question but I waved at him to keep quiet and pressed on. 'That stone orb then triggered my synaesthesia – my brain is wired to literally see certain sounds as patterns in my vision. And I managed to activate the orb, which turned out to be a control triggered by an acoustic note. The next thing I knew, a holographic map of our universe appeared. It showed an alien ship on its way from Tau Ceti towards Earth.'

Mike blinked several times.

Now to hit him with the most difficult thing to swallow. 'Using the control orb, I managed to pitch myself and Jack into an alternative reality, where the real world became an-out-of-focus mirage. It was there that a tetrahedron-shaped UFO appeared and did the whole classic beam-of-light routine. You, unconscious, were deposited from it, landing at our feet. I managed to get us back to our own world so that Jack could try to revive you. The rest you know.'

Mike stared at me, every single possible emotion seeming to pass through his eyes. Then of all things, he whooped and clapped. 'Bloody hell, it all fits!'

'Fits what?' Jack asked.

'What I've been researching, guys. Something odd is buried at Skara Brae. I didn't want to tell you anything, Jack, until I was sure. But my acoustic tests revealed a dense mass beneath your site.'

Jack stared at him in the rear-view mirror. 'What sort of dense mass?'

Mike blew his breath out. 'You're not going to believe this, but it was a pyramid shape. A tetrahedron.'

I gawped at him. 'With how many sides, five?'

'Four actually, if you include the base,' Mike replied.

'You're shitting me,' Jack said, shaking his head.

'No more than you are me.'

'This has to be linked to everything that's been happening,' I said. 'The strange tremors, the spiralling patterns of crystal centring on Skara Brae, the weird slow-moving tremors...not to mention that Earth Song message you returned with, Mike.'

'I just wish we knew what it means,' Jack said.

'But we do,' I replied. 'I was talking to an old colleague, who told me that Earth Song is the name for a secret research project. You see, our planet creates its own sounds across multiple radio frequencies. It's normally a random noise, but that changed about a year ago when a regular recurring radio pattern first appeared. No one knows why, or where the source might be.'

'Shit, you're saying this artefact beneath Skara Brae might be the source?' Jack asked.

'I don't know, but it's too big a coincidence for it not to be a strong possibility.'

'OK, there's some sort of alien artefact buried there, which is melting my brain enough already, but there's one thing I really don't get, Mike,' Jack said. 'I've used ground radar on that site and seen nothing buried.'

'Don't forget you didn't spot our stone orb with it either.'

'True.'

'And actually it does make sense, because the kit I used to detect this mass isn't exactly standard,' Mike said.

'How so?' I asked.

'It's my own invention, using low-frequency vibrations to detect density variations beneath the ground. With my computer simulation I'm able to model things to a significant depth – certainly greater than current ground radar can achieve.'

'For an amateur, you sound like you're working on the bleeding edge of geophysics,' I said.

'I am. But geophysics is just part of what I do.'

'I thought you were a geologist,' Jack said.

'That's my day job. But this is what all my money goes into. You could say it's something of a calling. But before I go into all that I need a shower to warm up and something to eat. My brain is fit to explode with all this new information, not to mention the mother of all headaches.'

'You're not the only one,' Jack said.

'But there is something else I want to know – how does Alvarez and his mercenaries fit into all of this?' Mike asked.

'They belong to a group known as the Overseers,' I replied.

'And who are they when they're at home?'

'A lot of trouble...' I gritted my teeth as a stab of pain pulsed through the wound in my arm. 'I think I'm going to need some more painkillers, Jack.'

'We'll sort you out when we get to the caravan. Just down this road for a couple of miles and follow the turning for the beach, Mike, right?'

'You got it.'

I eased the pressure on the pad a fraction to see that the blood had congealed over the wound. 'How is your chest, Jack? It must be stinging like hell.'

'I'll live – nothing a few butterfly bandages can't sort out. Or failing that, superglue.'

'That is pure Jack Harper,' Mike said. 'Once I saw this big guy drop a rock on his foot, fracturing it. He didn't so much as swear.'

'So you're the strong stoic type then?' I asked Jack.

'Oh, don't you worry, if I have something to really cuss about, I let the world know.'

'You're certainly a handy guy to have around in a crisis.'

'You too it seems,' Jack replied with a smile.

'So what are you, Lauren? Ex-military like our Jack here?' Mike asked.

'Something even more badass, I replied. 'I was a radio tele-scope operator in my former life.'

Mike's eyes widened on me. 'Oh, I'd love to hear more about that, especially over a drink or three.'

'Watch him, Lauren. Mike here has quite the moves with the ladies.'

I snorted. 'Bless him.' Unfortunately for me, the guy I was actually interested in obviously didn't feel the same way.

I glanced down at the day bag cradled in my lap that was keeping the stone orb safe. Maybe with that and the information still buried in Mike's head, we'd claw our way to answering this mystery. And now we knew there was something – possibly even an Angelus crashed craft – buried beneath the site.

CHAPTER FIFTEEN

ALTHOUGH RAIN SWIRLED past the window, I felt completely snug inside the caravan, which had vastly exceeded my expectations. Far from a shabby white mouldy thing, it was a gorgeous silver Airstream. I wasn't normally into any form of caravanning, for which I blamed a disastrous trip with Aunt Lucy to Southend-on-Sea when I'd been twelve, but I'd definitely make an exception for this beautiful beast.

The Airstream was all flowing retro lines and American diner styling on the outside. The interior was another matter, with a serious sound system and speakers that seemed to be built into every surface. It was upholstered in black leather with red piping, and discreet LED strips cast soft blue light over the interior, giving it the appearance of a nightclub. All very cool, although slightly weird for me considering I was stripped down to my bra yet again as Jack the Viking stitched the wound in my arm. But Jack was a gentleman and hadn't so much as cast a glance at my cleavage.

'OK, you're done, Lauren,' Jack said as he cut the thread of the final stitch.

I braced myself and glanced down at the bullet wound. I'd been expecting to see an ugly stitched hole, but Jack's needlework was extraordinarily neat. The wounds on both sides of my arm from where it had entered and exited had been reduced to thin red lines.

'You shouldn't be left with much scarring,' Jack said as he taped a bandage over the top of his work.

'Could be the perfect excuse for a tattoo.'

'Never been a huge fan of those myself.'

I immediately found myself dismissing the idea...

Hang on, what was going on? I'd almost been shot and I was worrying about Jack's opinion about body art. The guy was not on the market and I needed to have a word with the part of my subconscious that wouldn't accept that obvious fact.

But there were also bigger priorities. Concern rippled through me as I took in Jack's shirt caked with his dry blood. I had tried to insist that he dealt with himself first, but Jack had refused.

'What about your own injuries, Jack?' I asked as I pulled my sports top back on.

'I guess there's no point putting off dealing with them any longer. Doctors make the worse patients.'

'Isn't that the truth.'

I felt my pulse quicken as Jack started to undo his buttons. But that endorphin rush was quickly replaced with worry as I took in the numerous stab wounds across his chest and stomach. They were even worse than I remembered.

Anger rose through me. 'We should have gone back and shot Alvarez when we had the chance.'

'Another time,' Jack said.

'Even with the Hippocratic oath?'

'I'll make an exception when it comes to Alvarez and his

mercs. He and his kind represent everything I despise.' Jack opened a box of butterfly bandages.

'I feel exactly the same, especially after it got so personal.'

Jack's gaze immediately sharpened on me. 'What do you mean?'

I still wanted to hold off telling Jack about Aunt Lucy. I wasn't here for a sympathy vote. 'It's personal,' was all I said.

Something unreadable passed through his expression. 'I understand.'

'Thanks...' And I meant it. It was easier to keep a lid on that part of my life rather than pick over old wounds, especially when I needed to be focused on what was ahead of us. 'Let me wash your wounds first with some antiseptic. You don't want them getting infected.'

'That would be a real help, Lauren.'

I crossed to the caravan's black lacquered sink and filled the washing-up bowl with hot water from a freshly boiled kettle. I threw in a good measure of disinfectant and Jack offered me a sanitised surgical white flannel. I dropped the cloth into the bowl before wringing it out, then held it up to his chest. My hand hovered over his skin. 'I'm afraid that this is going to sting.'

Jack stared past me into space. 'Like a bitch no doubt, but go ahead.'

My toes curled as I started to dab at the bloody mess of his body, but Jack only grimaced slightly and gave not so much as a whimper. Mike hadn't been exaggerating about Jack's stoicism.

He dried the wounds as I worked on them and pinched the edges together with the butterfly bandages, which held the wounds together perfectly.

The door of the small shower cubicle in the caravan opened and Mike appeared in a fresh T-shirt with the legendary slogan 'Totally Bogus!' scrawled across it, as he towelled his hair dry. Yes, so the surfer look.

'That suits you better than a hospital gown,' I said.

'Nobody looks good in a hospital gown,' Mike replied. He began to hunt through some drawers.

For the first time since arriving here, I thought of our conversation in the car. We needed to put together a plan and we needed all the facts for that.

'Mike, is now a good time to tell us more about your work?' I asked.

He turned to us, his expression wary. 'It probably is, but...'

'Reservations?' Jack asked.

'Yes, because I need you both to keep an open mind to this. Just remember, I didn't laugh in your face when you said I'd been abducted by a UFO.'

'Look, Mike, I've seen enough to keep me very open-minded about most things,' I said. 'So hit us with it. What's the full story?'

Mike opened the fridge, helped himself to a Diet Coke and sat down. He took a gulp as he gazed at us. 'Geophysics is just part of my playbox. A more accurate description would be maverick theoretical physicist working at the fringes of science.'

Jack gawped at him. 'Since when, Mike?'

'Since for ever. I just don't normally talk about it, especially after the backlash I suffered from the scientific community.'

'Why the backlash?' I asked.

'Because of the area of theoretical physics that I specialise in.'

'You're not part of the string theory gang, are you?'

'I wish. That would make life much easier, as string theory is an incredibly well-funded area. I certainly wouldn't have to work in a surf shop to pay the bills.'

'So what area is it then?' Jack asked.

'Best if I step you through. Let's start with Einstein's theory of relativity, and how it deals with the very large effects of gravity on masses such as stars and planets. Well, the related area is quantum physics, the study of the very small.'

'Are you looking for the theory of everything then? Something that links the theory of relativity to quantum mechanics?' Jack asked.

'Since when did you know anything about this?' Mike asked, looking impressed.

'Hey, I don't just dig holes in the ground. I also like to read about this stuff and catch the occasional documentary about cutting-edge physics.'

'Good. That should make explaining the new unification theory I've been working on a lot easier. One idea that's been gaining traction, even though no one is prepared to fund it properly yet, is called E8.'

'Oh, you're one of that lot,' I said. 'That figures, what with you being stuck out here rather than in some nice university lab.'

'As the only non-scientist here, would anyone care to explain what E8 is?' Jack said.

'E8 is based on the theory that there is an eighth dimension where all the real action takes place,' Mike said.

'Eighth dimension? That's a hell of a lot more than our three,' Jack replied.

'It certainly is,' Mike said. 'But the E8 theory is a thing of beauty as far as maths is concerned. And it neatly deals with all the missing parts of the puzzle that string theory has never been able to answer. Basically, E8 is a strong candidate for a workable theory of everything that at last unifies relativity and quantum physics.'

'So is this like the idea that we're living in a holographic universe projected by some sort of vast galactic computer?' Jack asked.

'You really have been watching some cool documentaries,' I said.

'Doesn't that fit your mental image of me then?' Jack asked.

'Something like that,' I replied with a grin.

'To answer your question of whether E8 is about our world being a simulation, a bit like in *The Matrix*, not quite, but it's close. It's based on the concept of a quasicrystal higher dimension.'

'Say what?' Jack asked.

'Maybe it's easier to think of it this way: our reality, everything we know, is just a shadow thrown by a quasicrystal in the eighth dimension.'

'Nope, still not following you there,' Jack said.

'Then try this... Like in *The Matrix*, the quasicrystal is the computer that runs the code for our reality. Here, let me show you.'

Mike opened a drawer, pulled out a thick notebook and began to draw. After a few minutes he held up a sketch for us to examine. 'Here we go.'

Jack and I looked at a symbol made up of lots of triangles rotated around a central axis and intersecting each other like a flower with a hundred petals.

'What are we looking at?' I asked.

'A mathematical representation of E8, seen as a two-dimensional image. Now imagine it in three dimensions, as a star-like object with lots of points.'

'A star that projects our reality from the eight dimension...' The thought struck me like a bolt of energy. I dropped the flannel I'd been using to bathe Jack's chest and raced across to my day bag. 'I'm going out on a limb here, but what you're describing, could it be related to this?' I withdrew the stone orb and handed it to him.

'This is the artefact you interacted with?' Mike asked.

'That's correct. The right sound triggered my synaesthesia and conjured up the galactic chart I mentioned.'

Mike's expression widened. 'An acoustic trigger... And this pitched you into an alternative world?'

'Yep.'

Mike blinked several times. 'And the UFO that dropped me off was definitely a tetrahedron – a four-sided triangular-shaped craft?'

'Yes, just like your buried mass,' I said.

'Holy fuck!' Mike said.

'That's significant?' Jack asked.

'Too bloody right it is. Do either of you know what a fractal is?'

'Of course,' I said. 'It's a triangular pattern that occurs in nature over and over again, in everything from fern leaves to coastlines.'

'Exactly. Well, a tetrahedron is a three-dimensional version of a fractal. In other words, a basic building block of our universe. And guess what repeated form makes up a three-dimensional E8 quasicrystal?'

I looked again at the E8 image in the notebook – the multi-pointed star made up of triangles. 'A tetrahedron?'

'Absolutely right. And the shape of that craft you saw can't be a coincidence, not to mention the dense mass you detected beneath the surface. Those shapes have to be somehow directly linked to the eighth dimension.'

'As crazy as that sounds, it does make some sort of sense,' Jack said.

'Damned right it does,' Mike replied. 'But if we want any more answers, we have to get back to Skara Brae right now. I need you to activate your stone orb and show me exactly what you experienced.'

Jack shook his head. 'But it will be crawling with MI5 – or worse, the Overseers – by now.'

'I don't know about anyone else, but I so don't care if this means we have a chance of saving our world,' I said.

Jack looked between me and Mike as he pressed the last butterfly bandage on to his chest. 'Then let's do this, guys.'

Mike scooped a smartphone with a cracked glass screen from the drawer.

'Hey, no modern phones. They can track us with those.'

'Relax, this is my mate's old phone and he's already removed the sim. I need a specific app on it.'

'For what exactly?' I asked.

'You'll see,' Mike replied with a smile.

I grabbed the Audi's keys and placed the stone orb back into my bag. MI5 and Overseers or not, I was determined to chase this particular rabbit all the way down to the depths of its crazy burrow.

CHAPTER SIXTEEN

WE'D BRIEFED Mike fully during the drive to Skara Brae about MI5 and what had happened at the hospital. He'd looked distinctly horrified as we'd filled him in about the extent of the reach of the Overseers and what they were capable of. When we'd arrived, we'd parked the Audi a good couple of miles away down the beach from Skara Brae to be on the safe side. Now the three of us were trudging along the shoreline through sheets of squalling rain.

Jack, burdened down by all the kit he was carrying, looked like a movie action hero for whom Christmas had come early. He'd discovered a weapon store in the Audi's boot where the spare wheel should have been. Thanks to that, he was now carrying half an armoury on his back.

'Is all that stuff really necessary?' I asked.

Jack patted the gun I'd been using, to which he'd bolted god knew what from the arms store. 'We need to be prepared for anything, so I've attached a grenade launcher to this HK416 carbine you managed to snag yourself.'

'Oh, is that what that type of gun is?'

'Hell, don't let any special forces officer hear you refer to it as just a *gun*. This is the Navy SEAL's weapon of choice and designed to take all sorts of attachments. The fact the Overseers are equipped with these would suggest that these mercs are experienced soldiers.'

'With infinite funds at their disposal, I wouldn't expect anything less,' I replied.

'And to take on MI5 agents shows that they really don't give a flying fuck about anyone standing in their way,' Mike said.

'Which is why I've had to stay off the grid,' I replied. 'Every time I've run into them, people have died...'

I made sure I didn't look anywhere in Jack's direction, but I saw him giving me a sideways glance.

'It's not too late to turn round,' he said.

'Could you really live with not knowing?' I asked. 'With Earth Song, whatever it's about exactly, we may have a way of saving our planet from an alien race determined to exterminate us.'

Jack shook his head at me. 'Yeah, there's no other option really.'

Mike nodded. 'MI5 aside, the thing I don't understand is why this island isn't crawling with special forces by now. There's no sign of any soldiers on the ground yet.'

'That's a good point,' Jack replied. 'You'd have thought blowing up a hospital would have initiated a serious military response from your government by now.'

'Nothing on the news either – at least going by what we heard on the way over here, guys,' I said. 'There must be a news blackout.'

'There's probably an operation underway, and the authorities are keeping quiet until all the Overseers soldiers have been neutralised,' Jack said.

'But surely Alvarez will have planned for a counter-attack?' I asked.

'However well armed the Overseers are, they can't hope to hold off a response from the SAS, who would no doubt be the first sent in to deal with a threat like this,' Jack replied.

'So maybe we'll find Robert with them and waiting for us,' I said.

'If this Alvarez guy is half the badass we think he is, I wouldn't be so sure.' Jack readjusted the metal tube slung across his back.

I gestured towards it. 'Is that what I think it is?'

'A rocket launcher,' Jack replied. 'Better to go in ready for anything.'

Mike shook his head at Jack and me, giving us a disapproving look. He'd made a point of not taking a pistol for himself when Jack had offered him one. He'd then given us a long speech about not believing in violence to solve problems. Over a year ago I would have been right there with him. But my run-ins with the Overseers had somewhat shifted my perspective. Not that I was happy about it, but it was just the reality of my new hardened attitude towards people trying to kill me.

'So how much further?' I asked.

'About another half-mile,' Jack said.

'And what's the plan when we get there?'

'If it's Robert, I say we hand ourselves over to his protection and be open about what we've discovered. Better the devil you know.'

'And if it's the Overseers?'

'Then we'll rely on our insurance policy,' Jack replied, tapping his gun.

'You were a field surgeon and not a frontline soldier, right?' I asked.

'Yep, but I did get to hang out with many injured special forces officers, which probably explains a lot of my attitude.'

I nodded as the mobile in my phone vibrated. I took it out and saw it was Steve's number, just as I'd hoped.

'Hey, what about your lecture about how easy it is to trace a mobile?' Mike said.

'This is an old phone without a GPS chip. Anyway, it isn't registered to me, so no one should think to check it.' I hit the call accept button before it went to voicemail.

'Hi, Lauren, I am the bearer of interesting news.'

'Something about Earth Song?'

'I'm afraid not. However, I did hear back from my friend at the IceCube Neutrino Observatory. It seems there was an atmospheric neutrino burst detected around the first of November.'

This corresponded with when Mike had disappeared. Now to confirm my suspicion. 'Any other neutrino activity since, Steve?'

'Yes, actually. They detected a fresh burst yesterday.'

'Don't tell me, around 11.30 a.m. GMT?'

'How could–'

'Don't ask. But tell me – how powerful was this burst in terms of radiation?'

Mike and Jack stared at me.

'Only just above background levels – not much more than you would receive flying in a passenger jet at high altitude.'

'So anyone close to the source would be OK?'

'Yes. Why? What the hell have you got yourself into this time, Lauren?'

'You know I can't tell you now. Maybe one day. Anyway, thanks, Steve. I've got to go.' I hit end call and turned the mobile off to be certain that Steve wouldn't call me straight back for an explanation.

'What was that all about?' Mike asked.

'One of the Overseers soldiers let slip that there had been a neutrino burst over Skara Brae. On a hunch I spoke to an old friend at Jodrell Bank. He made some enquires and confirmed what I already suspected. The unexplained neutrino events seem to have coincided with the trips over to the twilight zone.'

'So another part of the puzzle falls into place,' Mike said.

'But what caused them?' Jack asked.

'We said before that something had to be responsible for conjuring up that hologram. My guess is that the buried artefact has everything to do with it. If the stone orb is the control, maybe the buried artefact is what pitched us into the twilight zone and caused the spike in neutrino activity.'

Jack gestured ahead. 'We're nearly there, so we'll have to discuss this later. Look sharp, everyone, and keep quiet.'

I felt the prickle of adrenaline building up inside me as grey sand billowed from the beach and up over the Skara Brae site dead ahead of us. No obvious sign of activity, which was a good start.

We slowed to a creep and I took out my silenced gun – or actually, suppressed pistol, as Jack had corrected me. He'd also told me that this weapon Robert had given me was a Mossad .22 LRS pistol. Apparently the LRS was favoured by mercenaries because it was so reliable and unlikely to jam. He talked about weapons like other people talk about cars, but I wasn't sure I'd ever do the same. The one thing I did know was that it felt comfortable in my hand, even though it was surprisingly heavy. Jack had found a couple of extra magazines for it in the weapons store. Using it was fine in theory, particularly on Alvarez, but I still wasn't relishing shooting this weapon in anger again. I was already going to need years of counselling on the other side of all this darkness.

As we neared the Neolithic site, the sound of a heavy-duty drill drifted over to us.

Jack's eyes narrowed and he held his hand out flat to indicate we should keep low, then beckoned us towards him. 'It sounds like some bastards are ripping up my site, most likely Overseers. If I wasn't going to kill Alvarez before, I sure as hell am now.'

'Digging for your mysterious dense mass object, Mike?' I asked.

He frowned. 'I guess they could be.'

'In that case, I'd better scout ahead and find out exactly what's happening,' Jack said.

'I'm coming too,' I added.

Jack gave me a hard look. 'No way, Lauren.'

'Don't waste your breath, Jack. I'm coming.' I crossed my arms and waited.

'Damn, you're stubborn,' he said.

'It's one of my more endearing qualities.'

'OK, but if you're going to insist on doing this, at least keep your head down and try not to get shot.'

'I'll do my best.'

'British sarcasm, right?'

I raised my eyebrows at him. 'Something like that.'

'Well, if it's all the same with you guys, I'll hang back here,' Mike said. 'I haven't quite got the death wish you two obviously have.'

'Oh, you're no fun,' I said. 'But seriously, no problem. We'll come and get you if it's safe.'

'And if it's not?'

'If you hear things kicking off, run like hell back to the Audi and get yourself away,' Jack said. 'Then get the word out about what went down here.'

Mike nodded. 'You can rely on me for that.'

Jack and I clambered up a steep concrete slope – part of the sea defences on the shore protecting the area from erosion. First checking no one had seen us, we hopped over a boundary fence on to the site itself. There was no sign of anyone, but I could hear plenty of activity coming from within the mounds of Skara Brae.

'Ready for this?' Jack whispered.

'No, I'm scared shitless.'

'That's the right attitude. It'll keep you alert and hopefully alive.' He pointed to the mounds ahead of us and lowered his palm to the ground.

Following his lead, I lowered myself flat on the grass. Then together we shimmied up the nearest embankment.

I had to stifle a gasp at the first thing I saw – the MI5 woman I'd seen the previous day lying dead on her back, her face staring up at the grey sky, bullet holes riddling her body. Another officer was sprawled over the top of the opposite mound.

'It would have been anything but a fair fight,' Jack whispered to me with a grim face.

A swirl of nausea spun through me. This was the reality of what we were facing. It could be us soon.

I did my best to ignore the pounding of blood in my ears as we edged forward until we were able to peer down into the ruined rooms. The noise of drills rattling on stone grew louder as we saw exactly what was going on.

A number of Overseers soldiers were digging holes throughout the floor of the Skara Brae ruins.

I glanced across and saw Jack's knuckles white on the stock of his carbine. It wasn't surprising since this place was being irreversibly vandalised. His gaze narrowed on one of the mercenaries, who pushed an orange cart with a screen mounted into the handle.

'What's that machine, Jack?' I whispered.

'A ground radar system. But, like I told Mike, because of the density of the rock, they won't be able to image down much more than a metre below ground level.'

Colonel Alvarez walked into view round the corner of a wall and one of the soldiers immediately rushed up to him.

'Still no signal of the artefact, Colonel,' the man said.

'Find it or I will personally shoot one of you,' Alvarez replied. 'We're already running on borrowed time. Our people in the UK military command won't be able to delay the deployment of the SAS for much longer.'

'Shit, so they know,' I whispered.

'And that explains why they've turned my site into a jackrabbit's burrow,' Jack replied.

'If they have people in the UK military, that explains the lack of response at the hospital and the news blackout. Just how much power do these Overseers wield?'

'Way too much if they can pull the teeth of your government like this.'

'So what do we do now?' I asked.

'I'll create a diversion. Be ready for it – when the shit hits the fan, you and Mike will need to find out what you can on the site. But you won't have long.'

'Will you give me some sort of signal?'

'Don't you worry, you'll know. Afterwards, if everything goes according to plan, we'll rendezvous back at the car.'

'And if doesn't?'

'Let's make sure that doesn't happen.'

'Please be careful, Jack.'

'You too. You might have caused me more trouble than anyone I've ever known, but I can't deny life's interesting with you around. Just remember to aim that LRS pistol of yours at the head, and give it three shots to make sure.'

'Bloody hell, triple tap, seriously, as in first-person shooter games?'

'For real. A Mossad LRS is something of a stealth weapon,

but deadly if used in the right way. And I say that as a surgeon who knows his way around a head trauma.'

'Jack, I'm not sure I'm up for that.'

'I understand, Lauren. You haven't had any training and you're certainly not a soldier. But we're in the deep end of the pool together now and you need to do whatever it takes. Act now and grieve for the loss of your humanity later. After all, the Overseers will do whatever it takes to win, and so must we.'

My stomach cramped into a ball, but I nodded at his pep talk. 'You're right, Jack, even if I don't want you to be.'

'Just stay strong and you'll do fine.' Jack raised his chin at me and then crawled away.

My body grew icy cold at the prospect of what was coming as I edged back to where we'd left Mike.

CHAPTER SEVENTEEN

'WHAT'S GOING ON?' Mike asked as I reached him back on the beach.

'The Overseers, that's bloody what. It looks as if they really are looking for your buried artefact.'

'Damn it. How do they even know it's there?'

'They detected the neutrino bursts when first you and then Jack and I disappeared. That probably put them on the right track.'

'Just our fucking luck. It takes me months to find this site and then it goes and announces its presence to the world.'

'Those are the breaks. Jack's going to create a diversion to leave the site clear for us to investigate. What do you think should be our first priority?'

'I think we need to clarify what else the control orb can do. Understand that and we might be able to gain an insight into what it was designed for and how this site is connected to altering the Earth Song.'

'OK, but we'll need an acoustic sound to trigger my synaesthesia.'

'That's why I brought my mate's old phone. It's got a tone-generator app that he installed when he thought he was going deaf from listening to too much ear-bleeding drum and bass. I'm interested to see exactly what frequency triggers your synaesthesia. We'll need to gather as much information as fast as we can.' A wide smile filled his face. 'Then I'd love to take a quick trip over to the eighth dimension with you. Maybe even make direct contact with the entity that abducted me.'

'Not sure there'll be time for a joyride,' I said. 'I wonder how Jack is getting—'

I was interrupted by a bright flash coming from the visitor centre beyond Skara Brae, followed by a loud whoosh. An explosion shook the ground as an angry ball of fire rose from somewhere in the car park.

'Bloody hell, that'll be Jack and his rocket launcher then,' I said.

'Going by the size of the explosion, he must have taken out one of their vehicles,' Mike replied.

I could see Alvarez already racing over the top of the mound towards the explosion point as he shouted orders to his soldiers to follow him.

But Jack wasn't done yet, not by a long way.

Smoke grenades started to land all around the visitor centre and within moments it had disappeared behind a wall of dark fog.

'I think we can say that's one very successful diversion,' Mike said.

I nodded. 'Come on, let's get a move on.'

The sound of gunfire came from the fog but it wasn't aimed our way.

We crept up on to the mound and peered down. The site was clear, the ground radar abandoned, but we would need to move fast to pull this off. I grabbed the stone orb from my bag as we raced round to the steps and descended.

Meanwhile Mike already had his old phone out with an app powered up his phone's screen. 'I'm going to try out various frequencies until we hit the right one. Ready?'

'Go for it.' I checked again that the safety was off on my pistol and held the stone orb in my left hand.

Mike moved the slider on the phone all the way to the top and 1000 hertz was shown on his app's display. He pressed the play button and a modulating high-pitched tone whistled out.

'Anything?' he asked.

I shook my head.

'Right, I'll keep lowering the frequency and you tell me the moment you get anything.' He began to quickly move the slider downwards and the pitch lowered with it, all the way past 100 hertz, but still nothing. He kept going...all the way down to 40 hertz...and the world around me suddenly exploded with light. Then it blinked out again as the sound became too low.

'OK, back up a fraction,' I said as another explosion rocked the car park.

Mike nodded and slowly raised the indicator until 37.9 hertz was displayed. A flash of light and icons appeared round the stone orb.

'Stop, it's working,' I said.

Mike slapped his forehead. 'Why didn't I try that first – it's the same frequency I was using when I fell through into the twilight zone. I must have accidentally triggered something at this site. Can you try your stone orb out now?'

'OK. First I'm going to see if I can pull up the celestial map.'

I began to rotate the ball and the inner illuminated group of icons spun round until a symbol that looked like a spiralling galaxy appeared. That had to be what I was looking for. I rotated the orb until the icon was inside the selection square at the top.

Then I flicked my wrist forward and our solar system flared into existence before me.

'I know a lot of astronomers who would kill for this,' I said.

'So what are you seeing?' Mike asked.

'A map of our solar system. I'm going to see if I can gain some control over it.'

I experimented by moving the orb in a flat plane like it was a computer mouse. That panned the view out beyond the Kuiper belt as gunfire continued to crackle in the distance.

OK, so to zoom out...

I rotated the ball in my hand backwards and a circular scale appeared in it with an indicator that moved downwards as the view pulled back.

'I'm getting the hang of this. It works in three dimensions as I move the orb.'

'What about that asteroid ship you saw before?'

'Let me see if I can locate it again.' As I kept on zooming, the Tau Ceti star system was displayed near the outer walls of Skara Brae. Then something I hadn't tried before occurred to me. I tried to walk towards it and, sure enough, the star stayed put as I headed away from Earth to the other end of the site.

I peered down at the miniature Tau Ceti star with its four former M-class planets strung out from it. Further away on the system's ecliptic plane lurked three gas giants.

'This is seriously incredible,' I said. 'I can actually move around the hologram and it stays put.'

'And that ship?'

'Still working on tracking it down.'

A flashing red box just beyond the outer edge of the Tau Ceti system caught my eye. I moved towards it and saw the asteroid ship within the marker. 'Yes, it's here...'

One of the icons, a backwards arrow, was blinking as it hovered above the spiralling galaxy icon. Next to it was a circle icon and then another arrow pointing in the opposite direction. Both of the additional icons were unlit. What did that mean? Only one way to find out.

I selected the circle in the middle and flicked my wrist forward.

At once the planets orbiting the star sped up to a blur, replicated by the planets in our solar system on the other side of the ruins. I had to be accelerating time.

The asteroid ship raced out along the dotted line until it came to a dead stop about a third of the distance away from Earth. A bad feeling started to fill me. That could mean...

Shouts and cries came from around the visitor centre as the smoke started to clear.

I ignored the noise and Mike watching me intently as I tried the arrow pointing right. Sure enough, the ship jumped forward and it was in Earth's orbit. All sorts of red symbols lit up all over our planet.

I selected the middle circle icon again and the ship jumped back to the centre position between the two systems. My sense of dread deepened. That could only mean...

'Oh fuck!' Not the most profound thing to have said, but it pretty accurately summarised the situation.

'What is it, Lauren?'

'The ship that's coming to destroy us – you know I thought it was only just departing the Tau Ceti system?'

'Yes...'

'If I'm reading this right, and taking into account the time a ship would need to decelerate, it's actually only about five years away.'

'You mean it travelled six light years in a day?'

'I don't think so. If they had some sort of *Star Trek*-like warp drive, they wouldn't be messing around with solar sails. My best guess is that what I saw originally was a recording of where the ship was. I think I just selected an icon which updated its location to its real time position.'

'So you're saying that five years is all our planet has got left – unless we find a way to stop them?'

'Exactly. And I've watched way too many sci-fi movies to know that launching a few nukes isn't going to cut it.'

'But something implanted the message that Earth Song could save our world in my head, presumably from this threat. So maybe the answer to this is in there too?'

Before I could answer, Jack came sprinting over the top of the mound and leapt down to join us. 'We need to get out of here. Alvarez and his soldiers are on their way.'

'But we need more critical information,' Mike said.

'Not an option right now, unless you want to die.'

'Don't worry, we'll be back and then we'll work it out, Mike,' I said.

'OK, let's shift our arses then.'

We ran for the steps and had just crested the mound when Alvarez appeared running full tilt towards us, with at least twenty soldiers right behind him.

'Fire at will!' Alvarez shouted.

His soldiers dropped to their knees and began shooting. Bullets hissed over our heads as Jack and I returned fire. With no way forward, we backed down into the basin.

'Fucking hell, we're trapped in a killing zone,' Jack said as he loaded a fresh magazine.

Mike stared at me. 'No, we're not. Lauren, you have the way to get us out of here.'

He was right: dropping us into the twilight zone again was our only chance. Ignoring the thunder of gunfire, I spun the icons until the stacked three wavy lines were highlighted. A grenade came through the squalling rain and arced over the mound.

Fuck!

I flicked my wrist forward just as the grenade landed with a chink and we all instinctively ducked. The world turned into a wavering mirage and a ghostly explosion rippled out from the grenade.

'Where the fuck did they go?' Alvarez shouted to his soldiers as they crested the mound. They stared down into the ruins.

'They can't see us,' Mike whispered.

'You can speak up – he can't hear us,' Jack said.

'Welcome to the twilight zone of the eighth dimension, Mike,' I said.

He stared at me for a moment and then gave a wide grin.

A new icon lit up above the orb – a multi-pointed star.

Mike stared at it, now able to see the icons too. 'That looks like the symbol for E8...' His expression twisted as he grimaced.

Sudden searing pain surged through my body as the mirage of the world vanished and was replaced by glowing patterns of energy.

I tried to suck in air, my lungs burning as the air emptied out of them, as Jack and Mike clutched at their throats. A vacuum! A spinning sensation started to build inside me and my body began to dissolve like sand being blown from a dune.

The others stared at me, shock filling their eyes, as they disintegrated too. My mind tilted as we all evaporated into the ocean of energy around us.

CHAPTER EIGHTEEN

Ribbons of energy danced around me like I'd dived into some immense dark sea filled with luminous seaweed strands. A sense of vertigo spun through me as my now non-existent lungs clawed for air. Every fibre of animal instinct within told me that I was dying, that my body had been destroyed, that I, a three-dimensional being, wasn't designed to exist in this. But this *what* exactly? Not the twilight zone, but a full-blown reality of the eighth dimension. That was what that control icon I accidentally selected must have meant. And that mistake would mean I had killed the others and condemned Earth. I was going to feel a sense of utter despair before the flicker of my consciousness was extinguished. Fear – deep and primeval within me – screeched at the knowledge that I was about to be wiped out of existence.

But then a light began to appear out of the patterns before me and a voice, not my own, filled my thoughts.

'Don't be afraid, Lauren,' Aunt Lucy said.

I clung on to her words, just like I had as a small child when I'd been frightened, even as my being splintered apart. I felt Aunt

Lucy's unconditional love wrap round me almost like something physical. Gradually, my panic began to ease as somehow I knew I wasn't about to die.

The fibres of light weaved around me and from them shapes and forms coalesced. Walls, real physical walls made from wood, appeared to create a room...a room that I recognised... But it couldn't be...

My gaze swept around, eating up the details as they came into sharp focus. Closed deep-red velvet curtains hung from dull gold poles. Shelves lined most of the walls, filled to overflowing with books. A Christmas tree stood in one corner next to a crackling fireplace over which two stockings hung from hooks. A Persian rug with an intricate pattern filled the middle of the floor...the floor I'd often lain on as a child to read.

My mind started to rebel. This couldn't be real. An extension of the hologram technology maybe? But, no, because it was more than just a vision. The scent of cinnamon and pine cones drifted across from a bowl of potpourri to fill my nostrils. There was sound too – the clicking of an old clock on the mantelpiece as its regulator mechanism spun like two orbiting planets beneath a glass dome. I'd watched that clock for hours as a child, endlessly fascinated by the mechanism inside after my aunt had explained how it worked to me.

On the desk was a photo of a blonde woman with a lined face. Her glasses were hanging down from a chain round her neck. She was smiling at a nine-year-old me, all big eyes and teeth braces and grinning like a mad thing, as she spun me round her. The one and only Aunt Lucy.

That photo had been taken during our first summer together after she'd officially adopted me. My life had been going off the rails after living in a series of foster homes after my biological parents had been killed in a house fire when I was seven. After that I'd never felt that I belonged. I'd started to become a school refuser. And then, out of nowhere, Aunt Lucy had entered my life and everything had changed. She'd helped me turn my life round, investing the love and energy in me that I'd always dreamt a parent would do. I'd flourished with her support, surprising myself with just how academic I was. Aunt Lucy had been my best friend, my anchor. And now she was gone.

I caressed the photo frame with my fingertips... That older woman who had meant everything to me was no longer here because of Alvarez.

I blinked back sudden tears, now fully taking in this room. It was her flat at Christchurch College in Oxford where she'd worked as a lecturer. The happiest of my happy places for me. In this flat, behind the walls of the college, she'd given me a second chance at life. She'd pushed me hard, but I'd blossomed under her stewardship, pursuing my own academic career that had eventually led me into the world of radio astronomy.

But how I could be here? And then my mind caught up.

This had to be some trick of my dying mind, maybe creating my very own version of heaven. If this was what my afterlife looked like, it certainly beat any version of the pearly gates I'd dreamt of. But where was the finishing touch: the precious Aunt Lucy herself to welcome me in?

For the first time I noticed how wet I felt as a raindrop dripped down from my head on to the shoulder of my cagoule...

I stared down at my very real legs and the small puddle of rainwater that had fallen from me on to the polished floorboards.

For a fantasy this place had a lot of detail assailing all my senses. But was there an alternative explanation?

I crossed to the curtains and pulled them back. The answer stared me in the face.

Instead of Oxford's skyline of dreaming spires that should

have been visible from my aunt's attic room, I could only see the rippling energy patterns of the eighth dimension.

A shiver ran through me as I glanced at the door. It should have led to a spiral stone staircase snaking its way down the tower. But no way would I risk trying that in case I fell out of the safety of this room.

What the fuck was going on? If ever I needed a stiff drink it was now.

I crossed to Aunt Lucy's drinks cabinet and took out one of the more expensive craft gins she had loved. I poured myself a triple, not bothering with any tonic, and downed it in one. The smooth taste of high-quality alcohol had a steadying effect on the spinning sensation inside my head.

OK, think this through, Lauren. You're meant to be a scientist after all.

I hunted around the room, looking for any clues, anything out of the ordinary.

My eyes fell again on the Christmas tree. Beneath it were a number of carefully wrapped presents in white paper decorated with polar bears. A lump filled my throat – this was a very precise moment from my past.

I scooped up the smallest present from the top. My hand shaking, I began to tear open the paper. Within it was a red box displaying a silver shield and cross emblem. I lifted the lid and took out the brand-new Swiss army knife. I put my hand into my cagoule pocket and withdrew an identical but older knife. It was the same in every way apart from wear and tear.

The pang of loss strengthened inside me and a tear trickled down my cheek. Why did she have to die?

I breathed through my nose. *Come on, Stelleck, figure this out.*

Everything about this room pointed to it being a frozen moment from my past life, lovingly restored in every detail apart from seventeen-year-old me and sixty-year-old Aunt Lucy. So what was the purpose of this?

I pocketed both knives and felt the weight of the newer version nestling alongside its older sibling. This was beyond crazy. It certainly felt real. But maybe there was another explanation – that I'd simply been tipped over the edge of madness by being dropped into the eighth dimension?

But then my eyes fell on Aunt Lucy's journal on her desk. I thought of her search for M-class planets she'd helped pioneer with the blink technique, whereby a planet passing in front of its parent star caused the slightest dimming of light. It had been the breakthrough technique that had helped track down thousands of other planets outside our solar system. And Aunt Lucy had poured it all into her journals. She'd even written the odd note about me, usually after an argument, but nothing that I hadn't agreed with when I'd cooled down and sneaked a look. Aunt Lucy had referred to those journals as her 'brain dump conduit', an expression that had always made me smile.

I picked the blue journal up and began thumbing through it. But this wasn't like her original journals crammed full of notes, drawings and doodles. Instead, this was a pristine blank copy.

So why the difference in this otherwise perfect simulation? Was that significant?

I placed the journal open on the desk. I'd started to turn away when a shiver ran down my back. I moved slowly back round to see three words on what had been a blank page...

Who am I?

.   .   .

My skin prickled as I picked up the journal again. Those words definitely hadn't been there a moment ago. Was this some form of communication? If so, from what?

Was it something I could reply to? But how? Could or should I write in the journal? Or how about...

I cleared my throat. 'I can't believe I'm saying this like this is some sort of séance, but, Aunt Lucy, is that you?'

A sharp rap came from the door and I almost wet myself.

CHAPTER NINETEEN

MY HEART THRUMMED in my ears as I crossed to the door and reached for the handle. The knock came again and my heart crunched into a ball. My mouth dry, the brass knob slipping slightly in my sweaty hand, I opened the door...

Mike gawped in at me, behind him not the stairwell but a seedy-looking bar. My mind spun at this remix of reality.

There was a stage at one end where bright purple lights illuminated the instruments of a band that looked set up and ready for a gig. Then I noticed the unplugged electric bass guitar slung round Mike's neck.

I flapped my hands at him as if trying to put out a fire. 'What the hell is all this, Mike?'

He didn't say a word for a moment, but stepped past me into the tower room. He turned round slowly, spreading his arms wide. 'This place means a lot to you, am I right?'

'Yes, it does. This was my aunt's room back at Christchurch College and it's filled with happy memories for me.'

Mike nodded and gestured to the room through the doorway. 'That place is the same for me.'

'Any particular reason that bar is important to you?'

'Because of this.' He stuck his feet apart, flicked his hair back and thrashed the guitar's strings. They screeched like a cat. As the notes faded, they sent a brief flurry of red pops of light into my vision.

'And what's that meant to be?' I asked.

'My best rock-god pose. This is the student union bar where my band and I used to perform whenever we had the chance. And, oh, how the ladies loved us.'

'I think that last part was probably in your imagination.'

Mike gave me his best attempt at a hurt look, but then smiled. 'Almost certainly. But I still adored this place. When I performed here with my mates we were living the dream.'

'So in other words this is your happy place too?' I asked, using air quotes for 'happy'.

'Yes, at least the location is. But it doesn't quite mean the same without my mates here and no audience to watch us.'

'Nothing like the oxygen of a live performance, hey?'

Mike raked his hand through his hair and gave me a lopsided grin. 'Something like that.'

'Do you mind if I have a look around your inner sanctum to try to work out what all this means?'

'Knock yourself out.' Mike stepped aside and made a sweeping gesture with his arms.

I stepped past him into the bar.

The first thing I noticed was the smell of stale beer and maybe a hint of student male sweat, followed by the slightly sticky linoleum floor as I walked across it in my boots. It could have been a template for every other student bar across the country. It certainly brought back some hazy memories of too many drinks and a guy – because there always seemed to be one – trying their luck with me. I'd always quickly put them right.

I took in the blackboard – I guessed it'd been used for

detailing drinks on offer, but the area had been wiped down with a message written beneath...

Who am I?

My spine tingled as I pointed it out to Mike. 'The same words appeared in my room.'

'I thought it was just something scribbled by one of the philosophy students.'

'No, I don't think so. It's in both rooms and I literally saw it appear.' I gazed through the semi-opaque tinted windows of the bar at the flickering white ribbons of light rolling past outside. 'Is something out there trying to talk to us?'

'You're still thinking in three dimensions – that there's an "out there" and "in here". But they are both same thing when it comes to E8.'

'So why create these three-dimensional rooms for us?'

'Probably because we're simply not physically or even emotionally equipped to cope with existing in this higher reality. I don't know about you, but before I found myself within the safety of these walls it felt as if I was dying out there for a moment.'

'*Out there?*'

He flapped a hand at me. 'Too sharp, Lauren, but you know what I mean.'

'Yes, I do. I felt the same. So what are these rooms then? Our own little display boxes in some sort of E8 alien pet zoo where we can be studied?'

'No, I don't think it's anything like that. I think one of the more likely explanations is that these rooms form a conduit through which to communicate with us.'

'OK, so then how do we talk back to whatever it is?'

'A good question. But before we tackle that, don't you think we should find Jack?'

'Shit, of course we should.' Toe-curling guilt flashed through me. I hadn't so much as thought about Jack since we'd arrived here. But then again I had been caught in my own psycho drama.

'I hope he's doing all right alone. Before I found you next door, I was starting to seriously doubt my sanity,' Mike said.

'You're not alone there.'

He nodded and crossed to the stage and ran his fingers over the bass guitar with a wistful look on his face, then placed it back on its stand.

It wasn't hard to see that this time in his life meant a lot to him, just like the room next door for me did. But what really made it special for both of us were the missing people. A beautiful sparkling soul in the form of Aunt Lucy for me, and a group of drunken students for Mike.

'I haven't tried this way out yet,' Mike said as he crossed towards another door that I guessed should have led out to a university campus. He put his hand on the handle and slowly opened the door.

Golden sunlight flooded through the doorway to illuminate the dark bar. My mind scrambled to process the scene it revealed.

A golden beach with a gentle sea beyond. Large rocky outcrops were scattered offshore, waves foaming around their bases and framing the small bay. The only hint that this location wasn't really our world was the blue of the sky fading as it rose up towards the dancing lights of the eighth dimension.

My gaze was immediately drawn to the figure standing by himself, staring out to sea. Jack.

Mike stared out through the doorway and shook his head. 'Wow, that's quite a view.'

'Not just a pokey room for our Jack. His happy place is on a far grander scale.'

Together we stepped out, embraced by the gentle warm wind that sighed over the beach and rustled the tufts of seagrass covering the dunes sloping down to the shoreline. I glanced back to the door – the bar was sitting there in mid-air like some surrealist painting. All it needed was a melted watch draped over it.

I turned away and Mike and I followed the trail of footprints that led over the sand towards Jack. As we neared the sea, the smell of ozone filled my nose, and I marvelled at the attention to detail in these scenes once again.

But even before we reached Jack, I could tell that something wasn't right. He was too still, too rigid, in the middle of this otherwise beautiful setting.

'Are you OK, mate? Mike called out as we neared, obviously sensing something was off with Jack too.

Jack's shoulders dropped, but he didn't turn to greet us.

'What's wrong with him?' Mike whispered.

My instinct was already kicking in. I could almost feel the pain radiating off the guy as he stood in the shallows, the bottoms of his jeans soaked through by the sea.

I glanced at Mike. 'Let me deal with this.'

He nodded. 'OK...'

I walked forward until I was alongside Jack. But still he didn't turn. When I stepped in front of him and peered at his face I saw exactly what I'd intuitively expected: tears streaming down his cheeks. I gently placed my hands on his shoulders and he flinched.

'What's wrong?' I asked.

Jack broke his gaze away from the sea rolling over the beach. 'I haven't been back here... This was where she...'

'Who?'

His eyes glistened as the air sighed out of his nose. 'My wife, Sue. She died here.'

In this impossible place, I finally understood why Jack was alone working at a dig on Orkney.

I gestured around us at the beach. 'But this doesn't make sense. Mike and I both found ourselves in places from really happy moments in our lives. So why would whoever is behind all of this chose somewhere that is so painful for you to return to?'

'But this place, Big Sur, is the happiest place in the world for me.'

'I don't understand...'

'It's like this. Sue was a military trauma surgeon like me, and we both witnessed awful things during our tours of duty. But Big Sur was our sanctuary, the place where we healed those shared scars. When we were here we explored the whole coastline – canoeing, swimming, fishing and doing the things that people in love do. I proposed to her on this very spot.'

'So why the tears, Jack?' I rubbed his arm.

'Because it's also the most painful place in the world for me to return to. Sue and I came back here for our tenth wedding anniversary. The trip was us trying to recapture the old magic after we'd started to grow apart. There was less love maybe, but plenty of fishing and canoeing...and we talked more than we had for years...' His hands clenched and unclenched.

'Something happened?' But I didn't really need to ask the question. My instinct was already screaming at me that it had.

Jack waved a hand towards the ocean. 'We were about half a mile out in our canoes. This idiot in a speedboat tore through here, showing off to his woman.' Jack hung his head. 'The prick ploughed straight into Sue's canoe... A few weeks later I was scattering her ashes at this same spot.'

I stared at him for a moment, now understanding the sharp edges I'd first encountered. The guy was a widower whose heart had been shattered forever on this beach one summer day. And years later I'd crashed into his life, judging him without any right to do so.

Jack's shoulders shuddered as fresh tears rolled down his face.

In that moment I didn't care that I hadn't known Jack so long. All I wanted to do was take his pain away. I wrapped my arms round him and held on to him as he shook.

Mike watched us, mouthing to me, 'What's wrong?'

So even though he'd known Jack a while he still didn't know his friend well enough to know the significance of this place. I gave him a slight headshake and held Jack until I felt the tension start to flow out of his muscles as his grief eased and the tears slowed.

After a few more minutes he gently pulled away from me and pinched the top of his nose. 'Sorry about that. I normally manage to keep a lid on it, but this place is too much.'

'Sometimes tears are good, Jack.'

'I know, but once those floodgates open I feel as if I'll be swept away with it all.'

A hollow feeling filled me. I knew exactly what Jack meant. When I'd lost Aunt Lucy, my own personal anchor in this world, it had felt like the sun would never rise again. It had of course, but it'd taken me a long time to feel its warmth again.

'I understand,' I said.

Jack smeared his tears away with his arm and turned towards Mike. 'So we're not in Kansas any more, Dorothy?'

Mike gave him a small smile. 'It would seem so, mate.' He gestured down at the beach and for the first time I noticed the message written in the wet sand.

Who am I?

. . .

'What's that about?' Jack asked.

'We think it's whoever is responsible for all this – their way of trying to communicate with us,' Mike said.

'The thing is, we need to figure out a way of talking back to them,' I added.

'I see.' Jack nodded at the bag slung on my back. 'Have you tried the stone orb yet?'

I stared at him and ground the palm of my hand against my head. 'Bloody hell, how stupid am I? You're right. If the orb can bring us here, it follows that it could easily double up as a communication device.' I quickly took the stone ball out of my bag.

'You'll need my tone generator,' Mike said. He started to fish his phone out of his pocket.

I wasn't sure why I did it, maybe an instinct kicking in, but I'd already started to squeeze the orb. At once, icons etched from light appeared in the air around the orb. So wherever this was, I obviously didn't need to trigger my synaesthesia.

'Looks as if we're good,' I said.

Jack and Mike both gazed at the symbols floating around the ball. So they could see them here too, just like when we'd been in the twilight zone.

Mike squatted on his haunches and examined the icons. 'Hey, Lauren, have you tried this icon yet? The way it's pulsating suggests you need to activate it.'

He was right. There was triangular symbol strobing with blue light. I rolled my hand sideways until the icon was in the selector window, then I flicked my wrist forward.

A tetrahedron-shaped UFO plummeted out of the sky and came to a dead stop further along the beach from us.

A blinding ball blazed from it, casting long shadows from our bodies that stretched away across the sand as we shielded our eyes.

The light began to fade and I looked up to see the craft had vanished. But something else was there instead...

A woman ran towards us. She was in her mid-thirties and wearing knee-high leather boots, a short skirt and a biker's jacket. Her long, blond hair, scooped over a shoulder, bounced as she sprinted across the sand.

The air caught in my chest. It couldn't be...

There wasn't a wrinkle or grey hair to be seen on her. I stared at this younger version of Aunt Lucy as she came to a stop before us.

She grabbed my arms. 'You have to get back there before they kill me, Lauren!'

I exchanged startled stares with the others. What the fuck was going on?

CHAPTER TWENTY

MY STOMACH FLIPPED over a dozen times as I took in the apparition of Aunt Lucy.

'Did you hear me? They're trying to kill me!' the woman said as she shook me.

I glanced at Jack and Mike. 'You're seeing this too, right? I'm not hallucinating this?'

They both nodded.

'Who's trying to kill you, mam?' Jack asked.

'That's no *mam*, that's my Aunt Lucy,' I said and glared at the woman. 'At least *supposedly*. So who or what the fuck are you really?'

'Cool it, Lauren,' the impostor said.

I shook my head and turned away from Aunt Lucy to the others. 'This is obviously another conjuring trick of the sim we're in.'

The thing that was pretending to be Aunt Lucy gave me a puzzled look. 'So who am I?'

Mike, Jack and I changed meaningful looks. Her choice of words couldn't be a coincidence.

'Someone, for some twisted reason, who is impersonating my dead aunt.' I tilted my head to one side. There was another possibility... 'Unless you're telling me you're a ghost?'

The woman reached out and enclosed her hand gently round my wrist. 'No, I'm as real as you are, Lauren. At least I think so.'

'In which case you have to be some sort of entity from the eighth dimension,' Mike said. 'You've had to take on this human form so you can communicate with us, right?' He gestured around us at the beach. 'You're probably responsible for all of this too.'

'I am?' Aunt Lucy chewed her lip.

'You mean you don't know?' I asked.

Aunt Lucy shrugged. 'I'm not sure how I got here, Lauren.'

'But you said someone was trying to kill you. Who?' Jack asked.

She stared at him with her lips pinched together. 'I did?'

'Yes, you did, mam,' Jack said.

'I'm sorry, my memory is so fragmented. But I do remember Lauren here clearly. I remember how much I love her.' She gave me a wide smile and reached out for my face.

I instinctively flinched away.

'You must remember something about where you come from?' Mike said.

She screwed her eyes up tight as if trying to pluck out a memory that wouldn't come. Then her eyes snapped wide open. 'Yes, a fragment is coming back to me. A team of soldiers at Skara Brae is about to destroy my matrix.'

'Your what?' Jack asked.

But Mike was nodding. 'Matrix, as in a crystal matrix?'

'Yes. So you're not just handsome but smart too,' she replied. 'If they destroy it, the best hope for your world will be to die with me.'

'Is it something to do with Earth Song, Aunt Lucy?' I said before I could stop myself using that name.

'Lauren, you're old enough to call me Lucy now, especially in front of these two rather gorgeous guys. You need to introduce me properly.'

I gawped at her as she pouted at Jack and Mike. This was pure Aunt Lucy – the biggest flirt I'd ever seen, despite her age, and especially with a gin or three under her belt. She had been the regular party animal when she'd got going. And this was a younger model. God help Jack and Mike – and any other man she came across.

Shit! I shook my head at myself. Once again I was thinking about her as my real aunt.

'Sorry, you said our world's only hope would be about to die?' Jack said, seemingly impervious to this Lucy's charms.

'I'm so sorry, everyone. I realise I'm not making much sense. The problem is, I have only splinters of memory available as something disrupted my neural net.'

'Hang on, so you're some sort of eighth-dimensional computer running this sim?' I asked.

'I...' Her expression brightened. 'Yes, Lauren, my bright little sunflower, that's exactly it.'

Mike snorted. 'Sunflower...'

I gave him a look that made him pale. 'So...Lucy,' I said, forcing myself to use this computer's chosen name, 'do you mean that Earth Song is our planet's best hope, like the message Mike received? Something to do with a possible defence against the asteroid spaceship coming from Tau Ceti?'

Lucy clapped. 'That's it! The Kimprak are a self-replicating scavenger race. They're on their way to your planetary system to harvest it for resources and...' She shook her head. 'Sorry, my memory has failed me again.'

'That doesn't sound good in any way, shape or form,' Jack said.

Lucy frowned. 'I'm afraid it isn't. But somehow I know that I can help you to fight them, I'm just not sure how.'

'Do you remember anything about the significance of Earth Song in this?' Mike asked. 'You see, there's a good chance it was you who abducted me and planted a message in my head.'

'I'm really sorry, but I have no idea about that. Although I'm fairly sure I didn't abduct you, but instead you managed to activate part of my sub-code routines and that's how you fell into the eighth dimension. I had to take rapid action to save you as you wouldn't have lasted long, and you fell into an unconscious state before I could stabilise a three-dimensional reality around you. Unfortunately, if I implanted anything about this Earth Song in your mind, I have no memory of it.'

So this computer entity – perhaps an AI like Sentinel but more advanced – had saved Mike. And she'd also rescued all of us from the same fate. Maybe I needed to cut her some slack.

A distant rumble of thunder came from the clear blue simulated sky and a tremor shook the beach beneath our feet.

'Damn it,' Lucy said.

'Problem?' Jack asked.

'They're attempting to move my core matrix and severing my remaining neural links to your world.'

A second tremor rattled the ground, much stronger than the first, and threw the sea into a fury of swirls and eddies.

Lucy clutched her head, pain twisting her features. 'Links being broken—' Her words broke off as her body shattered into particles that swirled away until there was nothing left of her.

'What the fuck just happened?' Jack asked.

'Nothing good,' Mike replied.

The beach began to vibrate beneath our feet as the sky started to grow darker. 'Shit, this feels bad.'

'You think?' Jack said as he fought to keep his balance, the vibration starting to intensify.

'You need to get back to your world,' came the disembodied voice of Lucy from above us, as if some sort of omnipotent sky god.

'Try the stone orb again,' Mike said.

I took the ball out and squeezed it in my hand. No icons appeared. 'Fuckety fuck!'

'The Empyrean Key is being affected by the actions of the team at Skara Brae as well,' Lucy said. I guessed by Empyrean Key she meant the orb.

Jack shouted up into the air as wind whistled around us. 'So how the hell do we get back there?'

'I'll open a portal for you whilst I still can,' Lucy replied.

Another burst of light blazed along the beach in the growing night. But rather than a figure appearing as Lucy had, this time a shimmering rectangle of light hung in mid-air just above the beach. Through it we could see Skara Brae.

My mind scrambled to make sense of the scene.

The portal showed Alvarez and his mercenaries peering down into a large hole in the middle of what remained of the Skara Brae ruins. The site had now been almost totally destroyed. Standing in front of a yellow digger, Alvarez was smiling and talking to his team, though it was playing out in perfect silence for us.

'Fuck, will you look at what those bastards have done?' Jack said.

'As bad as that is, it's going to be the least of our worries if Lucy is right,' Mike said. 'If she dies, so does any hope for our world to survive this invasion by the Kimprak.'

The rumbling tone emerging from beneath the sand ratcheted up to a steady roar. The ground began to buck under our feet as we struggled to stay standing.

Alvarez was gesturing to a guy in the digger. A metal chain had been lashed round its bucket. The other end of the chain disappeared down into the deep hole. The colonel gave the driver a thumbs up and the digger started to raise the bucket, the chain attached to it tightening.

I gasped as the thing tied to a harness at the other end rose into view.

We all stared at the tetrahedron-shaped crystal, about two metres tall and wide. Shimmering blue light blazed at its heart. Fibrous glass-like roots came from it, disappearing into the surrounding ground – just like the other crystal symbols over Orkney. One by one the roots stretched out and snapped as the digger raised the crystal clear of the ground.

'That's Lucy?' Jack asked, pointing at the crystal.

'It has to be. She said that her neural connections were being broken,' I replied. 'My money is on those root-like things being everything to do with that.'

Lumps of rock from the outcrops plummeted into the sea creating huge plumes of water. With a boom, a massive crack zigzagged along the beach. A moment later it had grown several metres wide, revealing a swirl of E8 energy patterns within it.

'Go through whilst you still can or you'll die here!' Lucy's voice shouted from the rapidly disappearing sky.

Jack hoisted his carbine and loaded a magazine. 'They're going to be right on top of us the second we appear. So I'm going first, then follow after me.'

'This so isn't going to end well,' Mike said.

'We've no choice, Mike,' I said. I unhooked the LRS pistol from my jeans and slipped the safety catch off. 'You heard what Lucy said. Maybe there's an outside chance we can persuade them to stop if they know the fate of the world hangs in the balance.'

'I'd say that's so statistically improbable that I'd dismiss it as a data rounding error,' Mike replied.

'Maybe, but we're still going to try,' Jack said. 'It's our only play here.'

The beach started to tilt towards the growing fissure.

'See you on the other side of this!' Jack shouted over the scream of the wind. He leapt through the doorway, which blazed with light and obscured what was happening to him on the other side.

I raised the LRS pistol and nodded to Mike as I stepped through. My vision exploded with blinding whiteness and I felt hard ground smack into me. The blurred shapes of soldiers and Skara Brae swam into focus as vertigo rolled within me.

My head spinning, I struggled into a kneeling position, panning my pistol round to look for any target as gunfire and shouts buzzed in my ears. My vision had started to clear when Mike appeared out of thin air and almost crashed into me. At last my fog of confusion faded and I registered what was happening.

Jack was over by the digger, using it as cover, and trading fire with the Overseers soldiers. Sparks flew from the vehicle as the driver cowered in the cab. The crystal swung in its harness, just one stretched glass tether left connecting it to the ground – the AI's last neural connection to our world. If I had any doubt Lucy was in trouble, the now only faint shimmering blue light within the crystal confirmed it.

We needed to stop this – whatever it was.

I took aim with the LRS at the guy pinning Jack down with a barrage of automatic gun fire. The guy spun away, grabbing his leg as blood sprayed from it and he collapsed to the ground.

'Hold your fire!' Alvarez shouted to his soldiers, making a show of holstering his pistol.

The men surrounding us hesitated, giving each other sideways glances.

'You heard me, lower your fucking weapons,' the colonel repeated. 'This may be our only chance of retrieving an Angelus artefact intact.'

The soldiers did as they were told, but glowered at Jack who still had his carbine raised at them.

Alvarez spread his hands wide at us. 'I'm sure you're as anxious as we are not to damage the artefact.'

'It's probably the only thing we're going to agree on,' I replied. 'But if you don't want to damage it any further, you're going to have to stop what you're doing. You're killing it.'

'OK, I may be open to your suggestions,' Alvarez replied. 'Especially after our previous attempts to recover a working Angelus crystal.'

Talking was good and Alvarez was being reasonable which made an unexpected change. At least that meant they weren't firing at us. But I was having to fight my instinct to shoot the bastard in the head.

I took a steadying breath. 'First of all, answer me this. This crystal looks the same configuration as the other tetrahedron-shaped craft that have been spotted around our world. I'm guessing this is one and the same?'

'Yes it is, but how do you know about those other craft?'

'Let's just say an old mutual friend of ours gave me a tip-off.'

'Ah, of course, the Angelus AI, Sentinel.'

'Yes. He was here to help us but you tried to seize him anyway. And now you're trying to do the same thing again. Just tell me why? What motivation can you possibly have?'

Alvarez shrugged. 'The oldest motivation of all – money and power.'

'How so exactly?'

Alvarez shrugged and smirked at me.

'Then let me guess. You can make a vast fortune reverse-engineering UFOs?'

He gave me an impressed look. 'Very perceptive of you. And yes indeed, although admittedly the workings of this Angelus craft – and others we've recovered – are far beyond humanity's current understanding of physics.'

And others. So it sounded like all the rumours of captured UFOs, including Roswell, were true. If we survived this, the implications would be huge.

I raised my chin towards the suspended artefact. 'But you don't understand. That crystal is sentient.'

Alvarez gave us a wolfish smile and took his pistol back out. 'In that case, step away from the artefact. It's rather in the line of fire at the moment and you wouldn't want it harmed, would you?'

Jack sighted his carbine straight at Alvarez's head. 'And neither do you, buddy. Seems to me that we have ourselves a good old Mexican stand-off here. So...' He swivelled his weapon towards the crystal. 'You take one step towards us and I swear I will put a bullet straight through the heart of that artefact.'

I clenched my fingers on my pistol as the soldiers' fingers twitched for their weapons, all looking to Alvarez to give them the order. 'Jack, you can't – you heard what Lucy said.'

Alvarez's eyes snapped back to me. 'Lucy? Who's that? Someone from wherever it was you suddenly just appeared from?'

'Wouldn't you like to bloody know,' Mike said.

'I admire your spirit, all of you, but trust me there is nothing that some specially crafted torture can't elicit from you at a later point.'

Mike glanced at me. 'Tell him what's at stake here, Lauren.'

'Tell me what?' Alvarez replied.

'This crystal is some sort of Angelus super computer.'

'Like Sentinel you mean?'

'Not exactly, but that doesn't matter for now,' I replied. 'The key thing you need to know is that this crystal's AI told us that if she's destroyed, the last hope for our world will die with her.'

'Last hope from what?'

'A huge asteroid alien ship on its way to this system,' Jack said over the barrel of his carbine.

'I see...' Alvarez's tone softened a fraction.

Maybe we were getting through to him. 'Whoever you work for surely has to be interested in the fate of the world. They're not going to be happy if there's nothing left of it for them to exploit?'

'Of course they care about the world. One of the Overseers' key objectives is to keep this world safe from enemies that the public know nothing about. We have certain technologies far beyond anything that is known. Plans were put in place decades ago to create an armed response to any extra-terrestrial threat to our planet. Our organisation is very resourceful.'

I thought of how this very man had tried to seize the Angelus Sentinel AI and shivered inside. This guy sounded almost cocky about defeating the Kimprak, a mechanised race that had wiped all life from the face of another planet. Just how advanced was the Overseers' secret tech?

Alvarez gestured towards the crystal. 'I can assure you that if this thing is destroyed, yes, it would be an unfortunate loss of a potentially major asset, but it also isn't a problem.'

'But Lucy is an ally,' I said.

'An expendable one if it comes down to it,' Alvarez replied.

'Look, maybe we can work together on this,' Jack said. 'No one needs to get hurt if you just leave the crystal where it is.'

'Maybe...' Alvarez replied.

It must have been the tiniest micro-movement in his eyes that alerted me – suddenly my instinct was screaming at me that we were in danger.

Before I could shout out a warning, there was a hiss and Jack staggered forward. He stared down at the dart sticking out of his chest. Then Mike crumpled to the floor too, a dart sticking out of his shoulder.

Too late, I spun round to see Patrick, the old guy from the ferry, of all people. He was pointing a fat-barrelled pistol straight at me.

'Fancy running into you again, Lauren,' he said.

Before I could respond, a dart hit me in the neck. As I started to topple forward, my finger involuntarily squeezed the LRS's trigger. A single shot flew out, punching straight through the heart of the crystal.

As my head hit the ground, I saw the crystal's surface round the bullet hole crazed like a cracking mirror. The blue flickering light inside died.

Alvarez and his soldiers rushed towards the dying crystal as my head lolled to the side and unconsciousness rushed up to claim me.

CHAPTER TWENTY-ONE

MY EYES FLUTTERED open and I found myself on a bed in a room with round porthole windows along one wall. Prints of stylised flowers decorated the expensive-looking wood-veneered walls. There were a couple of designer chrome and black-leather seats at the sides of the emperor-sized bed I lay on, its frame made from scrolled golden metalwork. It might have been comfortable, if I hadn't been tied to the bed as if auditioning for a part in someone's kinky sex video.

My head ached like a rhino had been stomping on it. That had to be everything to do with the tranquilliser dart Patrick had shot me with. So much for him being a harmless old guy. So much for trusting people. Clearly Patrick was an Overseers spy who'd been sent to keep an eye on me. At least I was alive, but what about Jack and Mike? I fought the twist of panic inside me.

Through the porthole I could see the Skara Brae shoreline a few hundred metres away. So I was on some luxury boat moored just offshore. Probably Alvarez's private plaything if the Overseers paid him as well as I suspected they did.

I scanned the room for any clues and noticed my possessions

laid out on a table. The stone orb was there along with the detritus of my day bag, including two Swiss army knives...

Two?

In a rush I realised the significance. That meant our journey across the E8 had been real and not just some sort of simulation beamed into our collective minds. The fact there was a second shiny version of my Swiss army knife next to the old one meant there had been an actual physicality to those locations. And the implications of that were huge – Lucy could quite literally create reality.

I yanked against the ropes binding me to the metalwork. My bonds didn't budge even a millimetre. I tried to pull my feet but they'd been lashed to the footboard. Whoever had tied me up had obviously once been in the Scouts if their knots were anything to go by.

A murmur of voices grew from beyond the door. A moment later, it opened and there stood Alvarez and the duplicitous, back-stabbing Patrick smoking one of his roll-ups.

'Good, you're awake. We can get on with this,' Alvarez said.

'You can start by bloody untying me and letting me out of your pervy prison,' I said.

'As feisty as ever, Lauren,' the colonel replied.

I glowered at him, which usually had the effect of making people back off. But this guy just crossed his arms and the corners of his mouth curled up. Bastard.

I turned my head towards Patrick to see if my powers worked any better on him. 'And what's your bloody story, Patrick, or whoever you are?'

He smiled too. I seriously needed a heavy object to wipe the looks of amusement off their stupid smug faces.

'You mean you haven't worked it out yet, Lauren?' Patrick said, now with a London accent. The Scottish one had clearly been an act. 'I have to say I'm somewhat disappointed. I had you penned as a far brighter woman.'

'You obviously work for the Overseers based on the fact that you turned up at Skara Brae and shot all three of us with darts. Talking of which, if you have done anything to either Jack or Mike, I will personally rip your intestines out and use them to throttle you.'

Patrick just sighed, but Alvarez's hand blurred out as he struck me, the stinging blow slapping my head to the side.

I turned back to him and slitted my eyes as I licked the blood from my split lip. 'Has anyone told you that you're an utter dickhead?'

'Frequently. And you can view that slap as a tiny down payment on what's to come for so successfully screwing my mission up. We had an intact Angelus device before you shot it.'

His words were like a hammer blow to my chest. 'I destroyed it?'

'Oh yes, you did quite the number on the artefact, Lauren. Your bullet wrecked the internal crystal matrix and demolished the AI it contained. And that's something that my superiors are somewhat worked up about as we needed a functional Angelus device to analyse their technology.'

'So that crystal is definitely a ship then?'

'*Was* a ship. An ancient probe that buried itself at the Skara Brae site according to our carbon dating. And thanks to you, it's ruined.' Anger flashed through his eyes and he raised his hand to strike me again.

Patrick grabbed his arm. 'Colonel, I promise you that my methods will be more effective in getting answers from our prisoners if they remain conscious.'

So was this guy was some sort of torture specialist? If so, it figured. But at least Patrick had just given away that the others were still alive. For how long, for any of us, was another matter.

'I wouldn't have thought working for the Overseers was an old man's game, Patrick?'

'Oh, you'd be surprised. I'm a deep-cover operative who works independently of the other Overseers teams in the field. And my age is an asset in that respect. After all, who would suspect an old harmless man, hey, Lauren?'

I scowled at him. 'Quite.'

'Anyway, my dear, I've been keeping an eye on you since the Sentinel incident back at Jodrell Bank. Unfortunately for you, you've been a person of interest to the Overseers ever since.'

'What's that meant to mean?'

'I was tasked with monitoring your activities and have been keeping an eye out for you on the off-chance you might lead us to Sentinel. But you'd dropped off the map until one of our agents spotted you heading for Orkney.'

'But you did pick up my trail, didn't you, Colonel Alvarez, six months ago?'

Patrick peered at me and then Alvarez. 'You were investigating Lauren too?'

The colonel shrugged at him. 'Let's just say you aren't the only ones with people out in the field. I was tipped off by one of my people that Lauren here was investigating a UFO sighting on Exmoor. I thought it would be an ideal opportunity to deal with her personally after she'd previously got herself in my way.'

Patrick stared at him. 'And why am I only hearing about this now?'

'You don't share your intelligence with me, so why should I?'

I glowered at him. 'You utter sack of shit. Because of you my aunt is dead.'

Alvarez raised his eyebrows at me. 'So? Just a shame I didn't finish the job with you.'

'Fucking bastard!' I yanked at my bonds, desperately wanting to grab him by the neck, but once again they held me fast.

The colonel just grinned at my antics. He deserved every-thing that was coming his way.

Patrick gave Alvarez an unreadable look as he turned his attention back to me. 'Look, Lauren, we need to know why you turned up here in the first place. I imagine your arrival must have been something to do with Sentinel giving you some key informa-tion about Skara Brae?'

'Actually, that was all me. Sentinel just showed me that there was a very real conspiracy about UFOs.'

'I see. And the fact you found your own way here shows how resourceful you are, something the colonel here knows to his cost. And that's why when I realised you were on your way to Orkney I thought I'd arrange a casual meeting on the ferry to find out what you knew. Although it turned out that wasn't a lot – at least that's the impression you gave me.'

I rolled my eyes at him.

'I for one would have appreciated being informed that you were joining us on the Orkney mission, Patrick,' Alvarez said.

'I'm sure you would, but my role, as you well know, is to maintain my cover to get answers that your more vicious methods often fail to elicit.'

'I find them very effective,' the colonel replied.

'Even failed unauthorised assassination attempts?'

Alvarez slitted his eyes at the other man.

Patrick took a long drag of his cigarette. 'And then of course you nearly shot your prisoners in a firefight. Very commendable, I'm sure.'

'I had the situation under control.'

'It didn't look that way to me. It's just as well that I did. You should be thanking me, Colonel. If I hadn't shot them with tran-quilliser darts, we wouldn't be having this cosy little chat with Lauren now, would we? Now with the help of an appropriate drug, she will sing all her secrets to us like the proverbial canary.'

If my hands hadn't been tied I would have given him the finger. Instead, I had to settle for jerking my chin up at him.

'What secrets would those be?' I asked. 'I make a mean mai tai, but my recipe's my own and not for sharing.'

'Don't play dumb with us, Lauren,' Alvarez said. 'You three vanish into thin air and then reappear in the same way. I've already heard that both events coincided with brief neutrino bursts.'

'So you want the truth? We've been practising this incredible stage magic show. Good, isn't it? We're thinking of touring.'

Before Patrick could stop him, Alvarez slapped me across the face again, hard enough to loosen a filling. I sucked at it, fresh fury coursing through me. I really needed to keep a lid on my snarky attitude in a situation like this, but I couldn't help it.

I glowered up at him. 'Do your worst, Alvarez.'

A twisted smile had filled his face. 'Oh, I intend to.'

And I knew he meant every dribbling syllable of that statement.

Patrick stepped forward. 'You're no longer in charge of this situation, Colonel. From here on out, I'm the field officer in charge and I need Lauren awake if the sodium pentothal is to loosen her tongue.'

'You mean, as in the truth drug?' I asked.

'The very same,' Patrick replied. 'And you may think you can hold out on us, but you really can't.' He inhaled from his cigarette and blew smoke into my face.

'If I wasn't tied down I'd start by giving you each the knee in the nuts that you both so richly deserve. I'm not going to tell you anything.'

'We'll see about that,' Patrick said.

He opened a case and withdrew a syringe. 'What is it with you lot and your bloody thing for sticking needles into people?' I asked.

Patrick just smiled. 'I suggest you don't try to resist this, Lauren, as there's really no point.'

I yanked on the ropes. 'In your bloody dreams.'

Alvarez grabbed my arm and pushed it down flat on to the bed as I struggled against him.

I watched helplessly as Patrick plunged the syringe into a vein. Within seconds a warm woozy feeling spread through me like when I'd had one margarita too many. Despite fighting it with every fibre of my being, I felt my muscles relax and my mind following rapidly.

Alvarez released my arm and both men stood back. Patrick looked at his watch as the sensation of being deeply pissed took hold of me.

'Good – the drug should be in full effect by now,' Patrick finally said.

The room softened around me like somebody had placed a soft-focus filter over my eyes.

Alvarez loomed into view above me. 'Where did you and the others disappear to?'

Before I could stop myself answering, the words flowed out of my mouth. 'To the eighth dimension, silly.'

The non-pissed part of my brain groaned.

Alvarez's eyes widened.

'That's very good, Lauren,' Patrick said. 'And what happened when you travelled to this eighth dimension?'

'I was in Aunt Lucy's room at Christchurch College.'

Alvarez glared at Patrick. 'She must have been hallucinating.'

'Possibly,' Patrick replied. 'Try her with another question.'

Part of my mind registered annoyance that they were talking about me as if I weren't there. Or more precisely as if I were some sort of lab rat experiment, which I supposed I was. My consciousness was no longer in control of this situation and it was starting to feel like an out-of-body experience.

'Does travelling to the eighth dimension have something to do with the Angelus device?' Alvarez asked.

Again the answer sprang from my lips. 'Yes, we think so.'

'Interesting, very interesting,' Patrick said. 'So that confirms what our scientists have believed for some time – that these Angelus craft are extra-dimensional.'

'Yes, but the question is, how do they traverse between the higher dimension to ours and back again?' Alvarez said. 'It would seem that Lauren and the others have stumbled on a way to do that. If we learn how, the potential could be enormous for advanced stealth fighter craft. Even cloaked soldiers. Our employers would pay a lot for that sort of technology.'

The colonel leant in closer, his breath hot on my face. 'So, Lauren, tell us how you travelled there. Was it something to do with your synesthesia by any chance?'

Bloody hell. So they knew about that. Of course they did. If they'd been tracking me, they would have fully researched every aspect of my life.

The part of my mind that was watching this like a stage play was getting seriously pissed off by now. I fought my desire to point to the stone orb on the table.

'I...'

You can't tell them!

'I...'

Desperation swirled through my subconscious as I struggled against the woozy effect of the drug, trying to regain control. I clenched my hands hard, driving my fingernails into my palms.

'I won't tell you,' I said through gritted teeth.

Alvarez's lips thinned as his false smile dissolved faster than the sun on an English bank holiday. 'Patrick, you need to administer a second dose. We need that answer.'

'But another dose so soon will probably kill her.'

'She's of no use beyond the information she holds in her head.

And if she doesn't crack and your damned truth drug kills her, whatever you say, I'm going to use my tried and tested torture methods on the other two. So give her the fucking injection and let's get on with this.'

Patrick turned round, his back stiff. He crossed back to the case and took out a second syringe.

The world blurred again as Alvarez grabbed hold of my arm once more. I'd nothing left to fight with.

I felt a sense of powerlessness as I watched the syringe slide into my arm. But this time, rather than a sense of drunken warmth, a deep chill surged through me. Then every single muscle in my body spasmed as if I'd been wired up to the mains.

My hands clawed the air as a feeling like a nail being driven into my heart pierced my chest.

'She's going into arrest!' Patrick seemed to shout from far away.

My eyes rolled up into my skull as I felt hands pressing down on me. Then molten pain exploded in my skull and the room started to dim. The part of my brain still alert registered disbelief that I was going to die like this. And then the darkness came.

CHAPTER TWENTY-TWO

I FELT SO COLD, so utterly cold, colder than I'd ever been in my life... So this was what death was like, locked in a freezer cabinet? Hang on, I could feel something beneath me, soft and supporting. Maybe I was laid out on a cloud in a version of heaven more suited to a film. There'd be a guy along any moment now with a harp and a welcome cocktail.

But as I listened all I could hear was the gentle slap of waves against a hull. How could that be?

I cracked my eyes open and I found myself still in the bedroom on the boat. There was no sign of Alvarez nor Patrick. What the hell was going on?

I felt completely washed out and barely had any energy to lift a limb, as if Patrick had injected lead into my veins. But I was alive...I was bloody alive! OK, my head felt like a jangling box of nails and I had an epic hangover, but I was still breathing.

Through sheer willpower, I raised my hands to touch my face to check this wasn't a dream. My hands rose into view along with red burns ringing my wrists...and a distinct lack of rope binding them. I'd been untied?

My head swimming, I pulled my knees up into a foetal position and rolled on to my side, my muscles protesting.

Maybe this was some sort of trick. Alvarez and Patrick would
leap out of a wardrobe any moment and shout, 'Surprise! We had
you going there for a moment. Now back to the torture.'

Yet when I swung my legs over the side of the bed, my limbs
feeling like frozen blocks of ice, still no one appeared.

My thoughts started to order themselves. Who was I to look a
gift horse in the mouth? I shakily stood and shuffled across to the
table, my circulation slowly beginning to return.

My possessions, including the orb, were still laid out on the
table, my boots beneath it. Even my LRS pistol was there too.

OK, I was delusional. I had to be. Maybe they'd pumped me
with a psychotropic drug and were watching what I was doing
through a two-way mirror. But the only mirror in the room was a
freestanding make-up one. I could see no obvious camera
observing me with a blinking red light. If this was a hallucination,
it was every bit as real as Aunt Lucy's tower room over in the
twilight zone. And if this was real...

I placed the orb – what Lucy had called the Empyrean Key –
back in my bag, along with everything else with the notable
exception of the pistol, which I kept in my hand. So help Alvarez
if I ran into him.

My mouth felt bone dry. I seriously needed something to
drink. I helped myself to some bottled water from a small fridge
in the corner of the room. The water tasted like nectar and made
me feel a lot more human.

My mind cried out for answers. What had happened?

Maybe Patrick had left me for dead, thinking the drug had
killed me. But why the second injection of sodium pentanol
hadn't finished me off was anybody's guess. They'd probably left
me untied, ready to throw me overboard when they headed out to
sea, my body weighted down with rocks and never to be seen

again. The LRS pistol had probably been left there to dispose of in a similar fashion. They definitely wouldn't want any clues I'd ever been here left behind. Yes, it had to be something like that.

My immediate priority was finding out if Jack and Mike were still alive – please god they were. And if so, I needed to work out how to rescue them.

I reached for the door handle and opened it a fraction. I peered out through the gap into a white wood-panelled corridor lined with gold railings. Most importantly, it was empty.

My mouth dry again, I crept out of the room and closed the door behind me, my heart clenching at the click of the latch. I strained my ears for a response, but still nothing.

At the far end of the corridor a set of steps lit with blue LED strips led up to what I guessed was the deck. There were other doors off the corridor before that – hopefully other bedrooms where I'd find Jack and Mike, but even if I was right I needed to prepare myself for the worst.

I moved as quietly as I could, my weapon forward and ready to shoot if anyone so much as stuck a nose out of any of the doors. But I reached the door next to mine without incident and put my ear to it. A groan came from inside the room. Whoever was in there didn't sound in a good way.

So how to play this? I had no idea if the person in there was alone.

Taking a deep breath, I knocked on the door and stood back with my pistol aimed at it. The seconds stretched away, but still no one appeared.

LRS at the ready, I slowly turned the handle with my other hand and opened the door.

The first thing I saw was Mike hanging by his wrists from a beam, feet dangling off the ground, head slumped to his chest. For a terrible moment I thought I was too late. But then he slowly looked up at me through his dark fringe.

'Lauren?' he said, his voice barely audible.

I was with him in a second and slicing through the rope binding him with the newer version of my Swiss army knife. As Mike dropped free, I grabbed hold of him. I shuffled him over to the bed and lowered him on to it. Then I took a glass of water from a decanter on a side table and gave it to him.

He downed it in one, water running down the sides of his mouth.

I gently rubbed his back. 'How are you doing there?'

'My arms feel like they have been almost torn out of their sockets, but I'll live. What about you?'

'Oh, I had a regular party with Alvarez and Patrick.'

'Who?'

'The old guy who shot us all with his bloody tranquilliser darts.'

'Oh yeah, that git.'

'And what about you?' I asked.

'Alvarez was about to set to work on me when he received a message over his radio. Something about them being almost ready to ship out the Angelus crystal.'

I sighed. 'I don't suppose it matters much now. I managed to destroy it.'

Mike stared at me. 'You did? How?'

'I fired off a bullet by accident. The next moment the blue light inside the crystal died.'

Mike shook his head. 'That doesn't mean the crystal isn't still useful to them. They could tear it apart and analyse the tech inside it.'

'Right... But we can't let that happen, Mike.'

He rolled his shoulders. 'Why am I not surprised to hear you say that?'

'Because you've got to know the real Lauren Stelleck.'

'I guess I have. OK, I'll sign up to another of your suicide missions, but there's the small matter of finding Jack first. Not to mention dealing with any guards we run into before we can get off this boat.'

I brandished my LRS. 'Leave that to me, Mike. Are you OK to walk?'

'I'll have to be, won't I? Although I could really do with a good massage to loosen up my back.'

'You can book yourself into a spa if we live through this next bit.'

'What, you're not offering?' he asked with a feeble grin.

'Only in your dreams, Mike.'

He gave me a lopsided smile. 'I thought you might say that.'

At least his sense of humour was returning.

We made our way back out into the corridor and headed for the next door. I couldn't hear any sound coming from the other side of it. I knocked once. Nothing.

I slowly pushed the door open a crack to see Jack tied to a chair, his face badly swollen with bruises, his eyes shut. We both rushed inside and Mike shut the door behind us.

I checked his pulse. 'Thank god, he's alive.'

'I'm guessing, by the state of his face, he didn't talk,' Mike said. 'But whatever happened we need to wake him and get out of here. Especially if you're serious about trying to stop the Overseers shipping that crystal out.'

I handed him my pistol. 'You watch the door and shoot any bastard who dares to come through it.'

'But you know about me and guns,' Mike said.

'You need to get past that, Mike, just like I've been forced to, especially if we have a chance of coming out of this alive.'

'I guess.' Mike screwed up his nose as though the gun was something rancid as he took it. He crossed to the door to stand guard.

I gently took hold of Jack's shoulders. 'Jack, I need you to wake up.'

His eyelids trembled, but didn't open. Perhaps he was dreaming, or more probably reliving a nightmare about being tortured.

I gave him a firmer shake. 'We need to get out of here, Jack—'

His eyes sprang open wildly and his hands shot out and locked round my neck. He stood, lifting me from the floor and starting to throttle me.

As I gasped for air, Mike rushed over and tried to prise Jack's hands loose. But Jack struck out with his elbow straight into Mike's solar plexus and sent him sprawling.

I squeezed what breath I had between my lips as I grew light-headed. 'Jack...it's Lauren, stop it...you're killing me.'

His eyes locked on to mine and confusion swirled through them. 'Lauren?' Then he let go of me and I collapsed to the floor.

As I snatched in a lungful of breath, Jack stared at his hands with horror before looking back at me. 'Shit! Are you OK, Lauren?'

I rubbed my neck. 'I'm going to have one hell of a bruise tomorrow, but I'll live.'

'Goddammit, I'm so sorry.'

'It's OK, Jack. That was just animal survival instinct kicking in before you knew what you were doing.'

He nodded, but gave me a haunted look.

I stood up. 'Look, honestly, it's all right.' I gestured to his face, bruised and swollen like a boxer's. 'Did Alvarez do this to you?'

'Yes, and he only stopped because that old guy turned up and said it was time to get to work on you. The last thing I remember is Alvarez punching my lights out. If the colonel had come back to finish what he'd started, I doubt I'd be talking to you now.'

'I don't think any of us were meant to get out of this alive,' I said.

Jack nodded. 'But how did you both escape?'

'Good question, which we can discuss later on – first we get out of here,' I said. 'But we need to do one last thing.'

Jack fixed me with a wary gaze. 'What?'

'We need to stop the Overseers shipping out the remains of the Angelus crystal, if only to make amends for me destroying it.'

'You killed Lucy?'

'Can you not refer to the AI like that? It only makes the guilt trip worse for me. Yes, by accident with a bullet when we were tranquillised. But because of my stupidity, whatever Alvarez thinks they can do to stop it, I've put the future of the whole planet in danger.'

'No, that's already on the Overseers' shoulders,' Jack replied. 'So what's the plan to recover L— I mean, the Angelus device?'

Both Jack and Mike gave me an expectant look.

'Hey, when did I get put in charge?'

'Well, you were the one who got us into this situation, so it only follows that you should be the one to get us out of it, especially as Jack's in a bad way and I don't want the job,' Mike said.

'We'll have an argument about your logic there later. But there's no time to discuss it – we need to get off this boat and back ashore. We'll work out the rest from there.'

'In other words it's a seat-of-your-pants plan,' Jack said.

'Something I seem to specialise in. But this is going to be tough. To start with, there's bound to be at least one Overseers soldier on this boat.'

Jack shook his head. 'There'll be a lot more than that, trust me. I know that much about these guys.'

'I so didn't want to hear that,' Mike said. 'But I agree that getting the crystal is a priority, even if this mission sounds like a death wish.'

'Well, we'll definitely be dead if we stay here,' I said.

Mike scraped his hand back through his hair. 'Good point, so lead the way, our illustrious leader.'

'If you insist.'

Jack stood and swayed slightly. 'Sorry, still groggy here.'

'Let me help you,' Mike said. He looped an arm under his shoulders.

I led the two of them shuffling behind me out into the corridor towards the steps at the far end. As we neared, I crouched and, signalling to the others to stay put, crept ahead. I gazed up at the top of the steps and the closed door there. Our luck had run out. Through a window set in the door, I could see the back of a man's bald head.

'There's a guard outside the door,' I whispered.

'Any other way out of here?' Mike asked.

'Not obviously. The portholes are too small to crawl through.'

Jack took a shaking step forward and extended his hand for my pistol. 'I'll deal with the guard, Lauren.'

I shook my head at him. 'No, you won't. Look at the state of you. A fairy's fart would probably knock you off your feet at the moment.'

'Interesting mental image you painted there,' Mike said with a smile.

I raised my eyebrows and narrowed my gaze on Jack. 'Anyway, do we understand each other?'

He held his palms up. 'Hey, I'm not stupid enough to argue with you, especially when you're the one holding the pistol.'

'Good, then I'm glad we understand each other.' I tried to smile, but couldn't quite manage it.

Jack sagged again and Mike quickly moved to support him.

Despite my bravado, sweat trickled down my back as I crept up the stairs.

The guy's face was illuminated by his phone and whatever app he was using on it – Tinder going by the number of women he was left-swiping on. Beyond him, I could see the rear deck and past that a line of lights blazing a few hundred metres away on the shore in the darkness.

I returned my attention to the guard. His carbine hung from its strap on his right shoulder, its barrel pointed downwards.

For a moment, I considered shooting the guy in the back of the head. But apart from making me feel sick to my core, the silencer wouldn't negate the sound of breaking glass, which might draw unwanted attention. One guard could quickly turn into a dozen. And hadn't Jack said it would take three shots to make sure? I shivered. That meant I only had one other choice...

My heart pumping hard within my chest, I took hold of the handle and turned it as quietly as I could. Slowly I raised my pistol ready to slam the butt of its handle on to the back of the guy's head with all the force I could manage. I just hoped that would be enough.

I started to gradually open the door but my guardian angel must have nipped off for a quick cigarette because the tiniest, almost inaudible squeak came from the top hinge. It was enough.

The guy spun round, already raising his carbine towards me.

Time decelerated. Adrenaline hummed through my body as I squeezed the trigger of the .22 pistol with a hiss. A fierce look filled the guy's face, morphing into one of surprise as blood bloomed from his stomach.

Before I could do anything else, Jack was by my side, presumably powered enough by adrenaline to forget his injuries. He grabbed the LRS from me and clamped his hand over the guy's mouth. He placed the gun to the guy's heart and squeezed the trigger...three times.

The guard's eyes widened as he slumped on to me. I held him, feeling the life leave his body, his blood soaking through my clothes as I lowered him to the ground. Utter numbness filled me as I disconnected from reality. Yes, I'd shot someone before, but the proximity of this guy's death made this far worse. I stared down at the blood pooling beneath him.

Jack crept out on to the deck and peered up before doubling back. 'Are you OK, Lauren?' he whispered.

'Physically yes, emotionally I'm a car wreck. But I'll deal with that later, along with everything else.'

Jack nodded and unhooked the man's carbine from his body. He beckoned to Mike, who crept up the stairs to join us, his face paling as he saw the guard.

Jack put his fingers to his lips. Then he gestured for us to follow as we moved out from beneath the cover of the roof and on to the rear deck.

I tore my eyes away from the dead man's. When we joined Jack, he pointed towards the top of the boat.

The shadows of several people were silhouetted against the windows of the bridge. But at least no one was looking down at us.

'We need to get off this boat as quietly as we can,' Jack whispered.

I gazed off the back of the boat towards Skara Brae. A launch had been pulled up on to the shingle of the beach. That must have been how Alvarez and Patrick had got back ashore.

'It's not too far to swim,' I said. I tried to inject some humour into my voice and gestured to my blood-soaked clothes. 'I could certainly do with a bit of a wash.'

'You continue to astonish, Lauren Stelleck,' Jack said, shaking his head. He handed my LRS back to me and I strongly resisted the urge to throw it into the water.

'We need to get our arses in gear before someone discovers what's happened,' Mike said.

Jack nodded and pointed at the dead guard. 'First, we should deal with this guy before anyone spots him.' He slung the carbine over his own shoulder. 'Mike, give me a hand.'

Together they heaved the guy to the side, whilst I watched the bridge. They slowly lowered the guard into the water and let go. As he floated out from the boat, he rolled on to his back, arms moving into a crucifixion position. With eyes still staring in shock, he slipped down beneath the surface of the black water.

I shuddered, doing my best to ignore the nausea churning inside me. I would never forget the look on that man's face.

Jack took the lead and quietly stepped down a ladder into the water first. I stuck the pistol into my belt as Mike followed Jack down into the gentle waves. They treaded water as they waited for me.

So much death...

I gathered what resolve I had left and I lowered myself in after them. At once the icy grasp of the sea wrapped round me like a cold fist. My senses snapped alert as the chill cut through my numbness.

With our heads up, the three of us struck out for the shore, the hum of activity from Skara Brae growing steadily louder.

CHAPTER TWENTY-THREE

DAMN, I was cold. The swim had not only been exhausting, it'd almost sapped me of the will to live. In one sense it was a blessing, because it had stopped me thinking about the guy we'd just killed. That and trying to imagine a hot bath with lots of bubbles and scented candles. Yet the reality of the situation won the fight, especially now I was trailing water behind me as we headed up the beach, an icy night wind snapping at my back.

I was beyond shattered both physically and emotionally. God knew how Jack managed to keep going after everything that Alvarez had put him through. His reserves of energy must have run all the way to the core of the planet.

The one saving grace of our current situation was that it wasn't raining. The Milky Way was as brilliant as I'd ever seen it. The clear band of white dipped towards the horizon directly over Skara Brae. On any other night, I would have stood and drunk in this breath-taking scene to the bottom of my astronomer's soul. But now wasn't that moment.

Mike gestured towards the beached speedboat as we skulked

past it. 'We could call it a night now and just get the hell out of here on that.'

'You know that's not an option,' I said, trying to stop my teeth chattering.

'I know...' he replied.

I raised my chin towards the raised bucket of the digger visible above the mounds, a taut chain still hanging from it. Presumably that meant the dead crystal was still connected to the other end.

Jack's gaze tightened on me. 'You do realise we'll probably be throwing our lives away by attempting this, don't you?'

'That may be true, but if we let the Overseers take the Angelus device, that will be the end of it. And, you never know, there may be a way to fix it.'

'It sounds to me as if you're clutching at straws there, Lauren,' Jack replied.

'Maybe, but it would haunt me for the rest of my life if we don't try everything possible to revive Lucy. Even if that's only the five years until the Kimprak arrive.'

Mike smiled.

'What?'

'Just that's the first time you've referred to the AI as *Lucy.*'

'Whatever, but my point stands.'

'You really are a stubborn woman,' Jack said.

'Like you wouldn't believe,' I replied.

'Oh, I'm getting there, trust me.'

'Well, we've only got two weapons between us, and no grenades this time round to shake things up,' Jack said. 'So if we're going to throw our lives away on a lost cause, let's do this sensibly.'

'And what does that option look like when it's all dressed up?' Mike asked.

'If possible, let's try to make this a stealth mission and locate the crystal without engaging anyone,' I replied. 'Once we've done that, we can work out the next step from there.'

'That sounds suspiciously like another one of Lauren's famous seat-of-her-pants plans,' Mike said.

'Hey, you don't want life to suddenly get boring after we've been having such a great time so far, do you?' I asked.

'With you around there's little danger of that,' he replied.

Maybe Mike had a point.

We crept round the edge of Skara Brae. I could hear talking and even laughing coming from the other side of the few remaining mounds that hadn't been flattened.

There was a distinct lack of cover, but thankfully the arcing lights beaming down over the site cast the surrounding beach and countryside into dark shadow, helping to hide our presence.

An engine rumbled into action and, like a spider emerging from its lair, the digger began to reverse up a slope, its caterpillar tracks churning up the ground.

Jack immediately stiffened. 'The vandals are at work again.'

We ducked down and watched as the broken crystal, now strapped on to a metal pallet, started to swing in its harness as it was carried away. Several of the Overseers soldiers immediately hung on to the pallet, dampening the pendulum swing. Alvarez and Patrick followed behind.

My heart lurched as I took in the perfect bullet hole in the heart of the crystal. I knew it was an accident, but that didn't stop my growing guilt.

Stupid, stupid, stupid...

The digger rumbled down the other side of the mound and came to a stop.

Alvarez's words reached us as he addressed his soldiers. 'The priority is to get this Angelus artefact to the airport where we have a private jet due to touch down in thirty minutes. I want this crystal on-board and out of this damned country before the SAS turn up and make this day so much worse.'

'Understood, Colonel,' a blonde female soldier replied. She slapped the side of the digger and it started forward again, trundling towards the car park.

Alvarez turned round and headed back to the site with Patrick.

A moment later, the colonel's shouted instructions echoed around what was left of Skara Brae. 'We're not going to waste the great cover story MI5 created, so I want those C4 charges set. When we blow it up, all evidence of our work here will be destroyed too and MI5 can blame it on their unexploded bomb.'

We heard his soldiers laugh.

Mike raised his eyebrows at me and tilted his head towards Jack, whose knuckles were going white on his carbine.

I nodded. 'I know how you must be feeling, Jack, but we haven't got time to stop them blowing up your site and to grab the crystal.'

'One of the most important archaeological sites in Europe is about to be decimated and you expect me to do nothing?' he replied.

'We haven't got any choice, not really. If you go in there all guns blazing, we won't stand a chance. You said that yourself.'

'I know...' Jack hung his head. 'The list of stuff I want to make Alvarez and the Overseers pay for is getting pretty damned long.'

'For you and me both,' I replied.

Jack sighed and I could almost feel the electricity of his tension relax slightly. 'OK, let's play it your way, Lauren.'

Mike gave me a discreet tight smile.

We followed Jack and kept to the shadows as we made our way towards the car park.

We edged round the visitor centre and crouched behind Jack's old Land Rover. From its cover, we watched the digger manoeuvre the crystal until it was suspended over the rear of a pickup truck.

'What next, Jack?' Mike asked.

'Odds are against us taking out that many soldiers without raising the alarm.'

'So why don't we make it easier for ourselves?' Mike said.

'How exactly?' I asked.

'They're bound to have someone guarding the gate. We could give that individual a little visit and then intercept the pickup truck as it's leaving. It will even up the odds if nothing else.'

Jack exchanged a look with me. 'This guy has a good head on his shoulders.'

'Rumour has it,' I replied. 'But first let's make sure they can't follow us in any of the other vehicles.' I got out the Swiss army knives and handed one to Jack. 'The tyres.'

He nodded and, sticking to the shadows, we stuck the blades into the tyres of the other Overseers vehicles parked near the Land Rover.

'All good?' Jack asked me as we returned to Mike.

'All good. Let's go,' I replied.

As the Overseers started to lower the crystal on to the truck, we skirted along the low wall together. Moving at a snail's pace, ready to respond to any challenging cry, it felt like a lifetime later that we eventually reached the gate. But thankfully, Mike's hunch was right. There was just a single soldier guarding the closed gate.

Jack turned to me. 'Lauren, do you mind if I borrow your pistol? My carbine hasn't got a suppressor.'

'I can deal with him if I have to.'

'I know you can, but this one's on me and I don't want you to go there unless it's absolutely necessary.' I registered the flat tone in Jack's voice, once again hinting at a man with a difficult past.

Yes, he was a surgeon, but everything suggested he'd seen his share of action on the battlefield.

I held my LRS out to him.

Jack took it from me and checked the magazine. He began to edge forward quietly, like a cat on the hunt for its prey. This guard had none of the casualness of the guy back on the boat. Instead, there was a deadly stillness to this man, his eyes scanning the road constantly. But despite the guy's razor-sharp alertness he was looking the wrong way. Jack closed to within ten metres of him and raised the LRS.

I didn't dare breathe or even blink. Mike clenched his hands into fists as the unbearable wait dragged on. Jack stood still as stone, completely focused.

Then he pulled the trigger.

The hiss of the first bullet was followed by two more and the guard crumpled to the ground. Just like that, another life was snuffed out. And worst of all, I barely felt a flicker of emotion. It seemed the Overseers were becoming a generic enemy to me, rather than individuals with lives and families. Maybe when I looked back at this later, I would realise that the guard on the boat dying right in front of me, even if I hadn't pulled the trigger, had been the moment I'd crossed some sort of line, a line that was now rapidly receding behind me.

'Come on,' Mike whispered, breaking into my thoughts.

We joined Jack to help him drag the guard to the verge.

Jack slipped a hand under the man's jacket, withdrew a pistol and held it out to Mike.

'No, I'm sorry, I can't,' Mike said, staring at the weapon.

At least one of us was doing their best to hang on to their humanity tonight.

Jack nodded and handed my LRS back to me, his eyes probing mine. Then he nodded like he somehow knew exactly what I'd been thinking. He got it and so did I.

Jack helped himself to the man's black baseball cap and put it on. Then he stuck the guard's pistol into his pocket.

'It shouldn't be much longer before that pickup trucks leaves,' Mike said.

Jack nodded. 'When the truck gets here, I'll deal with the driver. Lauren, can you take out the passenger?'

'Right...'

'So you're not even going to bother trying to take them prisoner? Mike asked, looking between us.

'Afraid not,' Jack replied.

I nodded. 'This is a full-blown combat mission and we need to move as fast as possible. I know it sounds callous, Mike, but anything else will slow us down and get us all killed.'

Mike just shook his head.

I knew like Jack obviously did that this was a kill-or-be-killed situation. I was increasingly thinking like a soldier.

A rumble of tyres heralded the pickup's approach as it headed towards us from the car park.

'Take your positions and pray this works out,' I said, then I ducked down behind the wall, my thumb almost wearing a groove in the stock of the LRS as I listened to the vehicle approaching.

I heard a squeal of brakes and the whine of an electric window being lowered.

'Get these fucking gates open, Sam, we're on the clock here,' a man's voice said. 'Hey, you're not—' The hiss of a bullet cut his conversation dead.

I sprang up ready to fire as the driver slumped forward on to the steering wheel and the horn blared out.

Fuck! I didn't have time to think anything else, because the passenger door flew open and the female soldier we'd seen back in the car park rolled out, her training kicking in as she reacted to our threat. The woman sprang to her feet, bringing her own pistol to face me. Too late I started to swing my weapon round, yet there was the crack of stone on a skull and the female soldier toppled forward.

Mike stood behind her and lowered a rock.

'Thank you!' I said.

'At least I didn't have to kill anyone.' His eyes slid away from mine.

That told me, but I got where he was coming from completely.

Jack heaved the driver from the vehicle and the horn stopped dead, but it was too late. Shouts were coming from the car park and moments later Alvarez and at least ten soldiers were sprinting towards us.

'Time to get out of here,' I said.

Jack leapt into the driver's seat and Mike jumped into the back. As I clambered into the passenger seat, sparks flew from the tailgate as several bullets struck. In response, Jack stamped his foot on the accelerator. The pickup truck surged forward and smashed through the gates. Jack hauled the wheel over and we slid, fishtailing on to the road as another bullet smashed the side window. Jack corrected the skid and straightened the vehicle.

'Is everyone OK?' he asked.

'Physically yes, but in somewhat of a state of shock,' Mike said.

'I'm good,' I added, which was almost true.

A distant boom rattled the vehicle. I turned round to see an orange fireball rolling up into the sky above Skara Brae. There went the evidence.

Jack glared at the rear-view mirror. 'Bastards!' he shouted as we sped away into the night.

'So where are we going?' Mike asked.

'Oh, I know someone who may be able to help,' I replied with a thin smile.

CHAPTER TWENTY-FOUR

JACK HAD STOPPED ONCE during the journey to check for any tracking device, but couldn't find anything. Despite that, I'd spent most of the journey looking over our shoulders for any sign of pursuit. But at last we'd reached the house of the person I thought might be able to help. Luckily for me Jack knew Greg, the amateur smuggler I'd met in the pub, and where he lived.

We screeched to a stop behind Greg's yellow Punto, which was parked outside a lone bungalow on the edge of a field. An overflowing rubbish skip filled the driveway and several of the bungalow's windows had been boarded up with sheets of plywood. To complete the run-down look, a rusting, half-dismantled motorbike had been abandoned on the front lawn.

'Are you sure about this guy?' Mike said as he eyed the dilapidated home.

'Greg's OK, just not always on the right side of the law,' Jack said. 'But the guy's got a good heart.'

'I second that, based on my experience with him,' I said. 'Greg looked out for me when I got the cold-shoulder treatment from the other locals in a pub.'

'But can we really be sure he isn't another Overseers stooge like that Patrick guy?' Mike asked. 'After all, he had you fooled.'

'I'd strongly doubt that. He's lived his whole life on Orkney,' Jack said. 'He's a local through and through.'

'I agree,' I said. 'Without taking anything away from Greg, I can't imagine him being picked up by the Overseers' recruitment radar.'

'OK, let's do this then,' Mike replied.

We clambered out of the truck and began to pick our way past the strewn bags of rubbish to the front door. A pool of light from a hallway lamp shone through the floral-patterned glass.

Before I even tried the bell, frenzied barking started up somewhere deep in the house.

'Oh, that's just great. I so don't get on with dogs,' said Mike.

'Don't worry, it's only a pit bull,' I replied, trying to suppress a grin.

Mike narrowed his eyes at me as Jack rapped his knuckles on the door.

The sound of barking grew louder, followed by the shadow of a man hanging on to the collar of a dog on the other side of the frosted glass.

Mike stepped behind us with an apologetic shrug. 'As I said, I'm not good with dogs.'

The door opened a crack on a chain and Bambi promptly stuck his snout through the gap, making Mike flinch.

'Who the hell is it?' Greg's voice came from inside.

'It's Lauren. You helped me out with a lift from the pub.'

'Oh, it's you, cool. Hey, quiet, Bambi. Don't you recognise a friend when you see one?' Greg closed the door and we heard it being unlatched before swinging open. Greg's gaze passed over Jack and Mike with a pinched expression, as Mike peered out from behind me at Bambi.

'You found your Viking then,' Greg said.

'I did, thanks to you,' I replied.

Jack stuck out a hand. 'Long time no see, buddy.'

Greg shook his hand vigorously. 'You too, mate.'

'So how are things? Still managing to keep out of trouble with the police?'

'You know me.' Greg winked at him and then his eyes settled on Mike. 'And you are?'

'I guess you could say I'm a part-time beach bum.'

'Nice.' Greg raised a fist and bumped Mike's with his. 'So I'm guessing you haven't all turned up for a cheap case or three of Highland Park?'

'Another time, maybe,' I said. 'But right now we need somewhere to lie low until we can find a way off Orkney.'

Mike hitched his thumb over the shoulder. 'We also need to get our vehicle off the road before someone spots it.'

'It's hot then?' Greg asked.

'Baked potato toasty,' I replied. 'But more than that, it belongs to some seriously dangerous people.'

'Shit! OK, bring it round the side and we can stash it in my garage. Then we can share a drink and talk over how best to get you off Orkney.'

'What, you're going to help without even asking who's after us?' Mike asked.

Greg shrugged. 'That's your business. I don't need to know. I've been where you are, so I'm glad to help. Karma and all that.'

'You, Greg, are a saint,' I said.

'Maybe one with a very crooked halo, hey?'

I snorted as he headed past us. Bambi followed, all doggy smiles at Mike, who was still keeping his distance.

Jack backed the truck on to the driveway as Greg pulled up a wooden garage door riddled with rotten holes. Its hinges screeched in protest as he opened it.

'Must get those runners oiled,' Greg said.

'Along with a thousand other jobs around this house,' Mike whispered out of the corner of his mouth to me.

I gave him a hard look to shut him up.

Inside the garage, Greg flicked a switch. With a series of clinking sounds, a neon tube flickered into existence. The garage was illuminated before us, an open door on the right side of it leading to the main house. But it was what it was jammed with that made this garage unlike any other I'd ever seen. Most of the high shelving that lined the walls seemed to be filled with cigarette boxes and several large fuel jerrycans. Apart from one section on the left-hand side stacked full of boxes labelled 'Highland Park'.

'You must be a thirsty guy,' Mike said, pointing towards the whisky.

'Let's just say I have a few clients who prefer not to pay any customs duty.' Greg tapped the side of his nose.

The garage flared with the red brake lights of the pickup as Jack cautiously backed the vehicle into the garage, squeezing it between the boxes.

As soon as the truck came to a stop, Greg closed the garage door. His eyes locked on to the bulging shape under the tarp on the back of the vehicle. 'So what have you got there?' He started to reach out for it.

I shook my head. 'Greg, it'll be safer for you if you don't.'

Too late. Greg had already peered under the tarp and whistled. He threw the cover back to reveal the crystal on its pallet. He stared at it slack-jawed. 'Shitting hell, that's one hell of a bauble you've got there. Tell me that's not some monster fuck-off diamond?'

I swapped looks with the others. Should we tell Greg the truth?

Jack seemed to decide for all of us, jumping in with, 'Nope.

But in many ways it's even more valuable. The future of our world depends on it.'

Greg gawped at us. 'Fuck me. Seriously?'

'Seriously,' I replied. 'You see...' As I patted the crystal the rest of the words I'd been about to say lodged in my throat. A rolling shock of energy surged through my arm.

I snatched my fingers away, shaking them. 'Shit, that really hurt.'

'You OK, Lauren?' Jack asked.

Thankfully the sensation was already fading away. 'I'll live. Just a static shock or something like that.'

Mike's eyes widened and he put his hands on his head. 'Or something like that... What if Lucy is still alive in there, Lauren?'

'You think?'

'It has to be a possibility – if there's still energy running through its systems.'

Fresh hope surged within me.

'Who's Lucy?' Greg asked.

'Our codename for this crystal,' Jack said.

That was certainly an easier explanation than going with the truth, which would have probably taken hours and several dozen diagrams.

'Anyway, how do we check?' Jack asked. 'I can't exactly feel for her pulse.'

'The Empyrean Key!' I said. I headed round to the passenger door and grabbed my day bag. Greg gave the stone orb and me a questioning look as I took it out.

'Another thing that would take too long to explain,' I said. 'Guys, we need to generate a tone to trigger my synaesthesia.'

'Hey, Greg, have you got a smartphone I could borrow for a mo?' Mike asked.

'Sure.' Greg fished an expensive-looking mobile, as thin as a sheet of glass, out of his pocket. He unlocked the screen and handed it over to Mike.

'Is it OK to download an app?' Mike asked.

He smirked. 'As long as it's nothing too dodgy.'

'It's just a sound generator.'

'For?'

'Let's just say it's a science experiment,' I said.

'Then knock yourself out.'

Mike's fingers flew over the screen. Within moments he had installed a tone generator and his eyes lifted to mine. 'Are you ready, Lauren?'

'Always...'

'OK. Just dialling in the same frequency that worked for you last time.' He hit play and a familiar low bass note hummed out of the phone.

At once, my vision exploded and I gasped. Strands of red light flew about the orb, coalescing into ruby icons hovering round the stone ball.

'Going by your expression, it worked then?' Jack asked.

'Absolutely,' I replied. I studied the shapes before me. 'There's a ring of red icons orbiting the Empyrean Key and an icon with four triangles facing inwards that's pulsing.'

'Then I say try that one,' Mike said.

'What the hell are you all talking about?' Greg asked, his eyes darting with confusion.

'Later, over one of your bottles of Highland Park,' I replied.

'It's a date,' Greg said with a wink.

I rotated the icons until the red circle one was hovering in the selection window and flicked my wrist forward. Every single icon blinked out.

'Shit,' I said as I instinctively shook the stone, but the light display didn't reappear. 'I think I just hit the off button.'

'It was worth a try,' Jack said.

'I really thought...' The whisky bottles began to chink on their shelves as a shudder passed through the garage.

Greg rushed over to steady a box threatening to vibrate over the edge of its shelf. 'What the fuck is going on, guys?'

Excitement surged in me. 'Something wonderful,' I said.

'2001 again, am I right?' Jack said.

'You really are my sort of guy,' I replied with a grin.

And then it got better.

A pulse of blue light appeared at the top of the tetrahedron and shimmered down throughout the crystal. Then the light moved back up like a photocopier scanning a page. That completed, the light concentrated itself round the bullet hole and the cracks spidering out from it.

'What's happening?' Jack asked.

Mike leant in closer and his frown was replaced with a wide smile. 'Lauren's right, this is amazing. I think the crystal is beginning to regenerate around the damaged area.'

'You mean it's healing itself?' Greg asked.

Mike smiled at him and nodded.

'Lucy's going to be OK,' I said. The tears came from nowhere and I had to blink them away.

'Shit, lass, you've got yourself a bit worked up over a bit of stone,' Greg said as he pushed another whisky box back on to the shelf.

I laughed. 'Hey, it is a very sparkly stone.'

The vibration faded away, but light still shone along the fissures in the crystal.

'How long is this self-repair going to take?' Jack asked.

Mike shrugged. 'Who knows? An hour, a day, longer?'

'Thank god we saved her from the Overseers,' I said.

Jack smiled at me. 'Yeah, seems you had a point.'

Bambi suddenly growled and stared intently at the garage door. His growl deepened, raising the hairs on the nape of my neck. I quickly pulled the tarp back over Lucy.

Greg dropped down to look Bambi in the eyes and put a finger to his lips. At once the pit bull stopped the sound dead. Greg picked his way over to the garage door and put his eye to one of the numerous holes.

'Fuck!' he whispered. 'Are you being chased by people wearing black combat gear and carrying guns, by any chance?'

I grabbed my gun from my bag. 'How the hell did they find us?'

'Crap. They must have hidden a tracking device after all and one that was hidden real well,' Jack said. 'All they had to do was look up our current position to find us.'

'But we can't let them take Lucy, especially now she's repairing herself,' Mike said.

'And we won't,' Jack replied.

'How exactly?' I said. 'They almost certainly have us surrounded. The moment we step outside we won't last long. And even if we could escape, they'll be watching all the ports and airfields. We'll never get off here.'

'Well if we stay here we're all going to hell in a hand basket,' Greg said.

'We're definitely dead if we stay and almost as likely to be shot if we go, but I prefer the odds of the second option,' Jack said. 'As regards a tracking device leave that to me because I have an idea.'

Greg rubbed his neck with his hand. 'Okay, I was going to say this later over that bottle of Highland Park, but if you need a way off Orkney, I may be able to help you out. I have a mate who works on an oil rig. If we can get you to it, if you grease his palm with enough cash, he can arrange a helicopter lift to the mainland for you and your crystal.'

'Don't look at me, I've got next to no cash left in the bank' I said.

'Well, I have,' Jack said. 'I'll sort something out for your mate later if that will work for him?'

'Guess I can vouch for you,' Greg said.

'I'd appreciate it.'

'Then consider it done.'

'And the small matter of getting to a rig in the middle of the ocean?' Mike asked.

'Not a problem. See, I have access to this big fuck-off speed-boat. It's owned by a wealthy mate who looks the other way when I need it for my off-the-book gigs. Talking of which we're going to need some extra fuel for the trip.' He grabbed two of the jerrycans and put them in the back of the truck next to Lucy.

I was about to reply when the light in the garage suddenly died. A split second later came the crash of breaking glass some-where in the house.

'That sounds like my fucking front door,' Greg said.

'So that's our cue to get out of here,' Jack said.

Mike jumped into the back of the truck. Greg followed him, dragging Bambi along. A second crash echoed through the house and Bambi tore loose from Greg's grip, speeding away through the open door into the bungalow.

'Come back here, Bambi!' Greg said, jumping out of the truck.

He was answered by frantic barking and a man swearing in what could have been Russian. There was the hiss of a bullet and Bambi's barking stopped dead.

Greg spun round to face us. 'And now they've killed Bambi!'

'We'll be next if we don't get our butts into gear,' Jack said. He opened his window and rested the barrel of his carbine on to the sill, pointing it at the door to the house.

I heard the sound of footsteps approaching.

'Quiet,' Jack hissed as the lance of a green laser flicked along the hallway, clearly looking for a target.

Jack raised his carbine and I raised my LRS. He nodded to me and together we fired off several rounds into the darkened house.

A hailstorm of bullets answered our shots, peppering the cab and smashing several boxes of whisky beyond the truck and the jerrycans that started to leak fuel.

'Fucking tossers,' Greg shouted. 'Invading my house and killing my fucking dog. I'll fucking have you!' He grabbed a bunch of rags from a shelf.

'Get in the truck now, Greg!' I pulled at his arm and shoved him into the back with Mike.

Greg lowered his window as I leapt into the passenger seat.

A shadow moved towards us in the darkened hallway. Jack fired off another spray of bullets and the shadow dropped to the floor.

'I'll fucking have you,' Greg repeated. He lit the bunch of rags and chucked the burning material on to the shelves that now dripped with whisky. 'Time to get out of here.' Greg grinned widely.

I wasn't sure even Greg could have predicted just how spectacular the results of his handiwork would be.

As Jack slammed his foot down on the accelerator, a whumping sound came from the dripping fuel mixed in with the whisky as it ignited. A huge gout of flame plumed around the pickup as we surged forward. The truck's bull bar smashed into the garage door, reducing it to splinters as we shot into the outside world.

For a split second a startled soldier was caught in our headlights. He didn't stand a chance. The truck struck him square on with a crunch of metal slamming into bone. Then the guy disappeared beneath the truck.

My stomach clenched at the sickening lurch from the rear left tyre as we bounced over him and on to the driveway.

Bullets from multiple unseen attackers surrounding the bungalow struck the vehicle from every angle.

Jack and I returned fire as best we could, whilst Greg made V-signs out of the window as flames billowed out of the garage behind us.

With a screech of tyres, we skidded on to the road and hurtled away.

'So that's how they got the drop on us,' Mike said. His hand appeared over my shoulder, pointing ahead.

About half a mile along, a black helicopter was parked in a field adjacent to the road.

'Sneaky fucks landed far enough away so we couldn't hear them,' Greg said.

And they would follow us if we didn't do something about it.

'Jack, can I borrow your carbine for a moment?' I asked.

He gave me a grin. 'Sure,' he replied, handing his weapon to me.

A moment later he'd slowed the truck as we drew parallel to the helicopter. The cockpit was empty.

'Thumb that switch on the right to engage full automatic mode,' Jack said.

I pushed the lever and it clicked into place. I planted the stock squarely on my shoulder, aiming it up and out of the window.

'This one is for Bambi...' I squeezed the trigger. A trail of bullets streamed towards the helicopter, sparking off its underside.

'Fuck yeah,' Greg said.

'And this one is for forcing Greg to torch his house to help us escape.'

I pulled the trigger again and this time kept it pressed, walking the bullets along towards the helicopter's engine at the rear. With a bang and a satisfying flash of light, the helicopter exploded, panels cartwheeling away as a fireball rose into the sky.

Greg whooped. 'Better than the fucking fifth of November!'

Jack snorted as he accelerated the truck hard away.

'So about that tracking device you were going to deal with, Jack?' Mike asked.

Jack turned to smile at him. 'Oh, don't you worry, like I said I've got a plan...'

CHAPTER TWENTY-FIVE

THE CONTRAST between Greg's bungalow and his mate's home couldn't have been starker. Under the starlit night sky we approached along the driveway that led us towards a large, ultra-modern, white, curved house surrounded by landscaped gardens. I suspected that the owner moved in very different circles to Greg.

'What is it your friend does again?' Mike asked, peering out of the window and obviously drawing the same conclusion.

'Jay is big in special effects for films,' Greg said. 'He works all around the world and that's why he isn't here right now. I keep an eye on the place when he's away.'

'How do you know him?' Mike asked, voicing the question I was silently thinking.

'Went to the same local secondary school and stayed in contact on Facebook and stuff. Even though he's struck it rich, the poor bastard can't shake me. You know how it is these days – some people stick to you like limpets.' Greg grinned at us.

'But you're good enough friends that he doesn't mind you borrowing his boat?' Mike asked as we neared the house.

'Sort of. What he doesn't know doesn't hurt him, am I right?'
I grimaced. 'Oh, OK.'

'So where's this boat of his anyway?' Jack asked.

'Take the gravelled track on the left side of the house and that
will lead directly to it,' Greg replied.

Jack did as he'd been instructed and we headed past a huge
kidney-shaped swimming pool surrounded by loungers. The
paraphernalia of the owner's expensive lifestyle included some
sculptures of naked men dancing together. I guessed this place
had seen quite a few crazy parties in its time.

'Special effects obviously pays well,' Jack said.

'Obviously,' Mike replied.

We skirted manicured terraced lawns towards a beach at the
bottom and pulled up by a metal jetty. A large speedboat with a
wooden deck and curved windshield was moored to it, with two
huge engines at its stern.

'Looks fast,' I said.

'Like you wouldn't believe,' Greg replied. 'Those twin Merlin
engines kick some serious arse out on the sea. It's the ideal choice
for me in case I encounter a coastal patrol boat during one of my
midnight runs.'

'It's really only whisky and fags you smuggle, right?' Mike
asked.

He held up his hands. 'No way would I have anything to do
with drugs or other dodgy cargo. Apart from anything else, I
wouldn't want to risk the serious jail time.'

'Good to hear,' Mike replied.

We all got out of the truck and Jack peered out to sea.

'How far offshore is your mate's rig then, Greg?' I asked.

'About ten nautical miles as the seagull flies.'

'In that case, let's get Lucy loaded on to the boat.'

'But there's no way we can manually lift Lucy, even with four
of us,' Mike said.

'Don't sweat it,' Greg said. 'There's an engine hoist in that outbuilding at the foot of the jetty. Can someone give me a hand to fetch it?'

'No problem,' Jack said.

Greg nodded and they strode off together as Mike and I headed back to the truck.

With Mike directing me, I carefully reversed the pickup towards the jetty. I parked up and as I got out Greg took the jerrycans off the back and loaded them on to the boat. Mike pulled the tarp up.

At once the tension I'd been carrying across my shoulders released. Half the cracks in the crystal had already disappeared as blue light continued to shimmer throughout it.

'Lucy's looking a lot more like her old self,' Mike said with a smile.

'Isn't she just?' I replied.

With a rumble of wheels, Jack and Greg reappeared pushing an engine hoist towards us.

A few colourful swear words from Greg later, we had the crystal on its plinth dangling from an engine hoist.

We edged the hoist as close to the edge of the jetty as we dared. If it toppled over into the sea, there would be no fast way to retrieve the crystal. Then, with a huge group effort of heaving and more swearing, we manoeuvred Lucy down safely on to the deck of the boat.

Greg pulled out a large key ring from his pocket and caught the surprised look on Mike's face. 'What, you thought I was going to hot-wire the boat? Fuck, talk about being stereotyped.'

'Sorry, mate.'

Greg snorted. 'Nah, you're good. I took a copy of the key the first time I used Jay's boat. Less obvious than having wires hanging out of the ignition.'

Mike laughed.

'I just need to do something – back in a moment,' Jack said. He jumped on to the jetty, opened the passenger door of the truck and took something out from the glove compartment.

'What have you got there?' I asked as I climbed back on to the jetty and started to unhook Lucy's pallet from the harness.

'These.' Jack held up two radio sets. He spun the dials on both and handed one to me. 'I've set up the radios on a different frequency to the one that the Overseers have been using.'

'And I need this because?'

'Because I'm heading off in the truck in a moment to draw the Overseers away – assuming they'll be following the tracker.'

'But how will you get back here?' Mike asked from the boat.

Jack shook his head. 'This is a one-way trip. The moment I'm gone, you're all to get the hell out of here with Lucy.'

I put my hands on my hips. 'You're a clown short of a circus if you think I'm going to let you do this.'

'This isn't your decision; it's mine, Lauren.'

I stared at him. I knew exactly what this meant. Once Alvarez got his hands on Jack, there was little chance he wouldn't be killed.

My resolve hardened and I made the decision before I even realised it. I grabbed the other radio from Jack and slung it away on to a shingle beach by the jetty.

'Hey, I'll need that to know that you've made it to safety.'

I crossed my arms. 'Then you can bloody go and get it in that case.'

'Lauren, there isn't time for your theatrics.' Jack ran back down the jetty and jumped on to the sloping beach. He began searching around in the darkness for the radio set. Just as I'd planned.

I leapt into the driver's seat of the truck.

'Hey!' Jack shouted as he spotted what I was doing and started to scramble up the beach, the recovered radio set in hand.

'You don't have to do all the heavy lifting, Jack, and I'm more than capable of doing my part,' I shouted through the truck's open window.

I ground the accelerator into the floor and the truck surged forward away from the jetty, past Jack and on to the gravel track leading to the house.

In my mirror I saw Jack raise the radio to his mouth.

The handset on the passenger seat squawked. 'Lauren, stop. I can't let you throw your life away.'

'Just like *I* can't let *you*.' I hit the mute button so I couldn't hear his reply as I accelerated hard along the track to whatever my imminent future had in store.

What the hell are you doing, Lauren? I thought to myself for probably the hundredth time as I weaved my way along the coastal road, trying to put as much distance as possible between myself and the others. I would have to have a serious conversation with myself about being so bloody impulsive.

At least by now the others would be well out to sea with Lucy. That was what really mattered.

The thought had barely passed through my head when I caught the flick of light from another vehicle in my rear-view mirror. There were two distant headlights behind me.

Relax, it's just a taxi driver or someone else heading home for the night. But when I glanced at my mirror again, the vehicle had already halved the distance between us. Bloody hell, it was fast, which probably meant... I pressed the accelerator all the way to the floor.

The speedometer climbed past a hundred miles per hour, but still my pursuer closed in. What the hell were they driving – some sort of supercar? As if in answer, one headlight suddenly pulled in front of the other and everything made sense. Not a car, but two high-powered motorbikes bearing down on me like bats out of hell.

I started to cut the corners, using both sides of the road for the best racing line, remembering the go-karting sessions from staff days out back at Jodrell Bank. But even as the world blurred past, still the bikers hauled me in relentlessly.

Fuck! I thought as they closed to less than a hundred metres. Then the fun really began as sparks started flying from the truck's tailgate.

Shit, shitty, shit!

A full-beam headlight shone through my rear window, lighting up the truck's cab. A glance in my wing mirror showed me that one of the two riders was just off the rear left wheel and the rider was aiming a pistol at the tyre. I veered away from him, the pickup's knobbly tyres bouncing over the verge and throwing up clods of mud into the biker's path. I saw the guy brake hard in my mirrors as he skidded back on to the road.

And then things got really serious.

In the fraction of time I'd been distracted by the first rider, the other had shot up fast alongside me. In the corner of my eye, I saw him aiming his pistol straight at me.

I ducked and my window shattered, glass flying over me. Cold air screamed into the cabin. I slammed the accelerator and hung on as the vehicle sped forward. Every minute I survived would buy the others more time...

The first biker sped alongside the other side of the truck as if playing tag team with his colleague and the muzzle of his weapon flashed. The front tyre exploded and the pickup lurched as it skidded sideways.

Anger surged through me. *If that's the way you want to fucking play it, arseholes!*

I yanked the wheel hard over to the right and slammed on the brakes. The vehicle snapped back in the opposite direction. The biker started to brake too, but not fast enough. The rear of the truck slammed into him and he swerved into the ditch.

I sped away, watching what unfolded in my rear-view mirror. The motorbike's front wheel dug into the soft mud, pitching the guy over the handlebars and catapulting him straight into a wall. He disappeared into the distance behind me as I fought to control the pickup fishtailing wildly with its now blown tyre.

The sound of metal grinding on tarmac buzzed through the vehicle as it went into a sideways skid on a bend. A barbed-wire fence was rushing towards the truck. With a *twang*, it sliced through the fence and down the steep slope on the other side. Then the world began tumbling past the windows and airbags exploded all around me, the sounds numbing my ears. Three bone-jarring rolls later, the pickup shuddered to a stop on its roof.

I hung upside down from my seat belt and dragged in a lungful of air as I stared out through the shattered windscreen. But part of my mind was already rebooting. *Move, Lauren!*

I fumbled for the release button of my seat belt, pushing it and dropping down hard on to the roof, barely registering the pain. But as far as I could tell, I hadn't broken anything, the vehicle's safety features having done their job of keeping me alive. For how much longer was another question – the other biker was still out there.

I grabbed the radio set that had landed next to me and crawled out through the shattered windscreen. The glass sliced into my palms as a single headlight bounced towards me over the field.

I laid flat as a bullet hissed past me. The biker slowed as he drove closer, his pistol raised as he aimed for a second shot.

'Are you fucking serious?' I shouted.

My hand fumbled at the rear of my jeans and I pulled out the LRS from my belt.

I rolled sideways as another bullet skimmed me. 'You so have this coming!'

I aimed at the rider closing in on me. I ignored the trickle of blood dripping from the lacerations in my hand and the burning pain from what was probably a cracked rib. Then, like a switch had been thrown, there was no pain, just complete and utter focus.

I breathed out slightly as I aimed and squeezed the trigger, just like I'd seen Robert do back at the hospital.

The rider jerked backwards as he toppled to one side, his motorbike tipping the other way, throwing him clear. The bike crashed to the ground, handlebars digging into the earth and dragging it to a stop less than ten metres away.

I hobbled towards the rider, my LRS ready for the triple tap. But then I realised his head was twisted at a sickening angle. The guy was already dead.

I turned off the mute on the radio and squeezed the talk button.

'Hi, Jack – are you there? Over.'

Just a crackle of static.

'Jack, please tell me you got away OK and this was all worth it?'

The speaker burst with gunfire. 'Bit busy here, Lauren.'

'What? How come? How did they follow you?'

'Sneaky bastards must have hidden a second tracker on Lucy's pallet,' Mike replied in the background over more gunfire. 'They turned up a few minutes after you headed off.'

'A few minutes? Why didn't you leave immediately as we agreed?'

'*You* agreed,' Jack replied. 'We're not going anywhere until you get your arse back here. We're holding our own for the moment, but hurry. Turns out Greg is quite the natural with a weapon in his hands – something about too many video games.'

I looked at the wrecked pickup. No way was I going anywhere in that thing anytime soon. Then I gazed at the motorbike. It was covered in mud, but the damage looked mostly superficial.

'I'll be back there in ten.'

'We'll hold out as long as we can. See you on the other side of this.' The radio clicked off.

I pocketed the LRS and glanced at the rider still wearing his helmet. I wasn't about to try to prise that off his broken head and deal with the splattered brains it probably contained.

The bike was an absolute dead weight as I tried to lift it. But I must have been running on pure adrenaline and somehow managed to heave it upright. Moments later, I was back on the road, speeding towards the others. I just prayed I wasn't going to be too late.

It took every gram of concentration, especially with my collection of injuries loudly complaining, to control the powerful motorbike through the twisting lanes as I hurtled along. If anyone had seen me zipping past with my hair streaming out behind me, they would have probably thought I was some sort of avenging dark angel. It was pretty much an accurate description of what I intended to do to Alvarez and his bloody Overseers if any of my guys got hurt.

At last I swept into Jay's driveway. Six assorted SUVs and pickups were parked out the front, with no sign of the occupants anywhere.

I slowed the bike to a crawl along the gravelled track. I just needed to get to the boat and then...

My thought trailed away as I spotted Overseers soldiers sprawled flat on the sloping lawn, their guns aimed out to the sea. My gaze swept past them along the jetty – towards the spot where the speedboat should have been. It was gone.

So they'd been forced to leave. I pulled up, unclipped the radio from the lapel of my jacket and pressed the button.

'Guys, please tell me you're speeding towards the rig?'

'Of course we're not,' Jack replied. 'We had to fall back to the boat whilst we waited for you. The Overseers were about to overrun our position.'

'Then what are you waiting for? Get yourself the hell away from here.'

'So not happening, Lauren,' Mike's voice said.

'Oh, for god's sake, what are you guys like?'

'We're not leaving without you,' Greg replied.

Despite the seriousness of the situation, I couldn't help smiling. 'You big-hearted bunch of softies.'

'That may be true, but this is what's going to happen next,' Jack said. 'Get yourself on to the jetty anyway you can and we'll make a high-speed pass and grab you.'

'That's far too risky for you,' I argued not even caring about the same danger to myself.

Two powerful boat engines roared into life somewhere out on the dark sea.

'Not listening,' Mike said. 'Here we come, ready or not.'

Two gun nozzles flashed with fire, illuminating their speedboat circling a hundred metres out. Their bullets sprayed the embankment where the Overseers were positioned.

'Return fire!' I heard Alvarez shout.

The world exploded with the crackle of automatic gunfire – no need for the subtlety of silencers in this firefight.

Picked out by the pops of light, I counted at least twelve soldiers. Those were bad odds. They'd be an easy target if they came too close to the jetty. We needed a better plan...

Maybe it was because I'd watched *The Great Escape* with Aunt Lucy way too many times over past Christmases that made me come up with such a stupid idea.

I clicked the radio button. 'Be ready to haul me out of the sea and make a rapid getaway.'

'Hold on, what are you planning to do?' Jack asked.

'You'll see.' I breathed deeply.

Behold the avenging angel...

A pistol in one hand, the other twisting the throttle as far back as it would go, I sped down the track, spraying gravel out like confetti behind the bike.

'Shoot her down!' Alvarez shouted from the darkness as I flashed past his soldiers.

Payback... My first wild shot went roughly in the direction of the colonel's voice, but I didn't hear any cry of pain. Shame.

I sped forward, weaving as much as I could, and managed to squeeze off three rounds before the motorbike reached the jetty. As the rear wheel traded gravel for the metal of the jetty, it gained more traction and hurtled forward. I lay flat to the motorbike, bullets flashing off the metal floor beneath me. Then there wasn't any more jetty beneath the bike and I was flying out over the water.

Oh, fucking hell!

As the motorbike started to pivot down towards the waves, I stood on the pedals and shoved myself off sideways.

The bike hit the water hard, sending a great cloud of spray into the air. The sea smashed into me like a solid brick wall as the speedboat's engines roared towards me. But I was sinking, sliding beneath the surface, the air punched out of my lungs.

Bullets lanced around me as the bike plunged into the darkness. Then a silhouetted hull loomed over me like a giant shark.

My hands clawed up towards it, but I'd nothing left.

The sea tightened its icy grip on me and I dropped towards the depths after the bike.

Strong hands clamped round me with a splash. I was being

hauled back to the surface. A moment later, more hands were helping me and my rescuer out of the sea and on to the boat.

'Get us out of here, Mike!' Jack shouted as he lowered me to the deck.

Tracer rounds skimmed over the boat. Greg was illuminated by his own gunfire as he shot back towards the shore. Mike spun the wheel and the speedboat surged out to sea.

I gulped in a huge lungful of air as Jack crouched over me.

'Who do you think you are, James Bond or something?' he said.

'Actually, I was going for Steve McQueen,' I replied. Then my abdomen cramped and I retched up a stomach full of seawater all over his boots as we sped away.

CHAPTER TWENTY-SIX

BELOW THE CANOPY OF STARS, the oil rig blazed with lights. It towered over us, rising from the sea on monstrous metal legs like a frozen kraken risen from the depths.

Greg, who'd taken over steering the boat, throttled the engines back that had been pushed flat out since speeding away from the battle at the jetty apart from when he'd briefly stopped to top up the fuel tank from one of the jerrycans. He tapped his hand on the dash. 'Well done, gal. Got us here nice and fast.'

'Too fast,' Mike said, wiping the corner of his mouth from his last bout of vomit that he'd spewed over the side.

Thankfully, my stomach had settled a while back, helped by the copious amounts of freezing night air and sea spray that had been driven into my face.

Jack stepped forward to the prow with a rope ready to tie us off as we edged in towards a landing platform at the base of one of the giant legs.

Greg set the engine to idle and we drifted closer, whilst Jack leapt up on to the platform and fastened the boat.

I peered up at the rig. The main deck seemed like several

miles above us. 'How are we going to get Lucy all the way up there, guys?'

'Don't you worry about that,' Greg replied. 'They have a winch on-board to lift the heavy stuff.'

A spotlight flared into life and swivelled down towards us.

'What the fuck do you think you're doing? This is restricted site!' a voice boomed out through a loudspeaker far above us.

Greg stood up, shielding his eyes from the intense beam playing over the boat and cupped his hands round his mouth. 'It's me, Greg, you idiot,' he shouted. 'Is Callum around?'

'Sorry, Greg, wasn't told you were making a run tonight – although our whisky stocks are getting low.'

'Always here to help!' Greg called back.

Laughter came over the tannoy. 'You know us way too well, son.'

'That I do. Anyway, can you shift your arse and drop a winch line over so we can get this cargo on-board?'

'No problem. Give me a sec.'

A moment later, a large hook was lowered from a small crane mounted on the side of the rig. Jack reached up and grabbed it, then walked it back on to the speedboat until he had it hooked up to Lucy's pallet.

I peered under the tarp covering Lucy. Nearly all her damage had disappeared.

'Looking good,' Mike said from over my shoulder. 'At this rate, she'll be fully operational any minute.'

'Thank god.' I pulled the tarp back down over Lucy to keep her crystal form hidden from prying eyes.

Jack jumped back on to the deck and grabbed a holdall stored in the back of the boat. I hadn't noticed it before.

'What have you got there?' I asked.

'Insurance, lots of insurance,' Jack replied.

'OK...' That almost certainly meant guns.

Compared to how difficult it had been to get Lucy on-board the boat, the next stage was a breeze thanks to the crane on the rig. Soon our precious cargo was being hauled skywards. We kept track with her as Greg led the ascent up a metal staircase on the giant rig leg.

By the time we reached a locked metal gate across the stairway, my battered body was complaining very loudly that I seriously needed to give it a break.

'Very welcoming,' Mike said, gesturing to the nasty metal spikes topping the gate.

Greg grinned. 'All part of their security precautions to stop undesirables like us getting on-board.'

Lucy reached the deck above us and was swung over the side to land.

We heard footsteps clanking down the steps as a guy wearing red overalls with a long, rocker-style ponytail headed towards us.

'Long time, no see, you bastard,' the guy said to Greg as he reached through the bars for his hand.

Greg shook it firmly. 'Only a month and you get all teary on me, Callum.'

Callum snorted. 'So who are your mates then?' His gaze took in everyone, but lingered on me. To make it worse, he did the whole north–south over my body until he finally brought his gaze back to my face.

I sighed inwardly and drew my coat tighter.

'So as nice as this visit is and everything, why are you lot here?' Callum asked. 'It doesn't take this many people to drop off a few crates of whisky.'

'We need to get to the mainland with some cargo,' I said.

Callum thinned his lips and peered at me.

'And I was thinking they could hitch a ride on one your helicopters when the next one arrives,' Greg added.

'Were you now?' Callum replied. He gestured at the rig. 'Does this look like a fucking public airport?'

Jack leant towards the bars to stare at him. 'This is real important and we—'

Greg put his hand on Jack's arm and shook his head, smiling. 'I've got this, Jack.' He returned his attention to Callum. 'An extra crate of whisky during the next run then?'

'Make it two.'

Greg grinned and stuck his hand through the bars of the gate. 'Done, you sly git.' He nodded to Jack. 'Which means the price has just gone up to you.'

Jack sighed. 'I figured it might have.'

Callum took out a key to unlock the gate. With a flourish of his hand he waved us in. 'Welcome to the Shithole Hotel, a one-star establishment with some less than savoury characters.'

'Ignore him. In the crew's heads this rig is a frontier town in the Wild West,' Greg said. 'But really this place is about as wild as a teashop run by sweet old ladies.'

Callum made to cuff Greg, but then chuckled. 'Cheeky bugger.'

'That's me,' Greg replied with a grin.

Callum handed each of us a white hard hat from a basket as we filed pass him.

Above us the oil rig's main drilling tower stretched up into the sky. Multiple buildings nestled on the superstructure, metal walkways linking them together. Lights picked out the spiderweb of heavy-duty pipework running everywhere. I could also see a helipad above mounted to one side of the rig. Not surprisingly everywhere smelled of oil that was starting to make my eyes sting.

'So how long until the next helicopter?' I asked as we headed up the stairs.

'You're in luck,' Callum replied. 'Some guys missed their connecting flight due to a storm over France. That delayed their transfer to the rig, so the helicopter had to wait for them. They're due in the next half hour. Better still, the chopper will be travelling back empty, so I'm sure the flight crew won't mind you guys catching a lift with them.'

'And our cargo?' I asked, pointing towards the pallet as we reached the main deck.

'You mean that isn't for us?' Callum asked.

'Next run, I promise, and I'll waive what you owe me from that last card game,' Greg said.

'I still say you rigged that.'

'Skill, pure skill,' Greg replied with a grin.

'If you say so.' Callum shook his head. 'Okay, lets call it quits and I'll let you ship whatever is under that tarp out on the helicopter. But please tell me it's nothing too dodgy. It'll only upset the pilot and that will make all our lives shit.'

Better to play on the safe side, I told myself, in case anyone decided to take a peek under the tarp. 'No, just a geological sample that we need to have analysed,' I replied.

'OK, no problem, lass. You can come and share a drink with me and the lads whilst we're waiting,' Callum said only to me, as if the others didn't exist.

'A seriously big pot of coffee would be more my speed right now, but thanks anyway,' I replied.

'Then you'll have that, pretty lady.' He gave me a wolfish grin.

Seriously? I raised my eyebrows by way of a response.

Jack frowned at Callum, who ignored him.

Greg leant in towards me. 'You mustn't mind Callum – he's all bluster and no trouser action, if you know what I mean,' he whispered.

'Good to know,' I replied.

I took in the main deck of the rig. Despite being the middle of the night, two people seemed to be replacing a valve on a large pipe connected to the drilling tower.

'Yep, this operation never stops,' Callum said, pointing towards the work crew. 'Twenty-four hours a day, three hundred and sixty-five days a year. This rig even operates on Christmas Day. Time is money and all that.'

'Sounds like a tough life,' Mike said.

'Well, the huge pay helps take the sting out, for sure. That and Greg's illicit whisky supplies.' He slapped his friend's back.

My eyes sought out Lucy. She was still covered with the tarp and had been safely stashed on a clear section of the deck on the far side.

'Who the fuck is this now?' said a guy standing by the railing directing a spotlight out to sea.

'What is it, Jim?' Greg asked.

'See for yourself.'

We all joined him on the railing to peer out. The profile of the approaching vessel sailing towards the rig at full speed through the darkness looked uncomfortably like the same luxury boat that had been moored off Skara Brae.

Jim swung the spotlight towards it and picked out the foredeck crowded with at least a dozen soldiers.

'Friends of yours?' Callum asked.

'Arseholes who shot my dog and made me blow up my own bloody house, that's who,' Greg replied.

'Fuckers,' Callum said.

'You can't let them on-board,' I said.

'You're not seriously suggesting they're about to storm the rig?' Callum asked.

'That's exactly what we're saying,' Jack replied as he shifted the weight of the bag on his shoulder.

As if in answer, a tracer round streaked up over the top of the rig and everyone instinctively ducked.

An amplified voice boomed out from the boat below. 'We are about to board,' Alvarez called out. 'And if we meet any resistance, we will shoot everyone on the rig.'

'Definitely prize bastards,' Jim said, spitting on the deck.

'Shit, we didn't mean to bring this trouble down on your heads, guys,' I said.

'Don't sweat it, lass,' Callum said. 'Jim here is our head of security. He will sort them out, won't you?'

'Aye, I'll use the pressure hoses to hold the fuckers off. You go and radio for immediate assistance, Callum.'

'You got it.' Callum headed off across the deck and disappeared through a doorway.

Meanwhile, Jim crossed to a hose nozzle mounted on a gimlet on the railing and opened a valve. With a whoosh, a giant jet of water shot from the nozzle in an arc over the sea. Jim rotated the water cannon down towards the approaching boat and, in an explosion of spray, the water jet struck the foredeck, immediately washing at least one soldier off into the sea whilst the others hung on for dear life.

Jim grabbed a mic connected to a tannoy. 'Take that, you wankers!'

The boat's engines churned the water as it began to reverse away from the rig.

'See, that was easy,' Jim said with a huge grin towards us.

Callum came running back through the doorway. 'Something is up with the radio. I can't raise anyone.'

'That means the people on that boat will be jamming all the radio frequencies,' I said.

'So we're on our own,' Mike said with a grim face.

Jack dropped his holdall on to the deck and unzipped it. 'We need to get ready.'

I nodded as I took out the LRS pistol from my pocket. Callum and Jim both stared at it.

'Just who the fuck are you people?' Jim asked. 'Terrorists or something?'

I shook my head. 'No, if anyone is a terrorist, it's those guys down there. They've already murdered dozens of innocent people back at a hospital on Orkney.'

'Shit, no way!' Jim said.

'I'm afraid so,' Mike replied. 'Those people are nothing but ruthless killers.'

Jack gazed at my pistol. 'Oh, on this occasion I think we can do way better than that, Lauren.' He pulled open the bag to reveal an assortment of grenades and a lot of ammo, along with three automatic assault rifles.

'Where did that all come from?' I asked.

'There was another weapon store in the pickup. I helped myself – I had a feeling it would come in handy.' He passed me one of the rifles. 'This will be far more effective than your pistol at long range.'

'Got it.' I took a magazine from him and slotted it into the stock.

Callum stared at me open-mouthed, presumably reappraising his first impression of the *pretty lady*.

Jack handed the other rifle to Greg. 'I could develop a taste for fuck-off guns like this, Jack,' he said. He swung it round, pretending to shoot invisible enemies.

I grabbed the barrel and held on to it. 'Ever heard of the expression that something isn't a toy?'

'You weren't complaining about that back on the shore. Just look at this beauty, I mean...' Greg's words trailed away as he caressed the gun.

'You'll be writing it poems next,' Jack said, shaking his head.

Greg snorted. 'Aye, I probably will.'

I looked across at the rig team hunkered down behind some machinery. 'What about all these people on the platform, Jim?'

'If this is turning into a clusterfuck, we need to get them clear.'

'Have you got an emergency evacuation procedure that you can kick into action?'

'Of course. We practise it regularly,' Callum said. 'The rig is equipped with three emergency lifeboats that we can launch directly from this deck.'

'This isn't going to be pretty,' I said.

Jim nodded. 'Shitting hell! I'll organise an immediate evacuation.' He hit a big red button on a wall and a moment later a siren blared out.

Within moments, dozens of people appeared on the deck, some half-dressed and obviously straight from their beds. At least one guy had nothing on but a towel. But with practised discipline they lined up by the lifeboats angled down towards the sea on yellow metal ramps as the craft were made ready.

Jim cupped his hands over his mouth, 'OK, everyone, this is not a practice exercise. I repeat, this is not a practice exercise. The platform is about to be attacked and we need to evacuate everyone as fast as possible.'

'This is a wind-up, right?' a big guy with arms covered in tattoos called back.

By way of an answer, Callum pointed to the automatic rifle in my hands. 'No, this is the real deal. If you don't get your arses into gear, this pretty lass will put a bullet in them for you.'

The crew all stared at the gun and then me.

I swear all I did was raise my eyebrows a fraction. Then, to a person, they all burst into action and began climbing into the lifeboats.

'I wouldn't mess with you either,' Jack said, grinning at me.

'Heads up, they're coming back in for a second attempt,' Jim called out from the railing. He directed the nozzle down at the boat once more as it sped in towards the rig.

A green spot danced on Jim's hard hat. 'Watch o—' I started to say.

Too late.

A single shot. Blood sprayed out from the back of his hard hat. Jim slumped down on to the deck, the hose tipping up into the sky before he let go of the handles.

Callum rushed to his side. 'Jim!' He rolled his friend over to reveal a perfect hole in his forehead.

'Fucking bastards!' Greg shouted. He held the automatic rifle up and fired a stream of bullets, creating splashes in front of the boat.

Jack grabbed his arm. 'Hold your fire, Greg. We need to make every shot count. That was a high-velocity sniper round and they are out of effective range of these rifles.'

'OK, OK, wait to see the whites of their eyes. Got it,' he replied, spit foaming on his lips.

From behind us came a whooshing sound as the first lifeboat hurtled off its ramp and dropped towards the sea. Like an orange projectile it hit the ocean prow first, sending a huge plume of water up around it before bobbing back on to the surface. A moment later the lifeboat's engine gurgled into life and the boat moved away at far too slow a speed for my liking.

'You realise that the crew still won't be safe,' Jack whispered to me.

'I know. The Overseers won't want to leave any witnesses. So that's why we have to make this count, Jack. We have to hold them off till that helicopter gets here. Worse case the helicopter will see what's happening and can go for help.'

'No, the worse case is there won't be anyone left alive when help eventually arrives,' Mike said as he joined us.

With another *whoosh*, the second lifeboat sped down its ramp and hit the water.

A guy was leaning out of the last boat and beckoning to the rest of us to join him.

I looked at Callum. He was still staring down at Jim, his hands clenched.

I rested my hand on his shoulder. 'You need to get yourself out of here. Let us deal with these people.'

'No way, pretty lady. I'm in charge of this operation and have a duty to protect this rig until every other option has been exhausted.'

'If you're sure.'

'I am, lass.'

'OK, but keep your head down.'

'We'll see about that...' He picked up a large spanner and cradled it.

I turned to Mike and Greg. 'You guys should go too.'

'No way, they shot my dog and I want some sweet payback,' Greg replied.

'Mike? I know you hate fighting, so if you want to leave, everyone will completely understand.'

'No, I'm in this with you until the end, Lauren. And besides, I don't have to use a gun to help you.' He crossed to the pressure hose, grabbed hold of it and redirected it back at the boat that was heading for the landing platform.

God, the guy had guts because he was just as likely as Jim to get taken out by a sniper round.

'Try to keep your head down,' I said.

'I'll do my best,' Mike replied.

'Go now!' Callum shouted to the last lifeboat.

The guy grimaced but nodded. A moment later, the craft shot down the ramp and ploughed into the water. With the propeller already spinning, it surged away to join the small flotilla churning towards Orkney as fast as possible.

'Time to make Alvarez regret picking this fight,' Jack said.

I nodded and clicked the safety off my rifle, thumbing it to automatic mode.

Jack loaded a grenade into the launcher beneath his carbine. 'Three, two, one...' He popped up and didn't so much as flinch as three shots whistled past him. With icy calm, he aimed and fired the grenade. The projectile arced towards the rear deck of the boat below.

We ducked as the round hit and exploded, tearing a hole through the deck. Flames billowed up from the boat as it started to dip sternwards and began to take on water.

Greg whooped. 'Take that, you bastards!'

Mike swivelled the hose away and answered my questioning look. 'I don't want to put that fire out, do I?'

I raised a palm to Jack. 'And as for you, good shooting, Tex.'

Jack stared at me, leaving me hanging. 'I'm from Oklahoma not Texas.'

'All right, but, hey, I know a musical about that.'

'God give me strength. If you start singing "Oklahoma!" in the middle of all this, I swear I may not be responsible for my actions.' He smiled at me.

In that moment of a shared joke within the darkness, it suddenly felt as if we might all actually live through it.

Mike peered over the railing. 'Hey, we're not out of the woods yet. Some of those soldiers made it to the landing platform. I can see Alvarez and that guy Patrick among the ones heading up here.' With Callum's help Mike tried to angle the hose towards them, but then he threw his hands up. 'Damn, I can't get the angle to hose them off the rig.'

'Looks as if it's down to you guys,' Callum said.

'Time to get up front and personal,' Jack said. 'Lauren and Greg, you're with me. We'll hold them off from the top of the steps.'

I shuddered as I thought about the guy who'd died at point-blank range. Any sense of lightness evaporated as stark reality rushed back in. How could I be so detached about all of this?

I peered over to see the boat starting to sink. Soldiers' bodies floated in the water around it. This wasn't a bloody game – this was a battle for survival.

Jack glanced across at me from the position he'd taken at the top of the stairs with Greg. 'Are you OK, Lauren?'

'I just had a reality kick up the arse that people are actually dead down there.'

'It's a moment that every soldier goes through. It means you're human.'

'Good to hear. I was starting to wonder.'

'It will get easier.'

'If we live through this.'

'So let's make sure that we do...'

We took up firing positions at the top of the stairs.

The drum of footsteps heralded the soldiers' imminent arrival. They must have made short work of the locked gate.

'Get ready,' Jack whispered.

A smoke grenade clattered up on to the stair landing below us and began to obscure them.

A shadow moved through the smoke towards us and Jack sprayed automatic fire in its direction. A grunt was followed by the sound of someone tumbling back down the stairs.

'Lay down your arms and this will go a lot easier for you,' Alvarez shouted from below.

'If you think we're going to surrender, you've got another thing coming,' I called back.

'Don't forget this was your choice,' the colonel replied. 'The RAF are on the way and I now have to destroy any evidence which includes you.'

There came several clunking sounds and three projectiles raced up over our heads.

'Grenades! Get down!' Jack shouted.

We threw ourselves flat as explosions ripped through the deck and lit up the rig. There was a hiss and then a fountain of oil gushed out from a ruptured pipe straight towards the fire.

There was a moment of absolute quiet.

'Oh, fucking hell...' Callum whispered as the oil splashed on to the flames.

A boom shook the entire rig and a huge ball of flame boiled up into the sky. Within seconds, the entire platform was on fire, flames quickly rising to the top of the drilling tower.

Callum rushed over to a button and slapped it with his hand. Sprinklers erupted fine spray all over the rig. He started to drag a hose towards the fire. He gestured to Mike. 'You're with me.'

'You've got it,' Mike replied and he rushed to help Callum.

Together they started to direct the hose spouting fire-retardant foam over the nearest flames.

But to me it looked as if fire had already taken hold. I wasn't sure it would be put out by conventional means.

A shouted order pulled my attention back. I dropped my head again as figures loomed from the smoke and bullets sprayed around us. The world erupted with our returning gunfire. As we fought to hold them off, I was dimly aware of the heat intensifying at our backs. There was only one way this was headed.

'We need to get out of here!' Mike shouted across. 'Callum says there's another lifeboat on the south side of the rig.'

'Not without Lucy we don't.' I glanced at her pallet to see flames licking towards it. 'We need to get her away from that fire.'

Mike nodded and, together with Callum, he directed the foam towards the crystal atop the pallet. Yet the fire still rapidly spread towards it. The tarp covering Lucy was already starting to smoke from the intense heat. I needed to help.

'Can you and Greg hold off Alvarez by yourselves?' I asked Jack.

In answer he launched a grenade down into the stairwell. A loud bang erupted and a soldier tumbled away over the side of the railing.

'Go!' Jack replied.

Greg gave me a thumbs up, a goofy grin filling his face as his rifle's nozzle blazed at the stairwell.

I rushed over to the others. Mike was directing the hose into the fire alone as Callum unspooled the hook from the winch.

'How can I help?'

'Connect this to the pallet and I'll winch it clear of the fire,' Callum shouted.

'On it.' I took the hook from him and dragged it towards the pallet, looping it over the pallet's harness.

Meanwhile, Callum sprinted back to the winch's control and pressed a button. The motor whirred into action and, with a graunch, the pallet was dragged over the floor. It had only slid a few metres towards the crane when I spotted the section of raised floor that had buckled upwards and was directly in its path. Before I could shout a warning, the pallet rammed straight into it and started to tip upwards.

'We need to get it clear!' Callum shouted as he killed the motor.

'Be ready to winch it again the moment I free the pallet,' I called back to him over the growing *whoosh* of flames. I grabbed hold of the pallet and, my muscles popping, just managed to heave it up over the lip of the bent flooring.

I turned round to give Callum the thumbs up, but a huge bang came from above me before I could. I looked up to seeing the drilling tower buckling and falling towards me.

Callum came out of nowhere, cannoning into me. I twisted away as I flew through the air and saw the tower falling where I'd been a second ago...where Callum still was, his foot snagged on a loose section of decking.

The remains of the drilling tower crashed down on him in a rain of girders and oil. Before I could move, fire erupted, turning the wreckage into a burning funeral pyre. Callum didn't make so much as a sound as he died.

I stared, frozen, as the flames intensified around me. Then part of my brain registered that the fallen tower had also cut me off from Mike and the others as the sounds of the battle beyond it intensified.

Surrounded by fire, I edged backwards towards Lucy. The deck started to screech as it heated up. In the growing furnace the soles of my boots began to melt.

Better to use a bullet than be burned to death. I held the assault rifle to my temple.

I started to squeeze the trigger, but then the world blazed with light.

CHAPTER TWENTY-SEVEN

My mind scrambled to process what was happening. I was standing back in Aunt Lucy's room. I dropped my carbine to the floor as I slumped into a chair, put my head into my lap and sucked in great lungfuls of cool air.

'Are you OK, Lauren?' Lucy's voice said.

I sat straight back up and turned to see Lucy by the writing desk that my real aunt had used to mark her students' papers. This younger version of Lucy gazed across at me with a concerned look in her eyes.

'You saved me?' I said.

'Only for a brief moment. I can maintain this bubble of your reality here in the eighth dimension for you for a short while. Unfortunately, the fire raging on the oil rig is about to permanently destroy the matrix of my micro mind and render it useless.'

'Micro mind?

'That's what the crystal fragment you managed to recover from what later became the Skara Brae site actually is.'

'How long does it predate it by?'

'Hundreds of thousands of years.'

'Holy shit.'

Lucy scowled at me. 'Language, Lauren.'

It was exactly the response I would have expected from my real Aunt Lucy. 'Look, I would love to talk about this, but right now I have bigger priorities – specifically the people who are about to be killed back on the oil rig.'

'You can relax about that for now. In this higher dimension, I control the laws of physics. Inside this bubble of your three-dimensional reality, that includes time. So give yourself a moment to catch your breath and have one of those hot cookies I know you love from the Covered Market in Oxford.' She pushed a plate of cookies towards me, which were oozing with melted chocolate chunks.

Despite everything, instinct took over and I found myself taking a bite before I even knew what I was doing. Yes, back in the real world I – or at least everything around me – was about to be burned to death, but here in this temporary sanctuary, the warmth of a freshly baked biscuit filled my mouth and dragged me away to a happier place for a moment.

I licked the melted chocolate on my lips as I submerged myself into the flow of this impossible situation. 'OK, so you know the way to my heart and everything, but can you tell me what a micro mind is?'

'It's a facet of the overall consciousness that creates my AI.'

'OK. And what about all the things you don't seem to know about? For an advanced alien computer, you seem to have only a vague understanding about a lot of critical information, including who you were when you first appeared to us.'

'That's because there's a problem with the sub-systems. For some reason, I've lost connections to my other micro minds buried around this planet. Everything I currently know are fragments of the bigger picture contained within this single micro mind that you managed to recover. Even that fragment has been partly damaged, so there is a lot of critical information that I'm missing.'

'Any idea why you lost contact with these other micro minds?'

She sighed. 'None whatsoever.'

'Perhaps it's just wear and tear. I mean, you're ancient by any human measure.'

Lucy shook her head. 'No, my systems are self-repairing, as you yourself discovered when you shot me.'

'Yes, sorry about that.'

'Please relax, I know it wasn't intentional.'

'Good. But one thing I've been meaning to ask you about is that mutilated cow. Was that you?'

'Of course not. For those responsible you have to look closer to your own world.'

'The Overseers?'

'Exactly. Whenever there's a genuine UFO sighting in your world – one that isn't simply a secret military test aircraft – the Overseers aren't far behind.'

'So should I take that to mean the Angelus aren't the only aliens to visit our world?'

'Correct. That critical piece of information is something the Overseers have always attempted to suppress. So for those sightings they can't easily discredit, they instead work on feeding people's paranoia.'

'You mean with cattle mutilations and abductions?'

'Precisely. That's why the mutilations in Orkney happened *after* the runes started to appear. The Overseers wanted to make people afraid of species who might visit your world and actually come in peace.'

I thought of the reception I received back in the pub after I'd first arrived on the island. It suggested the Overseers' strategy had more than worked out as planned.

'So if the Overseers are behind so much of this, could they also be the ones responsible for attacking your sub-systems?' I asked.

'Possibly, although I have no data to confirm or dismiss that.'

'So what about the Kimprak ship? They obviously aren't coming in peace.'

'Sadly not. There are always a few exceptions and the Kimprak are one of the most dangerous races in the universe.'

'You said you thought you could help us defeat them but you can't remember how. Is there any way you can find out that missing information?'

'Yes, actually. I was about to tell you last time – before we were interrupted by the Overseers at Skara Brae. You need to track down my other micro minds. Within them we should be able to discover the answer to defending your world.'

'And these other micro minds are where exactly?'

Lucy raised her shoulders. 'I wish I knew, Lauren. However, a beacon has been automatically activated after my repair program ran its diagnostics. According to my initial analysis the broadcast signal contains a protocol designed to re-establish contact with my other micro minds after an emergency shut- down. One by one they should now begin to wake in a chain reac- tion and go into a standby mode. The more of these micro minds that you successfully track down and bring back fully online, the more information I'll be able to remember.'

I gazed at the antique clock mechanism spinning within the glass dome behind her. 'All of this is going to be a moot point if I and the others get killed. Could you bring them here too and we wait for the flames to die down?'

'I would, but there is one major problem with that plan. If you're all here, there will be no one left to stop the fire and my micro mind crystal will be destroyed. I won't be able to maintain this bubble of your reality. And without that, you would all die here too. As your species would say, it's a catch twenty-two.'

'You really don't pull your punches, do you?'

'Did your real Aunt Lucy do that?'

'No, she didn't. She always told me it like it was.'

'Then I will too.' Lucy leant forward. 'But there is something in your power to alter the outcome of what currently seems inevitable.'

'What? I'll try anything.'

'You need to use the Empyrean Key again and activate a certain function within it.'

I slipped off my day bag and took out the stone. At once the ring red of icons appeared over it.

'Now what?'

'You will have to wait until you are back in your reality for this to work. In a moment, I'm going to return you to the rig. Once back, you will only have seconds before the fire over-whelms your position. In that small window of time, you'll need to activate the initiate protocol of my micro mind. Look for a concentric circles symbol.'

'And what's that going to do?'

'It will unlock the first stage in defending your planet. Unfor-tunately, that's all I know.'

'Then that will have to do.' I looked at Lucy as I stood and felt an unexpected ache in my chest. 'Please answer me this one thing before I go. Why model yourself on my aunt?'

'That's easy, Lauren. She meant everything to you and, because of that, she meant everything to me.'

Then the last thing I expected happened. Lucy stood too and rushed round the desk to hug me.

My body relaxed into the familiarity of her embrace, the experience heightened by breathing in the Chanel No. 5

perfume that my real Aunt Lucy had loved so much. Her hair tickled my nose just like it always had during all the hugs my real aunt had given me. I tried to say something, but the words wouldn't come as tears filled my eyes.

As Lucy stepped away, my heart snagged. I could see her eyes glistening too. I flapped a hand at my face. 'What are we like?'

'I know...' Lucy blinked through her tears and took a shaky breath.

I had to turn away, because I'd been about to tell this Lucy how much I missed her. But of course it wasn't really my aunt, just a facsimile. My head told me that, but my heart was a different matter. It yearned to fill the Lucy-shaped hole in the centre of my being.

I held the orb out in my palm. 'I'm ready whenever you are.'

Lucy's eyes tightened on mine for a moment as I raised my hand in farewell. She gave me such a loving look that my insides twisted. Then she nodded, a look of determination carving her features as if she had to do this before she changed her mind. 'Here we go...'

The world flared white and at once heat slammed into me, clamping round my body, so hot that I could barely breathe.

Flames boiled around Lucy's crystal micro mind and me, gunfire adding a staccato backtrack to the roar of the fire. My clothes were smoking as the tarp over the crystal ignited and began to burn away. I'd still nowhere to escape to.

I peered down at the Empyrean Key, my eyes drying to sandpaper in the soaring temperature. Then I realised the orb had no shimmering icons over it.

Shit, the tone generator!

I had to activate it, but with what? Despite the panic threatening to swamp me, some part of me took over and an absolute calmness flooded through my body. The answer came to me as if I'd known it all along. I didn't need a tone generator at all...

I coughed as smoke billowed around me. I so needed a drink of water to do this. I coughed again, trying to loosen the tightness in my throat. And then I began to hum a bass note barely audible over the roar of flames closing in on me and Lucy.

Nothing happened.

I tried again, dropping the frequency until the sound was vibrating through my chest. A glint of light flickered over the orb and I lowered my hum again, clenching my stomach into a ball to push the note out as smoke burned my lungs.

A flicker of light ignited around the orb and icons appeared round it. I kept the note going as the last air in my lungs emptied out, rotating the Empyrean Key until the concentric circles locked into the selection window. I flicked the orb forward...and everything changed.

A pulse of blue light blazed through Lucy's micro mind. With a crackle like stone shattering, glass-like tentacles exploded from the crystal and began racing out across the deck like snakes.

The last of my breath died in my lungs and my humming became a coughing fit. The icons died around the orb and the tentacles slowed to a stop. My skin began to blister with the heat of the flames licking towards me. I ignored the excruciating pain. I had to keep going, whatever was happening, for the sake of our world. I drew in another rasping breath of air and managed a wavering hum. The circle with the concentric lines blazed into existence again.

The tentacles started growing once more, now closing up the gaps between them and smothering the flames around me, swirling away into smoke. The heat immediately started to subside.

Other filaments from the crystal were already seeking out the other fires. If I had any energy left I would have whooped at being unexpectedly alive. The icon hovering over the orb turned dark and I tried to intensify my humming but it didn't make any difference. Whatever was happening now seemed to be running by itself. I let my humming fade away and as I suspected, far from halting, larger tendrils began to form as the smaller strands weaved together. They rushed towards the edge of the deck and curled away over it. Was this part of Lucy's phase one plan kicking in?

I rushed to the far railing to see what was happening.

The glassy tentacles slid towards the sea like giant probing fingers. They struck the surface, sending out the barest ripples as they disappeared beneath the surface.

A sudden shudder ran through the oil rig.

Had the crystal roots begun burrowing into the seabed like they had around Skara Brae? And if so, to do what?

The blue light within Lucy's crystal blinked faster and the vibration through the platform subsided.

I felt the tingle of static wash over my skin, tickling my scalp. With a roar, white light blazed from the crystal and out through the interconnected tendrils of glass down into the sea.

The ocean around the platform lit up as if gigantic under-water spotlights had been turned on. The light raced outwards beneath the waves at hundreds of miles per hour, heading towards the horizon in a band of expanding brilliance.

I was dimly aware of people shouting on the other side of the fallen drilling tower, which was now enclosed within the slippery glass-like roots.

Then a humming sound grew from the crystal and the oil rig began to shake again as electricity arced out from it and lanced on to the structure. I backed away and shielded my eyes as the dance of energy plasma converged together.

A lightning bolt of intense energy shot straight up into the sky. Immediately great curtains of aurora radiated outwards as the rig screeched all around me. Then the lightning stopped dead and everything fell silent, the only sound the lapping of the waves below.

For the first time I realised that the gunfire had stopped too.

But it wasn't over yet. The light within Lucy's micro mind began to change from blue to deep amber. I felt heat from the crystal's surface. What was left of the tarp burned and the nylon ropes strapping it to the pallet melted.

A fresh wave of static tickled my skin. But if I'd thought this crazy experience was finished, something even more impossible was to come...

The crystal started to float up from the ground in perfect silence, ignoring gravity. I watched in wonder as it rose to about five metres above the deck and started to rotate until one of the points of its tetrahedron faced downwards. The crystal exactly matched the UFO craft in the classified files that Sentinel had revealed to me.

A new sound began to emanate from the hovering crystal. It was like a haunting whale song, intensely beautiful and intensely sad. I felt my eyes prickle as it faded away.

Then Lucy's voice spoke from the crystal. 'Farewell, Lauren. Until we meet again.'

Before I could reply, a pulse of wind smacked into me as the craft hurtled straight upwards at an impossible rate of acceleration. A sonic boom shook the rig as the glimmering point of light disappeared into the sky and the aurora faded away as if it'd never existed.

I heard a shout, followed by Jack and Mike climbing over the tendrils of glass covering the fallen drilling tower. Greg fired back at someone as shots flew over his head and then his body jerked as he was hit with multiple bullets.

Jack and Mike immediately doubled back. But a moment later, grim-faced, they slid down the slippery slope of crystal towards me.

'Greg?' I asked.

Jack shook his head.

Mike wiped tears from his eyes.

'That poor—' I stopped as something spiralling over the barricade caught my eye as it came.

A canister landed and smoke instantly billowed out of it.

'Get ready!' Jack shouted.

It was then that I realised I'd left the carbine in Lucy's room.

I grabbed my pistol from my pocket instead as two soldiers loomed out of the smoke and slid down the barricade, firing as they came.

No time to think; no time for regret. Jack and I fired together, dropping both of them.

'Shit, that's me out of ammo,' Jack said.

A third soldier raced out, his laser sight already dancing over Jack.

I aimed and fired. He sprawled to the ground. And then two more figures appeared – Alvarez with Patrick behind him.

I pulled the trigger. A dull click came from my gun. 'I'm out too,' I said to the others.

Mike shook his head and raised his hands in surrender. We followed his lead. But at least the most important part of our mission had been completed. Lucy had escaped.

Pure hatred filled Alvarez's face as he stalked towards us. 'Where the hell is the Angelus device?'

'Didn't you see her fast exit?' I pointed skywards and smirked.

The colonel snarled and raised his carbine towards me.

I tensed for the end. But at least I would die happy, knowing that we'd done everything we could to save our world.

Jack stepped in front of me. 'You can start with me.'

Alvarez gave him a snake-like grin. 'If you insist—'

He was cut off as something struck him in the back of the neck. I'd almost forgotten Patrick was there.

Alvarez spun round, staring at Patrick and revealing the dart sticking out of the back of his neck. 'You fucking traitor!' The colonel swung his carbine up, but Patrick moved lightning fast, especially for an old guy, and kicked the weapon out of Alvarez's hand with a slick martial arts move.

The colonel's eyes widened as he tried to claw at the dart in his neck. Then he sprawled to the ground and became still.

Patrick gazed at us and raised his shoulders. 'Sorry for the late intervention, but I was trying to keep my cover intact.'

'You saved us?' I said, not able to stop myself stating the bleeding obvious.

'It would seem so, wouldn't it?' Patrick said with a smile.

Jack stepped up to him. 'And what did you mean by keeping your cover?'

'I'm actually a deep agent,' Patrick replied.

'You have to be kidding me,' I said.

'Not at all.' He glanced at his watch. 'And if you don't believe me...' He gestured towards the ocean.

A black shape appeared, skimming fast over the sea and heading straight towards the rig.

At first I thought it was Lucy coming back, but then I saw the shape was wrong and it looked more like some sort of helicopter. But, no, not a helicopter. As it drew closer I saw that the faceted cockpit was like something from a stealth fighter, but without any windows. The craft was making hardly any noise too. Then I saw why. Rather than rotors, it had at least a dozen small propellers mounted on its two stubby triangular wings. They gave the craft the distinct appearance of a winged insect.

'My real employer has organised this lift for us,' Patrick said.

The craft's wings began to pivot along their axis towards the vertical as it came to an almost silent hover over the rig's landing pad.

'What sort of aircraft is that?' Jack asked.

'An XA101 advanced stealth electric plane. I'm sure you have dozens of questions, but the time for that will have to be later as this situation is moving rapidly. The UK military has finally closed down the airspace. Within five minutes, two F-22s will be arriving to survey reports of a rig fire spotted from Orkney. We need to vacate this area as quickly as possible.'

I shook my head. 'I'm not going anywhere until we know who you're really working for.'

Patrick gave me a sharp look but nodded. 'A. Jefferson, CO of Sky Dreamer Corp.'

'You mean the guy who runs that private space asteroid mining company?' Mike asked.

'The very same. My employer is very anxious to meet you all. Jefferson has a proposition that I think you're all going to find highly attractive. But none of that will happen unless we get your arses on the XA101.'

I traded frowns with Jack and Mike.

Then Mike shrugged. 'I guess I haven't got anything better to do. What about you guys?'

Jack nodded. 'Why not? After all, I don't have a job to return to after the Overseers did the number on Skara Brae.'

Jack and Mike both looked at me.

'OK, let's do this, but I want some straight answers, Patrick.'

'And you'll have them and more, I promise you,' he said. 'Can we please get a bloody move on before those fighters turn up?'

'As you asked so nicely,' I replied.

Patrick herded the three of us towards the helipad as the XA101's electric-powered props began spinning, ready for a fast lift-off.

CHAPTER TWENTY-EIGHT

I'D RIDDEN in a helicopter once before – during a memorable visit to Victoria Falls with an old boyfriend. That ride had been exhilarating and deafening thanks to the roar of the rotors. By comparison, this electric-powered journey was whisper-quiet. But there was another notable difference that had spooked all of us upon entering the craft – with the exception of Patrick – the distinct lack of pilots.

After take-off, we'd learnt from Patrick that the XA101 was a fully autonomous aircraft that didn't need pilots but used AI to control it in the air. A flight path had already been programmed into it that would take us in a westerly direction before turning south to hug the Scottish coast.

According to Patrick, we were heading for a private airfield. Once there, a high-speed private jet would be ready to transport us to our final destination – somewhere in South America. The severe lack of windows, something to do with the radar stealth profile apparently, was made up for by the wrap-around monitors built into the cockpit's walls. They showed a live feed from the outside world, with flight information overlaid. Although exhausted, the geek in me was more than impressed.

I watched with building curiosity as Patrick dabbed some liquid on to his neck from a bottle. With a growing feeling of horror, I gawped with the others as he hooked his fingernails beneath a flap of crinkled skin and started to peel it off.

'Whoa there!' Jack said.

'Relax,' Patrick replied. With a tug he peeled the skin up from under his neck and followed that party trick by pulling the rest of his crinkled skin away from around his mouth and eyes, and finally pulling it free of his forehead. Patrick tugged his grey hair off to reveal a hairnet plastering dark brown, curly hair to his scalp. Next, he slid the contacts out of his eyes that had been hiding green irises.

The transformation of the old man I'd first encountered on the ferry to this guy – who I guessed was in his mid-thirties – was complete.

'You have to be kidding me, Patrick,' I said. 'You've been wearing a disguise all this time?'

He dabbed at his face with the liquid, cleaning away the paste that had glued the mask to his real face. 'Yes, but the name isn't Patrick, it's Tom – Tom Hester.'

'So who the hell is Tom in real life?' Mike asked.

'A spy who, on the orders of A. Jefferson, has been working under deep cover within the Overseers. Over the last five years I've been infiltrating their organisation to learn their secrets. I had little choice tonight but to throw away all that investment in time and money to save your lives.'

'Then I guess thanks are in order,' Jack said.

Tom shook his head. 'You don't need to thank me. It's a small price to pay. You are all far more valuable than any covert operation.'

'OK, I'm sure we're flattered, but what makes us so important to Jefferson? He has more money than god,' Mike said. 'He could buy whomever he needs to get whatever he needs done.'

'That may be true, but you have more than proved yourselves in the field and in an extreme situation. You are all remarkable and skilled people in your own rights. However, as a team you have achieved extraordinary things – things no one else has got close to replicating. In two days you managed to unlock the secrets of an ancient Angelus artefact and activate it. That is far more than I could ever hope to achieve – and I've been attempting it for years now. That makes you of considerable interest to my employer.'

'So does that mean Jefferson knows the Overseers are suppressing the truth about UFOs?' I asked.

'Yes. And Jefferson is also interested in the Angelus devices.'

'He knows about them?'

'Of course.'

I shook my head. 'So why not tell me at least part of this back on the ferry when you first saw me, Patrick? Sorry, I mean, Tom.'

'I apologise for the deception, Lauren. But I couldn't take the risk of you falling into Alvarez's hands and telling him what you knew. It was a threat that became all too real when I had to step in and give you a sedative on the boat to save your life.'

'You saved Lauren?' Jack asked.

'Naturally. And you and Mike as well. If I hadn't engineered a problem at the dig site, Alvarez would have killed all three of you. Fortunately, my deception worked. I even managed to return Lauren's LRS to her, and made sure she retained the stone orb, which I imagine is significant to the Angelus device?'

'It is...' I blew my breath out. 'Tom, thank you for everything.'

'I just wish I'd been able to let you know I was an ally. But you are a truly remarkable woman, Lauren. Ever since the

Sentinel event, you not only became of interest to the Overseers but of immense interest to Jefferson too.'

'Please tell me you weren't involved in that attack on Jodrell Bank in any way, shape or form? Good people died that night.'

Patrick held up his hands. 'I promise you that I had no involvement whatsoever, Lauren. However, as an Overseers agent, I was briefed about the event after the mission failed. Congratulations, by the way, for your role in that outcome.'

'It was quite a team effort. One that cost an MI5 agent, Kiera, her life.'

'I know and I'm deeply sorry. Even more so about the murder of your aunt. Once again I found out after that Alvarez had taken matters into his own hands.'

Mike stared at me. 'Alvarez killed your aunt?'

'I'd rather not talk about it.'

'Shit, I'm sorry, Lauren,' Jack said.

I nodded. 'Please carry on, Tom.'

'When I picked up your trail again, Lauren, and realised you were heading for Skara Brae, I thought it was too good an opportunity to miss. I was also intrigued by what information you might flush out. To say you exceeded my employer's wildest dreams would be a considerable understatement.'

'So Jefferson is against the Overseers?' Mike asked.

'Absolutely. My employer believes that no one should be suppressing the truth about the existence of aliens and the reality of UFOs visiting our world, including the Angelus.'

Jack narrowed his gaze on to me. 'So Roswell and the rest are true?'

'Let's just say there really is some top-secret military tech being developed, directly controlled by the Overseers, based on alien craft that have been recovered.'

'And Lucy would have been next if we hadn't have stepped in,' I said.

'Lucy as in your aunt?' Tom asked. 'I'm not sure I understand.'

'You're not the only one with a lot to tell,' Mike said.

'And it's a long story. Lucy's our name for the Angelus device,' I added.

'I see...'

Jack shook his head at me. 'Everything I thought I knew about the world has been ripped apart since I met you, Lauren.'

'It's the same for me, even if I'm the one responsible. I know I went after the truth and everything, but I had no idea just how big the lie the public was being fed was until now.'

Mike nodded. 'It's certainly blown my mind – and I'm a guy who believes reality is a shadow of crystals in the eighth dimension, which we now know to be true.'

Tom's expression sharpened. 'Is this something to do with your disappearance at Skara Brae?'

'You mean you don't know? Even with all the secret databases you must have access to?'

'No, I don't. That knowledge doesn't exist in any human database, which means the Overseers don't know about it either. However, there has been speculation for some time that the alien craft that visit our world are extra-dimensional in origin. Tell me more.'

'I think it can wait until after we've all had a chance to rest, since it's long and complicated, but I promise you it'll be worth the wait,' Mike said.

'Then I'll look forward to it,' Tom replied.

Jack leant forward. 'It's risky taking on an organisation as dangerous as the Overseers, even for Jefferson.'

'That's precisely the reason for my deep cover,' Tom replied. 'Even my employer wouldn't be immune if the Overseers realised Jefferson's direct involvement and decided to move against Sky Dreamer Corp.'

'It makes perfect sense to me that Jefferson would do something like this,' I said. 'After all, the guy has always been anti-establishment. He's also made himself a lot of enemies because of his disruptive innovations in the flight and space industry. It's little wonder that he's not a big fan of the Overseers.'

'Precisely,' Tom replied.

Over his shoulder I noticed two red diamonds appear, superimposed over the views of the sea moving past on the screens.

A synthesised female voice spoke from a speaker in the ceiling. 'Radar contacts confirmed. F-22 fighter jets have arrived at the oil rig platform.'

'And have they seen us?' Tom asked.

'Negative,' the voice replied.

'OK. Let me know if there's any change.'

'Understood.'

'So we're all good?' Jack asked.

Tom nodded. 'We're under no risk at this range.'

'Glad to hear it. Getting shot out of the sky by a missile right now would ruin a fun-filled day.'

'You can relax on that front. The XA101 has an even lower radar profile than a Lockheed F-117 stealth fighter plane.'

'OK, there is one thing I still don't understand, Tom,' I said. 'Why didn't you kill Alvarez when you had the chance rather than use a tranquilliser?'

'Ah, that would be because I'm somewhat like Mike here.'

Mike tightened his gaze on to me. 'In what way?'

'I don't like to take a life unless I absolutely have to. So I use my own techniques, which is something that my employer respects and supports.'

'The more I hear about him, the more I like this Jefferson guy,' Mike said.

'Oh, you two will definitely get on. Jefferson has something of a passion for theoretical physics too.'

'Definitely my sort of guy.'

Tom smiled. 'Just so.'

I frowned. 'So what does that make Jack and me then? Two people with a careless attitude to life?'

The agent shook his head. 'You both needed to do what you had to. No one is going to judge you on that.'

Apart from myself, I thought.

Tom settled back into his seat. 'Now, if it's the same to you, I'm exhausted. And if I feel like that, I can only begin to imagine how you all must feel. So I suggest you try to catch some sleep because when we arrive at the airstrip we'll have another long flight ahead of us.' He nodded to us and closed his eyes.

It wasn't long before Mike had stretched his legs out and was fast asleep too.

I should have passed out, but instead I found myself staring at the image of the sea skimming beneath the XA101. I jumped when Jack waved his hands in front of my face.

'You nearly gave me a bloody heart attack,' I said.

'Sorry, I couldn't tell if you were asleep or not. But as you're awake, how are you doing?'

'I'm going to need time – a lot of it – to get my head around all of this.'

'Yeah, that's pretty much how I feel too. The one thing I'm certain of is that my life will never be the same again after this. But maybe that's a good thing.'

'How so, Jack?'

'I was pretty much hiding myself away on Orkney at the Skara Brae dig. I needed space after...well, you know now...' His eyes slid away from mine.

I angled my knees towards him. 'After Sue's death, you mean?' I asked gently.

Jack slowly nodded. 'I still miss her every single day, Lauren. But she would have got a hell of a kick out of all of this.'

'I'm so sorry for your loss.' If ever there was an inadequate, clichéd phrase, that was it.

But Jack nodded. 'And me for you with your Aunt Lucy. I take it she meant a lot to you?'

'The world, Jack. She was my family, my everything. Before her I was with a string of foster parents. But no one wanted the troubled child who never smiled.'

'Why the lack of smiles?'

'Both my parents died in a house fire. They said it was a miracle that I survived beneath the rubble of our house, although it was hard for me to see it that way. I think I was still grieving for them when I fell into Aunt Lucy's sights during an astronomy talk she gave to our school. I sort of stalked her after that, sending her emails about space. And she answered every single one. Eventually after she found out more about me, she legally adopted me and helped me to turn my life around, surrounding me with love. She was my rock and now she's gone.'

'Like for me with Sue.'

'It's tough, isn't it, being the one left behind?'

'It always is.'

I nodded and gazed at the screens as the XA101 began to turn towards the shore. 'What have we got ourselves into with all this, Jack?' I sighed.

'Well, there's no going back. I wouldn't want to even if I could.'

'Me neither...'

Jack raised his shoulders. 'So maybe that's a good thing. Time to move on and all that.'

I resisted the urge to reach out for his hand. If ever I needed to be held, it was right then. But Jack turned away and closed his eyes, probably reliving his wife's death for the millionth time. The thirty centimetres between us might as well have been several miles.

On the screens I noticed a coastline fast approaching and in the far distance the lights for an airfield blinked on.

Whatever the journey ahead, I might not have asked for it, but I was certainly going to see it through. Apart from anything else, I was desperate to see the Angelus version of Aunt Lucy again.

LINKS

Do please leave that all important review for ***Earth Song*** here: https://geni.us/EarthSong

So now you've finished ***Earth Song*** are you ready for the next page-turning book in the series?

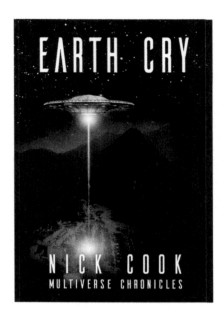

Pitched into a role she never asked for, Lauren soon faces decisions that will challenge the very core of her humanity. The secrets of an ancient civilisation are about to be unlocked, forcing Lauren, Jack and Mike into a desperate race against the Overseers to discover them, while the fate of the world hangs in the balance. Can Lauren find the strength within to become the soldier that the world needs her to be?

Earth Cry is available now on Kindle, in paperback and free within KU Unlimited. You can buy Earth Cry here: https://geni.us/EarthCry

AFTERWORD

Earth Song was an incredibly enjoyable book for me to write. As those who have read the prequel to this book, my novella *The Signal*, will know, Lauren's character came to life for me on the page. She is one of those rare author creations that just won't leave you alone, nagging you to give her a bigger role in your work. The only problem was, I had a separate trilogy to finish first, *Fractured Light*. Don't get me wrong. I loved writing the *Fractured Light* trilogy too, but I was also desperate to get back to Lauren and tell you the next part of her story. And now, at last, I have started to do that with the first full-length book in this new series, *Earth Song*. I can't wait to write the next books in this series following Lauren, Jack and Mike's continued search for the truth.

As always, there are many people to thank who helped with the creation of this book. To begin with, just as it should be, I must thank my wife Karen for supporting me in so many ways with my work. She is my Pole Star and my anchor in the storms that life throws at me. Yet another big shout-out to Catherine Coe for her ever-brilliant insights and amazing editing skills. My books simply wouldn't be as shiny without her. The other highly skilled member of my editorial team is Jennie Roman, who proofreads my books and spots all the errors I have missed. She is seriously brilliant.

I cover a lot of subjects in *Earth Song*, the core theme being UFOs and the question of whether or not aliens are real. As with all my books, extensive research has gone into this novel. Lauren talks frequently about chasing the rabbit down its hole in *Earth Song*, and that's exactly how I feel when I read the material I've collected about UFO sightings. (More about all thing aliens in a moment.) The rabbit phrase stuck in my mind thanks to *What the Bleep Do We Know!?* – a fantastic documentary film. It was this film that switched me on to the crazy world of quantum physics, a theme that regularly crops up in many of my science fiction books. It was this interest that also led me to another core strand in *Earth Song*, E8, and also the related emergence theory. If you hadn't come across it before, you may have thought that E8 was just a fanciful creation of a sci-fi author who'd probably drunk too much coffee. However, this is a very real new area of theoretical physics. The problem is that we humans, living in our three-dimensional reality, are simply not hardwired to understand something so inherently strange and weird to us. The E8 crystals mentioned in *Earth Song* really are a conceptual mathematical thing. And that's where we need a theoretical physicist such as Mike to come in to help us grasp it. If you're interested in finding out more, there is an absolutely wonderful documentary about E8 and emergence theory on YouTube called *Hacking Reality* that I highly recommend you watch. If you do, be prepared, however – as E8 really will blow your mind. Here's the link: https://www.youtube.com/watch?v=vJi3_znm7ZE

So back to the other hot topic of *Earth Song*: UFOs...

When I started researching them, I had no idea what was waiting for me. It may surprise you to discover that I was somewhat sceptical about the subject. And this was despite my personal experience of witnessing a strange craft in the sky one night with a group of astronomers, mentioned in the afterword of *The Signal*. To summarise, a group of experienced amateur astronomers – including me, a former pilot of light aircraft and microlights – didn't have a ready answer for what we witnessed one night near Cley Hill in Wiltshire to explain the glowing ball of light that accelerated at high speed towards the horizon in utter silence.

As I started to dig through the huge amount of material on the internet about UFOs, much to my own surprise I found myself leaning towards the belief that there really is something strange going on. I'm not here to try to convince anybody else about this, but if you have a moment, you might be interested in watching this video on YouTube about Bob Lazar – who allegedly worked at Area 51: https://www.youtube.com/watch?v=ZAeV3Vx4qeg

This, together with other even more convincing pieces of evidence, had me increasingly wondering whether there might be a real-life cover-up going on – not something I thought I'd find myself thinking when I first started writing *Earth Song*.

I am a science fiction author first and foremost and very aware of the human need to create stories about the world we live in – after all, it's what I do. Certainly I find the idea of UFOs being real highly stressful as it challenges many assumptions I have grown up with. I sincerely hope that the Overseers are just a fictitious creation on my part, but if not, it wouldn't be the first time that art has reflected reality, even if unintentional.

Anyway, back to the book! So what awaits Lauren, Jack and Mike in the next instalment, *Earth Cry*?

At the end of *Earth Song*, Lauren, Jack and Mike are travelling with agent Tom Hester to visit the mysterious A. Jefferson, on-board the XA101 electric prototype stealth craft. This vehicle is partly based on experimental electric aircraft that exist today, though obviously equipped with much better battery tech, and with a rotary wing design similar to the one the Bell Boeing V-22 Osprey uses for vertical landing. That's the factual side about my inspiration behind this craft. For those who follow my author Facebook page, you'll know that I have a strong love of classic science fiction films and series. And that little unpiloted sequence in the XA101 is my homage to a scene from an old favourite film of mine, *This Island Earth*, a great sci-fi movie from the fifties that I highly recommend. The scientists are picked up by a light aircraft, and it turns out it has no pilots. It's then that they start to realise something seriously strange is going on, giving them a taste of things to come...

I'm planning quite a few books in the *Earth Song* series, as Lauren is too great a character to resist. There will also be another series following *Earth Song*, about which I'm going to say nothing more other than that *Earth Song* is paving the way for it. Plus some way off in the future, I will one day write the sequel trilogy to *Fractured Light*.

Thank you for taking the time to read *Earth Song*. If you loved it, tell your friends. Word of mouth is so important for the success of any book. Another highly important thing is reviews. If you're reading on a Kindle, before you go do please take two minutes to click to the next page and leave an Amazon review. If you're reading a paperback, hop over to the Amazon or Goodreads website and leave a review. I will be eternally grateful, as every single review really helps me as an author.

Finally, to get exclusive cover reveals, writing and sneak peeks of my new books, you can subscribe to my newsletter here: www.subscribepage.com/b4n4n4

If you're ready to continue the Earth Song saga, the next book in the series, Earth Cry, is available via the link below. However, do please leave that oh so precious review on the next page before you go. https://geni.us/EarthCry

Nick Cook, February 2019

ALSO BY NICK COOK

The Cloud Riders Trilogy (Multiverse Chronicles)

The Earth Song Series (Multiverse Chronicles)

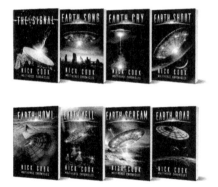

The Fractured Light Trilogy (Multiverse Chronicles)

Printed in Great Britain
by Amazon

27278880R00169